To..

Uncle

TIMES OFF

P McKimm

MINERVA PRESS
LONDON
ATLANTA   MONTREUX   SYDNEY

TIMES OFF
Copyright © P McKimm 1998

ISBN 0 75410 157 6

First Published 1998 by
MINERVA PRESS
195 Knightsbridge
London SW7 1RE

Printed in Great Britain for Minerva Press

TIMES OFF

About the Author

Peter McKimm was born in 1930 in Skerries Co, Dublin, and lived there until he was eight when his family moved to the Monkstown/Blackrock area where he has lived ever since.

As a child he spent a great deal of his summers at Seapoint and in his early teens fished from the West Pier and played tennis. Later his interests extended to game fishing, golf, travel, wine, music and recently writing.

He is a graduate in law from University College, Dublin.

He was secretary of the Irish Dairy Board until his retirement in 1990. His work in the Dairy Board, which is an international marketing organisation, precluded him from several hobbies so as soon as he retired he set about rectifying these omissions, which included writing short stories.

Business travel may give a taste for foreign countries but it seldom gives an appreciation for what these places have to offer. A hotel bedroom in New York does not materially differ from one in Frankfurt or Delhi. He and his wife have travelled extensively since his retirement, this time as tourists. As a result, many of the stories in *Times Off* reflect these travels, from trekking the Himalayas to wandering around Chile. They should cause the reader to think, but not to the level of being elitist or incomprehensible. They are primarily intended to be entertaining.

Acknowledgements

To my wife, Marie, who was charity personified; to my daughter, Lesley, who was brutally and refreshingly critical; to my daughter-in-law, Sharon, who at the outset presented me with a book on writing short stories; to the late Rose O'Rourke for her very thorough evaluation of the stories; to Gerry O'Reilly, whose encouragement and suggestions made for some enjoyable West Pier strolls; to those other friends, especially Liam O'Riordan, Lady Melanie Beaumont and Fergus Conway for the bones of three stories; to those relatives and friends who fled at the sight of another draft short story. I am glad to tell them to stop running, for now. To my sons, Andrew, who saved me from slaughtering my PC, Frazer, who helped to supply the graphics and Barry for chile.

Special thanks are due to Pearce Rayel for proof reading.

Foreword

In an age when television advertising tends to channel consumers' concentration to the gap between programmes, it seems a paradox that blockbuster novels, often heavily laced with technical or professional detail, are preferred to short stories. Of the list of the hundred best sellers for 1996, only three were books of short stories, which came forty-ninth, fifty-first and seventy-third.

Yet the short story has an illustrious history. One could arguably trace the genre back to the Old Testament's incidental short narratives (Joseph and his brothers or the story of Ruth and Naomi) and on to such writers as Defoe, Poe, Kipling, Stevenson, de Maupassant, Chekhov, Joyce, Jacobs, Henry, Maugham, Runyon, Saki, Thurber, O'Connor, O'Flaherty and Carver. The list is endless. The unusual number which flourished during the first half of this century raises the question, would all of them have even been published over the last quarter? Why have short stories apparently lost their popularity when people contend that they like reading short stories and for substantiation will cite examples of well-known stories? But most will admit their last short story was read in a magazine. Can that be the future for the short story? I hope not.

De Maupassant, that master of the short story, wrote that

'the public is composed of numerous groups
who call out to us:
"Comfort me."
"Amuse me."
"Sadden me."
"Move me to pity."
"Make me dream."
"Make me laugh."
"Make me shiver."
"Make me weep."
"Make me think."'

Short story practitioners and critics have never agreed on its
length or precise format. It would appear wrong even to
attempt to do so as that could shackle its evolution. Two
authors who had particularly influenced the genre,
Chekhov and Joyce, might never have become popular if
reactionary attitudes had been the norm. Of course, if their
style, art, craft, call it what you will, was not accepted by
their eventual publishers, and thus made accessible to
readers, they would have languished in relative obscurity,
but only for a while. Yet it is interesting to speculate, had
they emerged today as new authors, what would their fate
have been? Has this lack of encouragement from most
publishers pushed the genre into an obscure elitist corner
to be appreciated only by the few?

I have mentioned current commercial television which
contributes towards a shortening concentration span. An
ideal environment for short stories, one would imagine.
That is not apparently the case in spite of their popularity in
the past. In the short or long term genius will undoubtedly
succeed, but few short story writers are in that category,

which is not to say they do not have a marketable product. If Stephen Spielberg can so successfully refine the films of the Thirties and Forties for today's audiences then why cannot something similar be done for short stories. He came to the same conclusions as de Maupassant, namely, that people's desires do not change significantly. Modern marketing can turn customer desire into a hunger to buy or read.

For my own part, I have attempted to bear de Maupassant's words in mind when writing these short stories. My hope is that, at least to some extent, I have succeeded.

Contents

Seapoint

During the summer, me, Nedser and Lofty fished for stingoes at the slip at Seapoint, little fish which came up the side of the slip with the tide. When the tide was out we played rounders on the sand, or waded in the sea trying to stand on dabs, but we weren't good at that because they darted off too quickly in a smokescreen of sand. Older fellas waded out, carryin' a bit of wire with a sharp point for stickin' into them.

Fellas came from everywhere to fish for stingoes and crabs from the slip. If we arrived late there was no room except at the end of the slip where it was covered in green slippy seaweed. When the sea came in you had to move up, if there was room. If you tried to squeeze in you could get thumped, maybe even pushed into the sea. If I had to move I just gave up an' watched the others, 'cos I couldn't swim. That's how I became pally with Lofty. He looked like a giraffe even though he was only eight, same as us.

One day at the beginnin' of August I was late an' I had to fish standin' on the seaweed. It wasn't too slippy because the sun had been shining on it and dried it out. There I was, me leanin' over the side of the slip to see if there were any stingoes when two big Ringsenders, Ringers to us, gurriers to me ma, came along and pushed me, head first, into the sea. I shouted out 'Help' but they just laughed. As they were bigger than everyone on the slip, Lofty ran to get Tarzan, the corpo' man who looked after Seapoint. Tarzan came tearin' down, chased off the Ringers, and grabbed me by the back of the shirt, dumped me on the slip and squeezed me until I thought me guts would come out with the water.

'Look what ye did to me shirt. Me mammy will be raging,' I cried.

'He's lucky you called me,' said Tarzan to Lofty, ignorin' me. 'The way you are goin' on,' turning to me, 'I had good mind to leave ye there, ye ungrateful little bollocks.'

'I'm sorry Tarzan,' said I, knowin' he liked to be called by his nickname. 'Thanks a lot.'

After all, he did save me skin. We were friends with Tarzan, even goin' to the shop to get his Woodbines, 'coffin nails', me da called them. Sometimes we gave him a hand with the cleanin' up after the Jackeens were finished throwing their rubbish around. Nedser's da and he went to the same pub, often givin' us fish for Tarzan, big fish like ray an' cod.

After Lofty ran for Tarzan he and I became pals. Me best pal was Nedser who lived near us. His da knew all about fish since he worked on a trawler out of the Coal Quay. He took us down to the quay an' showed us the boat an' all the fish they had caught, massive fish, some as big as sharks.

Every year we had competitions for crabs and stingoes. Crabs were easier. All ye had to do was tie a barnacle to a string and, when the crab grabbed it, haul it up slowly. Pull too fast and the crab let go. Sometimes we got so excited when the crab was at the edge that it fell back in. Any caught had to be put back on the far side of the slip.

Nedser won last year an' I was second. This year a Ringer was leading the crab competition, with Lofty, me and Nedser next, ahead of a crowd of Ringers. We didn't really want the Ringers in the competition, but wha' could we do? They were bigger than us. So far, Lofty was ahead in this year's stingo competition. The rest of us had given up, but the Ringers wanted to win the crab competition. The two who pushed me in were a brother of the fella who was leadin' an' they thought I was second.

Crabs were gettin' scarce on our side of the slip an' we had rows about some not being thrown back in on the far side. Lofty said he saw one of the Ringers droppin' one of his crabs back where he caught it. The Ringer claimed the crab was a peal crab, which is a mother crab holdin' a baby, soft-shelled, crab underneath. He told us the baby came out from under its mother's belly and crawled over the edge of the slip. The mother followed.

'Wha's wrong with that?' he asked. We weren't going to call him a fibber seein' as he had his two big brudders around.

We were in the Tower, where Tarzan stored his stuff, talkin' about the competition when Tarzan said, 'Why don't yez go out to that place out there,' pointing to a place far out in the rocks. 'It's only clear at spring tide, which is now. It's full o' crabs. If youse go out with me bucka an' fill it youse can drop them under where youse are goin' to fish and then win your competition.'

'Can we go tomorrow?' we shouted.

'No, wait until Sunda' when the tide is as far out as it's goin' to be.'

Sunday was sunny and the place was full a Jackeens. Tarzan's spot was further out in the rocks than we had ever been. The rocks were around a pool at one end and stones at the other. We climbed down on to the stones and started lookin' under the brown bubbled seaweed for crabs. There were loads a them an' we were fillin' the bucket when we saw a huge red eatin' crab with massive nippers. Nedser shouted out, 'Don't touch it. Its nippers will take the finger offa ye.' He should a kept his mouth shut because the two big Ringers, who were lying sunning themselves on the rocks, jumped down to where we were claiming, 'That crab is ours. We were only keepin' it under the weed till we were goin' for our tea.'

They grabbed the crab and knocked over our bucket saying, 'sorry', an' laughing like jackasses. The green crabs ran all over the gravel, most headin' for the pool. What could we do but try and put them back? The Ringers leapt back over the rocks to sun themselves an' show the crab to their two mots.

We looked for more crabs, and when we found another small red one Lofty whispered, 'Stay quiet in case those two bollocks come back.'

Just as the water in the pool was gettin' higher with the rising tide we found the two big holes in the rock, about three feet up from the gravel and six feet apart. We could see water at the openin's an' red bloodsuckers around the front. We all looked in. It was dark inside. Nedser said he saw somethin' shinin' in there.

'Who's goin' to stick his hand in?' asked Nedser.

'I will,' says I, like an eejit.

I put my hand in, makin' sure to miss the bloodsuckers; in a good bit, I touched somethin' slimy that moved. Jeany Mack I got the fright a' me life, but didn't shout out after what happened with the crab. Instead, I leaped back standin' on Nedser's toe. He nearly gave the game away by his roar, but no one looked.

'Keep quiet, there is somethin' in there,' Lofty hissed.

We looked around, the Ringers were messin' with the two mots.

We then looked into the other hole, which was bigger, and saw two monster eyes staring at us. We got the fright of our lives. Lofty said it was a sea monster.

Nedser said, 'Don't be so stupid, it's a conger eel. It's massive, thick as your leg, Lofty.'

Lofty was impressed.

Slippy Burke had caught an eel on the slip and we thought it was big, 'cos it was six times the size of the stingoes. But this conger was somethin' else. We all thought if we caught the conger and showed it to the gang on the slip the competition would be forgotten.

'The Ringers would be mad,' said Lofty.

'How are we goin' to get it out? I'm not puttin' me hand in there, congers can bite,' said Nedser.

'The tide is comin' in again. Let's ask Tarzan what to do,' says I.

We went back to Tarzan who told us, 'I have a bit o' wire with a barb at the end, ye know for catchin' dabs. Its end is like a fishin' hook. Youse can come back tomorrow an' try an' stick it in him, an' pull him outa the hole.'

We went home talkin' about nothin' else. Me and Lofty could hardly sleep we were so excita. Next day we came back at half five and got the wire off Tarzan.

'Be careful with that yoke, I don't want any o' youse comin' back with it stickin' outa yez. I'll follow yez down when I'm finished here.'

We ran over the rocks, until Tarzan let a roar at us, so we slowed down. We were shakin' with excitement as we got near where the conger was, and fear when we saw the two Ringers with their mots, looking redder than ever.

They saw us and roared, 'If yez get any more eatin' crabs give us a shout.' Then they laughed like hyenas. Good for us the mots were there too which would keep them off our backs.

We pretended to be lookin' under the seaweed and rocks for crabs before lookin' into the holes. The Ringers and their mots were facin' inta the sun, with their backs to us. We were afraid the conger might have gone, but it was still shinin' in its dark cave.

'Jeaney look at the frigger,' said Nedser. 'It looks bigger than yesterday.'

We were squintin' through the two holes an' could see the shiny dark skin of the conger. Lofty bent down and started pokin' the wire in at it.

'It's no use, it keeps slidin' offa his back.'

'Here let me have a go,' says Nedser grabbin' the wire. He began pokin' like mad. The conger didn't move at first. All of a sudden he began to slide slowly out of the cave. Nedser stopped prodding. He jumped back pushin' the two of us behind him. Its head was huge, with two dirty, big eyes glaring balefully at us. It slid over the entrance, hesitated, its head movin' from side to side, still glaring at us. Then it slid slowly down the face of the rock.

Honest to God, he was as thick as me ma's leg. With three feet of him out of the cave, he looked as if he had a lot more to come. His head fell on the stones as his tail, a big flat thing, came outa the hole. Dark green he was with a white tummy. He was bigger than the snake in the Dublin azoo. The one that crushed people and animals and things.

'Jeany he is as long as me,' gasped Lofty.

Nedser put his hand out as if he was goin' to lift him. He got a hand on his back but Nedser's grip was too small and the conger was too slippy. Lofty said he was showing off, not for long. The conger turned his head as if to bite Nedser with a mouth fulla tiny teeth, like me ma's needles.

'Ah ah...' We all let out a yell of terror as we jumped back. It wasn't Tarzan who came, but the two Ringers from the rocks.

'Youse shaggers need the US cavalry an' here we are.'

The crab man jumped down, as if he were Flash Gordon, right in front of the conger which was slitherin' towards the pool. It didn't stop, so he put his bare foot on its back while the other fella made a grab at its tail.

'It's slippin',' he shouted. 'Put your foot hard on his back.'

The conger kept slidin' under his foot, at the same time turning his terrible head until he got his mouth on the underneath part of the right big toe of the Ringer. The conger musta had a big mouth because the blood poured out of the Ringer's toe like outa a stuck pig. Myself, I never saw a stuck pig but me da did an' ye know what I mean – it was like the time Piggy McGrath was hit on the nose by his brudder Mickser.

'Me toe, Jeasus, me toe,' he yelled. 'Looka wha' the bastard' done ta me.'

He was hoppin' all over the stones on one leg tryin' to hold his toe with his hand. Blood poured all over the stones an' rocks. He ran back, cursing something awful, to get his towel. We didn't know what to do, the conger was now gettin' near the pool which had got bigger with the tide. Once in the water he was gone.

Suddenly there was a roar from the rock above us, like from that fella Johnny Weissmuller who plays Tarzan in the pictures, except that it was our Tarzan. He fired a giant rock on top of the conger. 'That will halt his gallop,' he cried. It didn't, well it nearly did. He kept wriggling on the stones, except he didn't seem to know where he was going because he was now wriggling away from the pool. Tarzan hit him again with another rock. He just wriggled for a little while, going nowhere. The bleeding Ringer was sitting on the rock with a bloody towel around his right foot moaning.

'Served him right,' said Tarzan. Us, we were delighta.

We left the conger in Tarzan's store in the Tower until the next day. We didn't forget to take the bucket of crabs. We put them into the sea at the slip, where Lofty was going to fish on the Monday.

We showed everyone the conger the next day, telling them where we had got it. Tarzan wasn't there so we said nothing about his rock. After all, it was us who found the conger. The Ringers were mad jealous, much good that did them.

Lofty kept catchin' crabs, with Nedser and me complaining loudly that some people had all the luck an' it wasn't fair. He won the competition though.

The Ringers spent the rest of the holliers looking for congers all over the place, even as far as the Bull's Eye. Us, we just played rounders on the sand and stayed away from the slip. We were terrible sorry about the shaggers losin' the competition. Besides how can stingoes or crabs compare to a giant conger?

Last Métro to Austerlitz

The brightly-lit métro train quietly pulled into Gare du Nord just as Joe hurried on to a platform which, like the carriages, was almost deserted. At least he was not going to lose any more precious time, he thought, the French, unlike the Irish go to bed early. Not that nine-fifteen was late; wrong he realised, they were an hour different from Dublin, which made it ten-fifteen in Paris, hence the lack of passengers.

There were only two people in the carriage; a gum-chewing youth at the end and a pale-faced girl seated near the door. The wide choice of seats caused Joe to hesitate for a few seconds before he opted for the middle right-hand side. He placed his overnight bag near the window, and then sat down beside it. Out of sheer habit, he crossed his legs and carefully placed his folded black gaberdine coat over his knees. The doors closed and the metro left the station as silently as it had entered.

He was supposed to be enjoying himself on this journey, a birthday present from Patricia who had harboured the illusion that he had always yearned to travel overnight through France in a sleeper – a wagons-lits. That was simply because he had expressed such a desire when he and Peg were hurrying to the South of France in their car with the kids. He had only mentioned it on one evening when, fagged out driving, they were stopped at a level crossing to allow a series of sleeping cars to pass by.

Now that Pat was married in Toulouse she had promised herself that one day her father would realise her perception of his dream journey. It might have been nice if Peg was still alive, or even if he was a few years younger. At his age he would have preferred to go to Toulouse by plane. He knew only too well that Pat would have been very disappointed if he had opted for air travel. What was it Shakespeare said about it being better to give than to receive. He would have approved of this journey, he was both giving and receiving.

He could have done without all the fuss from the rest of the family though. You'd think he was travelling to the moon from the way they carried on. He hadn't even time to buy a copy of the *Irish Times* in Dublin. It was that bad.

Then the plane was an hour late leaving Dublin. To cap it all, that Aer Lingus crowd only gave newspapers to the club class. He looked out for an *Irish Times* as he left the plane. All he could see were French papers scattered over the empty club class seats.

'Were you looking for something, sir?' asked the hostess politely.

'Yeah, today's *Irish Times*,' he answered sourly, thinking it would be just his bad luck that one of his friends would die and he would not see the notice.

The métro train pulled up with a slight jerk at the next station, Gare de l'Est. He would always see the name in his mind's eye. A group of unkempt youths, five in all, tumbled into the carriage talking loudly in French. Somehow to Joe they didn't look French, Arabs maybe. They looked around the empty carriage before four threw themselves on to the seats across the aisle. The fifth sat heavily on the end of Joe's seat, facing towards his friends, with his back to Joe. They all looked around the near empty carriage, insolently, thought Joe, before recommencing their loud conversation. Meanwhile the young girl, followed by cat-calls, at the last minute jumped up and dodged through the closing door. Was she afraid of this lot, wondered Joe?

He resumed his brooding about the journey.

'I haven't got a *Times*. I have an *Irish Independent* though,' the girl had said solicitously.

'If that's all you have, sure beggars can't be choosers,' said he resignedly.

He got off the plane and went through those ridiculous futuristic tubes in Charles de Gaulle before he came to the enquiries desk. He just wanted to find out how to get to the RER. Even at that late hour there were a few people ahead of him. That silly overdressed French woman in front of him kept gabbling on until he was fit to burst. It was her fault he just missed the RER and had to wait about twenty minutes for the next.

The RER journey was depressing. The train appeared to pass through some of the worst wastelands of Paris. He just hoped it didn't break down in this Apache land. At this rate he would be cutting it fine to get to Gare d'Austerlitz for the three minutes to twelve wagons-lits to Toulouse. God, he could do without all this.

It was then Joe sensed a change in the background noise in the carriage. The five youths had stopped talking and were staring at him. They looked drunk, thought Joe, or worse, drugged. Avoid eye contact at all costs. Wasn't that the message for the New York subway? Funny he should remember that now.

He looked out the window to his right. Not that he particularly wanted to see anything pass by in the darkness but he could use their reflection as a mirror to see what they would do next. The smallest one was leering and pointing at him. He couldn't catch what he was saying. Not that it mattered. He couldn't speak the language anyhow. Whatever it was he bet it wasn't good. He strained his eye to catch a glimpse of what one of the others was doing. He looked as if he was trying to pull something out of the pocket of his blue denim jacket. It looked shiny and bulky. A big cosh maybe? He could see the carriage's only other occupant, the youth at the back, in the reflection of the window in front of him. He seemed totally unconcerned, his gum chewing jaw still moved in quick rhythmic movements. Joe turned his gaze back to the window beside him where he could see one of them still pulling at his pocket. Even with his distorted view he recognised a can of beer. Out of the corner of his eye he could just make out 'Kanterbrau'. He must have known he was looking because he lifted up the can in Joe's direction and leered, as if toasting his health. Joe was careful not to give any indication that he had seen him.

Then he got a hefty shove on his left side from the fellow sitting at the end of his seat. He had pushed his two feet against the opposite seat and heaved. This squashed Joe against his case and the window. Joe decided to put his bag on the seat in front which allowed him to sit up against the window. This appeared to cause the other to swivel around so that he was sitting beside Joe when he said something to him, in French Joe guessed or even Arabic.

The other four gave their full attention to Joe who could only look blank. The young fella beside him dug his right hand into his bomber jacket pocket and pulled out a flat half-bottle of brandy. It was a brand Joe didn't recognise, probably because it was rot gut. He took a messy slug and, with some still dribbling down the side of his mouth, offered the bottle to Joe. He probably figured Joe wouldn't take it. He has done this before, thought Joe. What would be their next move? Joe hesitated, uncertain as to what he should do, yet convinced he was in a no win situation. He thought about changing his seat. That could do more harm than good, to him that is. Drunks' humour can be fickle. Better to brazen it out.

He shook his head and said in English, 'No, thank you.'

The youth digested Joe's reply, sucking his teeth as if extracting the last drop of brandy from them. He knew he would get a refusal, thought Joe. The young fella continued to hold out the brandy out in front of Joe, his outstretched arm swaying slightly. He must have held it out for a full minute without saying a word, probably while his drunken mind cranked away, thought Joe. While he couldn't ignore the all pervasive aroma of the cognac he made his mind concentrate on what might be their next move. One thing was certain, he was definitely not going to be offered Martell or Hennessy. His companion at last changed his forbidding expression; he frowned, first at Joe, then at his brandy. Joe could feel the mounting tension in his body. Why in Hell's name did Pat get him on this? Without warning his companion's face broke into a smile. He put the bottle to his mouth and took another dribbling slug. He wiped his lips with his hand and began to laugh uproariously. Joe did not know what to feel. To confuse matters further the other four followed suit. He decided to force out a thin smile, despite feeling that he was in a carriage full of nitro-glycerine, one wrong move and vroom!

The train was slowing down. Should he make a dash for freedom at the next station? He dare not even look out to see if he could catch its name flashing by, just in case they guessed what he had in mind. The problem was that if he did get off he would probably miss the Toulouse train. Either way he looked likely to miss it so he may as well have a go. He tensed up, ready for the plunge. The name of the station appeared on the outside wall – Oberkempf. An appropriate one seeing as he was in a carriage with a crowd of neo-Nazis.

As if anticipating his next move his seat companion lifted his two feet and placed them on top of the opposite seat, effectively blocking his egress. Joe's mind was made up for him. Damn, he could say good bye to Oberkempf. Not the gum-chewing youth; he got off, leaving Joe alone on the train with this bunch of thugs. What to do? Before he could think of an answer the train moved out of the station. He now had a fellow feeling for the unfortunate Jews' last train journey.

Joe carefully turned his face to the overhead métro route map. He saw nothing of it. What he was looking for was an emergency lever of some sort to stop the train. He could see none, at least near enough for him to grab.

He spotted a glint of metal from one of their fingers. Was it a knuckle duster? He has always thought the expression about the hair rising on the back of ones neck was just that, an expression. It wasn't, he could distinguish, not just his hair, but every upright filament on his scalp. Maybe it was money they were after? He had about 500 francs, plus £200 in traveller's cheques. That should satisfy them. On the other hand if he offered them the lot they would think there was more to come, better to say nothing.

A nervous readjustment of his coat had caused the *Independent* to slide out of his pocket. He retrieved it from the floor, recrossed his legs, and with as much nonchalance as he could muster spread the top half of the newspaper across his knees, as if he was reading the headlines. He did his best to control his mounting panic. The last thing he wanted was for the newspaper to fall on the floor in case they hit him on the head.

One of the four said something to him in French. Christ, he would give anything now to have taken up Peg's suggestions that he learn some of the language. Then he recalled one sentence she had hammered into his head.

He offered it to them, '*Parlez-vous anglais?*'

The response was startling. They pointed at Joe and simply laughed uproariously again, each in turn mimicking his phrase. His seat companion solemnly replied '*non*' to each. Then one of them said something in French. Joe could only make out one word – 'Algérie'.

Jesus Christ, screamed Joe's mind, *you are in an empty carriage, in the middle of the night with cut-throat Algerians who are high on drink, if not drink and drugs.*

Joe tried to contain his terror. He had read enough in the papers about Algerian atrocities. Would they grab him and slit his throat? After all life was cheap in Algeria and there were no witnesses to worry about.

He could see the next stop on the métro was Bastille. Maybe he should make a run for it there, that is if he ever got there. The fellow on the far side emptied his can of beer and proceeded to crush it in his hand before throwing it on the floor. It was as if he had made up his mind about something, *me* thought Joe.

Come on Bastille, screamed Joe's mind.

Then his seat companion turned to him and said something in French. He picked up 'American'. They wanted to know his nationality. He ignored the query.

Then his companion said, '*Inglese – Eenglish?*'

'*No*,' almost shouted Joe, 'Irish.' The others looked blank.

Two from the far seat got up. One of them had that glint of steel in the fingers of his right hand. *Here it comes*, thought Joe, his fingers tightening on the *Independent*. For the first time in his life he noticed what was on the top right hand corner of the *Irish Independent*.

He was unable to communicate his nationality to them, yet he knew instinctively it was important to do so. He pointed at the name of the paper for the benefit of the one sitting beside him, nothing. He then pointed to a harp on a green background on the top right hand corner of the front page. He moved his finger to the word 'Ireland' in the script underneath the harp.

The effect was startling. His seat companion immediately jumped up, nearly causing Joe to have a heart attack.

Once up, he stretched out his right arm, closed his four fingers and with his thumb erect shouted, '*Irlande, Irlande.*'

The others crowded around to examine the newspaper before sticking out their fists in a similar fashion. One of them even took off a couple of beer can rings from his fingers and threw them away before giving the right arm signal. They were all smiling broadly. Joe's terror stayed with him for a few seconds before he realised he was no longer in any danger. He felt like crying with relief. Instead he managed a smile. They liked the Irish. Sure they were only a bunch of lads out for a lark.

The métro slowed down for Bastille and they all trouped out of the carriage, laughing and shouting farewells.

Joe, when they had gone, looked at his watch. He was okay for the wagons-lits so he turned over to the Deaths column in the *Irish Independent* to check if any of his friends had died. The trouble was some of them would only have their obituaries in the *Irish Times*.

Jack and Gillian
A Modern Fairy Story

'It's a paradox, Jack. That's what it is. You love Gillian. She loves you, but her heart's desire is to visit the Alps in a camper van. You hate camping. It's a dilemma with only one solution.'

George had been in his element, dishing out unpalatable advice to his friends, thought Jack grimly.

'An' what's that?' he had asked resignedly.

'Buy the bloody thing and go before you have a family. The alternative will be listening to Gillian pining for the Alps all of your married life.'

'I suppose you're right George, in fairness the Volkswagen camper van looks like a good buy.'

Jack was reflecting back to the beginning as he sat on a bench on the port side of the Calais ferry. Gillian was leaning over the rail in front of him absorbing her last glimpse of France. The sunshine and the thin summer dress showed off her figure to the full. Whilst her looks may not have matched her figure she had an air of serenity which captivated most men, especially Jack. He had to admit that George's advice, despite everything that happened subsequently, had proved spot on. Somewhere over that rail Gillian was still visualising her beloved Alps. Jack had a slightly different thought in his mind. *How can I get my hands on that bastard Percy Lawson for conning us into buying that blasted camper van; perfect mechanical order my ass.*

Jack had known nothing about camper vans and he had every intention of keeping it that way after a quarrelsome teenage family caravan holiday in the rain near Aberystwyth. That is until he and Gillian met smarmy Percy. He had been a failed suitor of Gillian's and knew all about 'her alpine fixation' as he liked to call it.

'Hi Gilly, I was thinking about you. If you still want to go to the Alps, a pal o' mine has a 1979 Volkswagen camper van. You'd love it Jack. Two other pals have just brought it back from a trip to Holland. Saved themselves a pile on hotel bills.'

'We are in a hurry Percy—' Jack saw trouble.

'Percival to you. You should know that Jack.'

'Jack, Percival is right. If we want to go this appears to be our best chance. Think of it Jack dearest, the freedom of the road from here to Switzerland.' Gillian was in full flight. There was no stopping her. Besides it would be churlish not to have a look at it.

'Okay, let's have a look,' said Jack unenthusiastically.

Percy's friend was a little cockney to whom Jack took an instant dislike.

'Look mate there's no risk to you. It's a snip. When you come back from the Alps you can sell the van at around the same price as you paid me for it. Is that a good deal or is it not? Think what those Swiss hotels would charge you. What's more, think of their awful grub. You'd buy the bleedin' van for two weeks in an 'otel.'

Neither Jack nor Gillian had been to the Continent before, but they had heard horror stories about their rotten food including snails, frogs and horse meat. There was no escape. At least he got £150 off the price, which made him feel he had got something over on those smart shysters.

'What about a guarantee?' Jack inquired.

Percival's friend looked as if they had been stabbed in the heart.

'Guarantee?' he said as if it was a turd. He quickly recovered his composure. 'Jack old man, what you see is what you get. Take as long as you like to examine the van. It has got a MOT certificate with a genuine 40000 miles on the clock. It's only been used for holidays each year. Any friend of Percival's is a friend of mine, so don't feel pressurised Jack. Ask any questions you like. At this knock down price you can't expect a guarantee.'

Jack couldn't see why not, but let it pass. He felt pressurised, largely because he knew nothing about these contraptions. Gillian on the other hand was depressurised. 'It looks fine to me. Maybe the red paint is a little faded but that should not affect its running. We can sell it when we get back as we may have a baby next year.'

Jack only heard the word 'baby' and that clinched it. A small price to pay for his heart's desire.

The following weekend they took the van for a trial run to the Cotswolds. Unused to driving a camper van Jack never exceeded 40 mph. The steering was a little loose and there appeared to be some noise which he assumed was normal. Otherwise, given its age, it appeared okay.

The campsite was a revelation for Jack. It had all services, even an adjoining pub. When they heard the sites in France were cheaper and better he began to look forward to their trip to the Alps.

A week later they were on the boat to Calais. Jack said nothing to Gillian about the van but he noticed on the journey to Dover that when he went over 45 mph there was a drumming noise, or rather a thumpty-thump, thumpty-thump. He just slowed down as they were in good time for the boat.

After a while in France she noticed the sound and said, 'Jack, is there something wrong? You look a bit tense. Is it that noise?'

'No. I'm okay dearest. I'm just getting used to the right-hand driving. The noise may be due to the fact we are in a van.'

'If you say so dearest,' she said, sounding doubtful.

They arrived at the campsite at dusk by which time it was almost full. The unoccupied emplacements were on a sloped part of the site.

'If I park the camper van sideways on the slope it will mean the beds will be fairly level,' Jack figured so he pulled the Volkswagen across the site and stopped short of a clothesline attached to an adjoining caravan. Gillian was a little uneasy at being parked so close to the line.

'Jack, I know its a still night but if the wind gets up at all those clothes could blow against the van.'

'Don't worry Gillian there will be no wind tonight. This is France. They don't have our winds here.'

It was indeed a balmy night and after the stress of the day Jack was now totally relaxed, sitting out drinking a beer whilst Gillian busied herself with their evening meal. He would get the noise checked out by a French garage in the morning. No point in dashing out too early in the morning, he thought.

'Maybe this camping isn't so bad after all, Gillian.'

Gillian's response from the van was unclear but the tone denoted agreement.

'Hey you, you are on my emplacement. Look a wha' you have dona to my wash.'

The loud words spoken in a foreign accent were accompanied by a pounding on the side of the van. Aggressive bastard, thought Jack, as he struggled to zip himself out of the duvet. Even in the darkness he could see some white clothing on the windscreen. He could also hear the wind had got up. A further pounding, just as he was throwing the duvet back, caused him to simultaneously bang his head off the overhead locker and his right hand jerked on to Gillian's throat.

He threw back the duvet forgetting Gillian was asleep beside him in the bunk bed. His annoyed 'Christ Almighty' was drowned by Gillian's scream, *'Jack*, there's a madman trying to strangle me.'

This brought on a flood of even more insistent knocking and Italian.

Jack managed to steer his six foot three frame to the door noting in passing that the time was half past five.

He was feeling half stunned from the bang on the head which had caused a trickle of blood from a scalp wound. Pulling over the door he was bought face to face with a young Italian with a drooping moustache. The Italian hesitated at first when he saw Jack's condition but then began waving a piece of his washing shouting, 'Looka, looka, wha you have dona to my wash, eeeet is filth.' He waved the other hand at the van.

Jack stepped out and followed his gaze to the front of his camper van which was covered in a colourful variety of rain soaked underwear. Woken by Gillian's scream, a growing band of silent campers had approached their van. An embarrassed looking Italian lady was going around collecting her washing from the ground whilst speaking in Italian to her husband. Gillian, hurrying out of the van, exclaimed when she saw the blood all over Jack's head and face.

She began to clean up the worst of the blood after which she said in a steely voice to the Italian, 'Do you think it right to go banging on people's vans, alarming everybody, just for the sake of some underwear? Look what you have done to my husband?' She pointed at Jack who was holding a bloodstained hanky to his head.

The little Italian's mouth opened and closed as if he were a landed cod. The audience looked at him expecting some violent reaction. There was none, but he was clenching and unclenching his hands while the blood rushed to his face. His wife read the situation better. They were the only Italians in the campsite and Jack looked in immediate need of medical attention. She muttered *sotto voce* to her husband who growled something back at her.

She obviously got her way because he turned away in disgust while she said in perfect English, 'You obviously made a mistake in parking your vehicle sideways. Nevertheless you should know the boundaries of your site, they are clearly marked. We are sorry my husband's knocking upset your husband.' Then half turning to the other campers she said, 'Perhaps you would help us to gather up our washing.'

Gillian knew when she was being put down, so she merely said, 'We are sorry. It was an accident. Let me help you with the washing.'

When they had all departed Gillian could see Jack's attitude towards camping had disimproved so she changed the subject. 'Jack, you know they launched the V2s directed at London from here.'

'And they were probably built by bloody Italians,' he said sourly.

Any chance of sleep was now gone so they made breakfast and departed under the smouldering eyes of the Italian.

The noise was giving Jack such a headache he decided he'd better have it seen to, sooner rather than later. They would never reach the Alps if they were to drive at no more than forty miles per hour. Jack pulled into a roadside garage. They knew no English and Jack in desperation motioned for the mechanic to accompany him in the van.

He soon reached the thumpity thump sound whereupon the mechanic exclaimed, 'Ah oui, je comprends.' He then motioned for them to go back to the garage where he drove the van on to his ramp. He made signs with his watch indicating they should return in an hour.

When they came back it was ready for them in the forecourt. The mechanic appeared and said it was the transmission, charging them a precious three hundred francs.

'Très bien... okay,' he volunteered with a big grin.

Thumpity-thump-thumpity-thump...

'Jack we should go back and demand back our three hundred francs. That was a waste of time and money.'

'No Gillian, our French is not good enough to take him on. He will only insist the part he put in was necessary and who are we to argue? I'm as mad as you but that fellow knows he will have us over a barrel. I have another idea. We will not stay at campsites for the next week. We can park overnight in lay-bys and fields. That way we'll recover most of our three hundred francs.'

Gillian did not want to argue so she agreed, on condition they make for a large English-speaking Volkswagen dealer and made sure he carried out a proper examination.

That evening they parked the camper van in a stubbled hayfield near Troyes, just off the N71, where the local farmer waved them into an out of the way corner. It was idyllic. The farmer had cut the hay and it was all rolled into large wheels which dotted the field like giant draughtsmen. The soft shadows created from each wheel by the setting sun gave a surreal setting, which Jack found unusually peaceful.

'Jack isn't this idyllic,' murmured Gillian as she looked out on the scene.

They laid out their table in the warm evening air and Gillian served up her first ever beef bourguignon which, washed down with a bottle of red Cahors, made for a memorable evening.

With the multicoloured sky for a backdrop Jack had to almost pinch himself to believe he was not at the pictures. They were at peace with the world and with wine inspired drowsiness Jack was looking forward to a good night's sleep.

'Jack, did you hear a sound?' Gillian's voice had an urgency which banished sleep.

'No Gillian I heard nothing. What was it like?'

'A sort of scratching,' whispered Gillian as if the wheels of hay had ears.

'Where?' said Jack wearily.

'Inside the van,' came the response.

'Would it be birds? On the roof. Their feet would scratch on the steel.'

'I don't think it came from the roof,' said Gillian defensively.

'Let's go back to sleep. I can't hear anything,' suggested Jack turning over.

'Jack, it's a mouse. Look at it, on the shelf in front of us,' said Gillian without hysteria, but not without a trace of alarm.

Jack carefully focused his eyes on the shelf. Sure enough there was a mouse standing on its hind legs examining the two humans with as much care as they were he. Suddenly he scampered off behind the fridge.

'My God Jack, what are we going to do? Imagine if that thing crawls over our faces in the dark,' and waxing stronger she said, 'and you sleep with your mouth open. Can you imagine?' said Gillian shivering at the thought.

Jack could not imagine. He had never been in a camper van before, so how could he know what to do about a live-in mouse? Still, he felt a positive response was necessary.

'We need a mouse trap,' he said firmly.

'What's the French for that?' said Gillian with natural female logic. 'Anyway,' she continued not waiting for an answer, and abandoning all logic, 'I could not bear to sleep here with a mouse. Even supposing I did, the thought of going to sleep with a trap going off and killing a poor little field mouse is not right. Could we not chase him out Jack?'

'And how do we do that?' said Jack fearing the worst.

'Take everything out of the van. Then he'll have no place to hide.'

'Gillian dearest we could spend all day at that, and still fail. Remember he went behind the fridge, which is a fixture.'

'Could we not empty the van and bang on the outside. The noise would frighten him out.'

Jack, without further comment, began to take everything out of the van and on to the cut meadow. When he eventually had taken everything moveable they had a large pile on the meadow. The only evidence of a mouse was its droppings.

'There's nothing else left to remove. I think he must be still inside,' said Jack.

'As I said, we have to open all the doors and bang hard, very hard,' said Gillian firmly to a unconvinced Jack.

They opened all the doors and, still in their night clothes, they began to bang on the side of the van with the flat of their hands. The noise was deafening. Their difficulty was they could not see if the noise drove the mouse out, nor could they appreciate the extent of the din they were creating on a calm summer's morning. The French farmer could though. He came running into his field to behold these two mad English people in their pyjamas engaged in what appeared to him to be an ancient ritual.

Jack saw him first waving his arms and shouting in French, '*Mon Dieu*, what is going on?' They both stopped the banging and tried to explain about the mouse, speaking loudly in the mistaken belief that the louder one speaks a foreign language the better it can be understood by non-speakers. The farmer looked at the pile on his field and was even more bewildered.

He raised his arms and eyebrows and said, *'Je ne comprends pas.'*

'I don't think he understands us, Jack. He thinks we are mad,' said Gillian.

'Mouse, what's the French for mouse?' hissed Jack urgently, 'if we could tell him that would be a help.'

'I don't know.'

'I know the word for rabbit, *lapin*, maybe if I called it a small rabbit and measured it with my hands he would understand.'

'Try it before he explodes,' cried Gillian.

'Monsieur… we have… *J'ai une petit lapin in la caravan.'* He staggered out the words, pointing at the van and opening out a three inch gap between his thumb and his forefinger as an indicator of size.

The farmer's eyes widened. He opened his mouth to say something then changed his mind. He nodded his head vigorously whilst saying *'oui, oui'* as he looked for the gate. Still waving he left the field.

'Jack, what if he has gone to get the police?'

'No, but just in case he misunderstood us we better fire the stuff back into the van and go. We can sort it out later.'

'What about the mouse? It may still be there. I don't fancy sleeping in the van tonight if we are not sure it's gone.'

'Okay Gillian,' said Jack unwilling to lose another night's sleep, 'we will drive as far as we can in the direction of Mont Blanc. We will get a cheap pension for tonight. No, no Gillian hear me out. We will find a suitable garage who will check out the cause of the noise and trap the mouse, if he is still there. Now how does that sound?'

'Fine Jack, but the cost?' said Gillian hesitatingly.

'Don't worry, Gillian. I had a few bob extra for emergencies.'

Jack drove as fast as he could until they reached a village near Mulhouse where they got a pension whose proprietor could speak English. He directed them to a garage who would do the work.

After a good night's sleep they went over to the garage. The owner came out with a mouse trap saying, 'Eet has keeled eet.'

Gillian looked sad on seeing the dead mouse. Jack just felt relieved.

Then he brought them over to the Volkswagen and said, 'Eet is the pneu, how you say eet, the tier.'

'The tyre,' said Jack.

'Oui, yez, eet take bigger tires. Them,' he said, pointing at the two front tyres, 'are *très grands* – how you say – big, *quinze*. I have got one *petit*, small, *quatorze*, and put eet on. There,' he said, pointing at the right hand tyre. 'The odder I have not got smaller but eet will be okay until you go to Angleterre... 'ome. The noise not *mal*... bad.' He smiled with pride at his command of English.

Jack asked him to repeat what he had said to the patron of the pension who in turn translated it for Jack. The two front tyres were too big, fifteen inch, and he had put on the only smaller, fourteen inch, one he had in stock. The noise would be less but that apart he could go as fast as he liked. He could get a second replacement when he got home. He also said the van had been in a crash but it had been very well welded. 'That bastard Percy, he knew that all along, and that's why it was so cheap.'

Then he asked the garageman what he owed him. He said, through his friend, he had the tyre in stock and it was obsolete and he did not want any payment. No amount of persuasion would make him change his mind. Finally he said that if they liked they could, when they got home, send him on some money. Jack was astounded but the Frenchman appeared pleased with what he had done so Jack thanked him warmly and they took their leave.

'They were two charming gentlemen. We were lucky we met them. I hate to think what that tyre cost. It would leave us short of money,' said Gillian.

Jack was puzzled. He had a feeling there was something odd about their generosity. It was unnatural, he thought to himself. Gillian was so pleased he kept his thoughts to himself.

Whatever their motivation, the van now gave half the thumping. He was relieved the problem had been diagnosed at last. Maybe after all they were wrong about the Continentals. Gillian was so enchanted by Courmayer she suggested they stop and have coffee in one of the expensive cafés overlooking the Alps. Jack managed to find a parking spot in the overcrowded car park and they walked up the steps to the café's panoramic verandah. All the tables were occupied except for one in the far corner, inside the glass door. To get there they had to tread their way carefully past the tightly packed tables. They were about halfway there when Jack noticed an elderly gentleman sitting alone at a table with his dog beside him, half blocking his passage. Just as he was stepping over the dog he bent down to give it a friendly pat. The dog, a black and white terrier of sorts, growled before making a lunge at Jack's proffered hand. He instinctively jumped back and crashed into the table behind him. In an effort to maintain balance he grabbed at the gentleman's table with his left hand. It collapsed under his weight, firing the elderly gentleman's cognac over the couple at the adjoining table. The table fell on top of the, by now, terrified dog which began to squeal in pain and fright. Amid shouts all round Gillian attempted to lean over the dog and give Jack a hand up. The dog, by now terrified, made to snap at Gillian's arm. She jumped back, lost her balance and toppled over on to Jack, leaving them both with their arms and legs waving amid total chaos in the restaurant.

The, by now, enraged elderly gentleman stood up, waved his arms and shouted in French, 'They have hurt my dog. How dare you. Imbeciles.'

This gave rise to a growing murmur of abuse at the crazy Englishman. Jack, by now recovering from the shock of events, did not understand a word. That did not stop him reading the hostility on the faces of the café's clientele. He reached down, pulled up Gillian and muttered to her, 'I don't think we are very popular here.'

Gillian, outraged at the reaction, hissed to Jack, 'But it's not our fault. It was that dog.'

Two waiters hurried over to restore order. They were followed by a dark-haired manager who, having heard a version of events from one of his customers, speaking in English very politely asked Jack and a protesting Gillian to accompany him to the door. He then asked them to leave, saying, as if it was a big favour, he would pay for the dog owner's spilled drink. Jack joined Gillian's outrage at the injustice of it all. Despite their protestations of innocence the manager was obdurate and stuck to his contention that it was better for them to leave.

'Look,' he said, pointing at his customers, 'you would not be happy here.'

'Christ, Gillian; how did I ever get myself into this land of dirty frogs?' Jack muttered viciously to Gillian when they were safely out of earshot.

'I don't know Jack dearest but this is Italy not France.'

The owner then followed them and politely expressed his regret. He explained the elderly gentleman was a retired local dignitary and a valued customer and was calling for their arrest. Gillian took it better than Jack. After all her fairytale had come true.

'Besides,' she said, 'there are plenty more cafés in the middle of the Alps. They found a campsite high up in one of the valleys with a view of Mont Blanc. There they could go for long walks. Gillian's enjoyment was so infectious that Jack was able to put the past behind him to fully enjoy the present.

Nevertheless, in light of the happenings on the outward journey, Jack was apprehensive about their return. It was uneventful, he even got used to the thumping of the wheel.

When they got home Jack decided to purchase a correct-sized tyre and change it himself. He would tackle Percy and his 'perfect mechanical order' claim. If nothing came out of his friend's offer to buy the van back he would simply sell it himself.

A couple of days after their return he jacked up the van and removed the tyre which to his surprise wasn't tubeless. As he pulled out the tube he felt something in it. It felt like a flat soft parcel. That's indeed what it was, with plastic wrapping. He ripped open the cover and found a number of small separate parcels all carefully sealed in opaque plastic wrappers. He opened one. To his astonishment it contained some £100 pound notes. When he had opened all the others he counted a total of £24,000.

Gillian, who had come into their garage in response to his call, gasped in amazement at the bundles of notes on the floor. Just then the phone rang. Gillian went in to answer it.

'It's Percival. He wants to talk to you. He says he has spoken to the previous owner who says he is willing to buy back the Volkswagen at the price you paid for it,' she said.

Jack's mind was elsewhere. Back in the garage near Mulhouse. No wonder the garageman was smiling so much. There must have been a parcel in the other tyre. He'll never sell a tyre at a better price.

'Jack, what will I tell Percival?'

He jerked himself back to his garage. 'What's that?' he asked. Gillian repeated the message from Percy. He thought for a moment and said, very deliberately, 'Tell him to shag off.'

Bougainvillea

Brett glanced at his rear mirror. There was nothing behind him on the highway, except slush and snow. He exhaled with relief, he had given them the slip, for now at least.

After the robbery he had taken Highway 395, then 88 when he saw the pursuing cop car. He had immediately jammed the Pontiac's accelerator into the floor which gained him some ground on his pursuers. As luck would have it he came to a bend where, just out of sight of the cops, he managed to pull off between a line of trucks into 89 and head for Highland Peak, not that he wanted to go into that unfamiliar territory. He just hoped the protesting horns of the truck would not alert the cops to his manoeuvre. They hadn't, so he could relax for a few minutes until he figured his next move. Highway 89 was steep and the combination of falling snow and slush signalled reduced speed. He reduced it further when he noticed the pristine white of the narrow mountain road ahead on his right.

Hell, he thought, *it can't be used much in this weather. If I take it slowly the snow should cover my tracks before the cops get up here.*

It seemed his best option, so he turned off the highway and started his slow climb up the winding road, taking care not to gouge out too deep a track in the snow. His spell in Folsom had taught him to be careful, but his stick-up of that store in Carson City was just plain careless; and shooting the guard in the leg wasn't clever. *Where the hell did he come from anyway? I cased that place pretty well and there wasn't a guard in sight*, thought Brett bitterly, as if he had been let down by the guard. Worse still the guard's appearance meant he could only grab a handful of bucks and run.

Jezz was I lucky they all stayed on the floor, he thought. *The roaring of the plugged guard musta delayed the chase.* Trouble was he then had to head south when he had intended to take the more familiar route to LA.

It seemed more of a track than a road, its edge so camouflaged by the snow that he was forced to drive on what he figured to be the centre of the road. Not the safest way on a road which was steep and twisting. As the Pontiac climbed the snow got thicker which made every bend dangerous. At one corner he almost skidded out of control when he came upon the red Chevy parked on the left hand edge of the road. Its zigzag skid marks were barely visible in the mounting covering of snow. He reversed and pulled his Pontiac behind the other car, just in case another one came down the hill. It was unlikely, thought Brett, but if a car came in the opposite direction he didn't want its passage to be blocked. He got out of his warm car. The freezing temperature nearly took his breath away. There was one person in the Chevy's driving seat, a white male slumped over the steering wheel. He seemed unconscious. Brett looked around to see what might have caused the swerve. Right on the bend there was a mound, under the cliff on the right hand side of the road. Brett scraped off some snow from it and, as he suspected, there was a large boulder underneath which had probably fallen down the cliff. The driver of the Chevy must have hit it, or maybe swerved to avoid it and skidded, leaving the front of the Chevy hanging over the edge of the road. The light wind caused the front of the car to rock slowly up and down. Each time it touched the ground some snow fell off the roof or bonnet. For Brett the car's red stood out against the snow like a gaping wound. Brett shivered again, as much to offset the hypnotic effects of the rocking car as against the cold. He looked over the edge hardly able to contain his violent shivering in the cold breeze. There was a ledge several hundred feet below him. Further down he could just make out, through the snow, trees and what looked like water; a river maybe? The guy in the car was either dead or unconscious. Brett didn't much care which as he wasn't about to go back and get help. He figured on the other hand if he was dead he might have some bucks on him, for which he would have no more use.

There was no way he was going to open the door of the Chevy and have it go over the edge, maybe even drag him with it. He first dug a couple of big rocks out of the snow on the side of the road and placed them on top of the boot of the Chevy. At least that stopped the rocking. Then he went back to the Pontiac, got a length of nylon rope out of its boot before carefully turning it and then reversing towards the Chevy. When he got about four feet from it he tied the rope to the rear of both cars. Now came the difficult part. He surveyed the two cars, satisfied himself that at worst the underneath part of the Chevy would get stuck on the edge and that any backward movement should prevent it from falling over the cliff.

He put the Pontiac into second gear and slowly, very slowly, took up the slack on the Chevy. It moved backwards with a scraping sound and then, to his surprise, came back cleanly on to the road. He leaped out, untied the rope and put it back into his boot. There was no point in leaving any evidence of his presence here. He opened the door of the Chevy and felt the side of the driver's neck for a pulse. There was none. *Dead as a door nail*, thought Brett, as he pulled him back from the steering wheel where he noticed a trickle of congealed blood coming out of his mouth, otherwise he was unmarked. *He musta had a heart attack*, thought Brett. He looked at the face of the dead man and then looked at himself in the mirror. *Jezz, if he hadn't got that moustache*, he thought, *he and I would look alike.*

Brett took everything out of the man's pockets and laid them on the passenger seat. He then took a briefcase from the back seat, removed the keys from the ignition and opened the Chevy's boot with one of the keys. It contained two chequered suitcases.

Musta been goin' on vacation, he mused. He then brought the dead man's belongings in to the warmth of his own car, noting with satisfaction that the tracks of the two cars were now almost covered by the swirling snow.

He sat down and began his examination of the belongings. The dead man's name was Craig Ryder. He was manager of a golf course in Sacramento. A letter about alimony indicated he was divorced. His briefcase contents included a passport with two airline tickets, one Dublin-London return, the other Frisco-London return. The departure date was in two days' time. There was about three hundred dollars in cash in the briefcase and two hundred and thirty four in his wallet.

Better than that goddamned hold up, thought Brett. Better still there was another two thousand dollars in American Express traveller's cheques in the suitcase. A quick run over a bundle of the letters and postcards showed he had befriended an Irish couple who had been inviting him over to Ireland for the last eight years. At last he was going, or rather, thought Brett, he had been going. There was no indication anywhere as to what he was doing seven or eight thousand feet up in the snow near Highland Peak.

He looked at his watch. It was thirty seven minutes since he had come across this accident. He'd better be going. Then it hit him like a flash. This guy, without his moustache, was a carbon copy of himself; not in every way, but enough. He could go to Ireland on his passport. He could easily get a false moustache in Frisco. These two hadn't seen Ryder for years. Even at that they had only met him at the golf club for an afternoon. Their image of him would not be that clear. If he studied the letters carefully and had a quick look at the golf club in daylight he'd have enough to get by on. He needed to get out, just in case the cops got a line on him. No way did he want to spend more time in the pen.

Once the decision was made he set about implementing it with gusto. Everything of his was put into the Pontiac. Then he set about the difficult task of taking off his clothes, undressing the corpse and dressing it with his own clothes. Halfway through he had to stop, his teeth were chattering so much. Then he remembered the Jack Daniels in the boot of the Chevy. He was careful not to take too many slugs. It did the job and he was able to continue, with the 'cross-dressing' as he referred to it in his own mind.

He then drove the Pontiac to the edge, with the body in it, taking care that none of Ryder's fingerprints were left on it. *Gotta be careful, Brett,* he said to himself. Ryder's clothes fitted him quite well; a little too big but not so as to cause attention.

Then came the most difficult part. How to get the Pontiac over the edge and not follow it himself in the Chevy. He got the Chevy on to the centre of the track and then drove the Pontiac so that it was facing the edge. Before he got out he put it into neutral then cautiously pushed it so that the two front wheels were at the very edge. Then he put it into 'drive' and got into his own, well not quite his own car, he thought. He started the Chevy and put it into first gear and pushed at the Pontiac whose exhaust creaked and groaned before it finally cleared and allowed the car to go over the edge. Brett cut the engine of the Chevy and leaped out to look over the edge. Just in time to see the Pontiac hit the ledge, bounce into the air before being flung out into the void. It disappeared from his sight towards the forest and the river. The silence appeared to last a long time before he heard a bang which was followed by an explosion and fire. It was as good as Brett could have wished. With any luck the body would be burned and the wreckage would not be seen for some time. He very carefully turned the Chevy around and drove back down the hill humming 'Whistle a happy tune' to himself. It was snowing heavily.

Dublin, Ireland – Two Days Later

The 737 touched down at Dublin Airport with a slight shudder, followed by the roar of the wind as the pilot raised the wing flaps. Brett's seat was by the window over the wing where the noise was greatest. He wasn't normally apprehensive about anything but the sudden combined din from the air and the reverse thrust generated a feeling of unease about the whole escapade. He kept telling himself he would be able to carry it off. Hadn't he learned the contents of the letters almost by heart? Among the tapes in the Chevy he had come across one where Ryder was talking to a group about grasses for greens. His accent was not unlike his own so he had practised until he felt they were almost the same, or should be to a European. It wasn't as if he didn't know how the other half lived. He did. Had he not spent two years studying medicine before he was thrown out. His old man had said to him 'Brett, you know what can happen to you? You could just become a drifter, if you are not careful.' Of course he was only half right. He had drifted right over the brink. He picked up his hand baggage and followed the stream of passengers off the plane.

Kathy Shanaghan was in the airport terminal also feeling apprehensive. They had only met Chris Ryder for about six hours in Sacramento Country Club eight years ago. She and Jack had called in on chance to see if they could play a game of golf. The guy in the office had told them the course was closed for a competition later in the day. Jack was disappointed; he had been told by a friend to make sure to play that course.

Craig had seen them wandering around and on hearing their Irish accents he came over and asked them if they had a problem. When they explained what had happened at the office he said, 'I've got to inspect the course to see if it is okay for the competition. Why don't we make it a threesome over the eighteen holes?'

It turned out his great grandfather had emigrated from Cork in the last century and he was curious to learn more about Ireland. Then to cap it all he insisted in standing them lunch in the clubhouse after the game. He would take nothing in return, other than to ask them to send a postcard from Ireland.

When they admired the bougainvillea in front of the clubhouse he took a cutting and had it specially vacuum wrapped for planting on their return to Ireland. Kathy took a picture from the balcony of Jack and Craig examining the bush in full flower. It was that photo which they used to monitor the progress of their own plant. It, as much as anything else, had helped to give continuity to their relationship. Kathy felt the least she should do was to invite Craig to stay with them in Dublin. She wrote that he could inspect their bougainvillea. Originally he was going to stay for a week, but he had rung, just before he left the States, to say that he had distant relatives in Hamburg who were insisting he visit them. He was very apologetic about the last minute change of course. Kathy was not too disappointed particularly as she and Jack had been wondering what to do with him for the week after he had mentioned his psoriasis caused him to wear gloves and that he could not play golf.

It was probably just as well he's going to Hamburg, thought Kathy, feeling a little guilty at the very thought. It was the moustache that first attracted her attention as he came out into the arrivals hall, plus the fact that he was staring at her, unsure himself, apparently waiting for a sign of recognition from her.

'Craig, Craig Ryder, it is you, is it not?'

'Why Mrs Shanaghan, you haven't changed a bit,' said a relieved Brett, holding out his gloved hand.

'Kathy to you, Craig. Jack sends his regards. He is on a business trip to Manchester. But he'll be back tonight. His software business has literally boomed over the past five years. So much so we moved house shortly after we came back from the States, to a Georgian place in its own grounds near Dublin.'

'I hope I am not causing you and Jack any trouble.'

'Not in the least. We have this big house and the two children, adults now really, have left home. So we have buckets of room, Craig.'

'I sure am lookin' forward to meeting Jack. How is his golf?'

'Not great. He is too busy working. The business is growing like the new time. Sorry to hear about your hands.'

'That's why I wear these gloves. Don't worry it's not contagious or anything like that; more of a nuisance. The doc said it is not big deal, just to keep them away from moisture.'

He followed Kathy to the car park where she stopped at a large new silver Mercedes. The driver hopped out and took his suitcase. Brett was impressed. *These people must have loads of dough*, he thought to himself.

When they drove up the winding drive and over the river he was even more impressed. The house was old and big. The front was covered in a Russian vine or some similar type climber. It looked to Brett like one of those houses out of a Hollywood film set. His bedroom overlooked the river which flowed through a field in which some horses were grazing.

Having washed and shaved he came down the old wooden staircase into the wide hallway where Kathy was waiting to bring him around the house and grounds. Then she showed him the bougainvillea. Brett did his best to congratulate them on their successful transplantation. He just hoped he got it right.

'It's Jack's pride and joy. You have no idea how he fussed when we had to transfer it, as a small scrub, from our old garden to here. It's a great topic of conversation, everyone is amazed at how he got a cutting from Sacramento to grow in Ireland. We have a special temperature-controlled greenhouse here with a sliding roof. He keeps referring to that photo, you know, the one with you and he looking at your one in Sacramento all those years ago. I'll have to take another one of the two of you looking at this, a sort of father and son; the trees I mean,' said Kathy laughing.

Some doll, thought Brett, *she sure has aged very well from those pictures of eight years ago.*

That evening Jack came into the sitting room like a whirlwind. 'Craig, it's great to see you. You look younger, fitter too, since we last met.'

'And you too Jack. I am very grateful to you both for your kind invitation.'

'Think nothing of it. We have never forgotten your kindness. I was delighted to tell Gerry I got to play the golf club, and to prove it I had that slip from your fantastic bougainvillea. You know, Gerry even remembered seeing it in front of the clubhouse.'

Jack was pleased with himself. Not as much as Brett who felt he could relax a bit more now that he had passed his most feared test.

Jack and Kathy had dinner with him in the dining room, a room as big as a barn to Brett. They even lit a log fire in his honour. After an alcoholic meal they adjourned to the study where Jack talked a lot about his business. Brett was interested to learn he was making a pile of dough.

'Craig, have you got any Irish punts, you know Irish money?

'Not yet Jack, I have dollars and traveller's cheque.'

'Look Craig, you mentioned getting a present for that German relation of yours. I'll get you some punts.'

Brett's loud and insincere protests were ignored as Jack leaped up and practically fell into the fireplace. He made for one of the paintings on the wall with Brett attempting to keep him upright. The painting swung back to reveal a wall safe. Jack dialled a code, SJ 547. Brett missed the last number, but that would not prove a problem. He hadn't been idle in the slammer with Georgie, the safer, as his cell mate. Brett wasn't going to miss this golden opportunity.

Jack got out a bundle of notes and pealed off several for Brett. 'There you are Craig, that will save you going to the bank. Anyway, the lazy bastards don't open until ten in the morning. You and Kathy can go straight to the shops in the morning. I am sorry I will be tied up all day. But don't worry I'll be free the day after tomorrow to take you on a trip,' he said in a thick voice as he closed over the safe. Brett was glad he had held back on the liquor.

They talked, or rather Jack rambled on, for a short while before they left for bed. Brett by now was tired, though not so tired as to be unable to decide on a plan of action. He had seen enough in the wall safe for that.

The next morning was sunny. Brett had got up early, supposedly to look at the river but really to get a picture in his mind of the overall early morning layout, including where the cars were garaged and how the servant gained access to the house. They had one girl who appeared to do everything. The driver, he learned, only came on request.

'Craig, come on over and have a look at the bougainvillea. We can slide the roof back for a few minutes.' Jack had caught up with him as he came around to the front of the house. He led him round to the side, which faced south, where they had a large aluminium framed greenhouse. They went in and Jack demonstrated the mechanics of sliding back the roof before proudly showing him the plant. Unfortunately it was not in flower and really did not impress Brett. He tried to sound as enthusiastic as he had the day before.

'In mid-summer it is nearly as good as yours.'

'I guess it will not get as big as ours,' offered Brett guessing.

'Maybe,' conceded Jack. 'There won't be one as unique as this in Ireland though. I have christened it "Sacra Boug". No one believes it started from a cutting at your club,' said Jack proudly. 'Before you go we must get Kathy to take a photo of us here. You know, like the one she took eight years ago in Sacramento. 'However,' he said, looking at his watch, 'that will have to wait. I must run if I am not to be late for this appointment.'

Jack made his apologies and tore off down the drive in a large car whose make Brett did not recognise. Jack was back for dinner that evening full of apologies for not being around. 'I am sorry Craig about this, especially as your visit is foreshortened.'

'Yeah, I've gotta go and visit these relatives in Hamburg, Jack. Once they heard I was comin' to Europe they insisted I go.' Brett did not want to stay too long, just in case his cover was blown. If Craig's body was discovered, and they cottoned on to the switch, it could lead to here. He had decided what he was going to do.

The dinner that night was early, due to the maid having the rest of the evening off. She wanted to get away early to visit her mother. Apparently she had the following day off. That suited Brett's plan. There would only be the three of them in the house that night.

They finished dinner early which left more time for drinking. Brett was not too taken with the wine and stuck to cans of Bud. That way he could drink less. He made sure to open more cans of Bud than he was drinking. Every time he went to the john he emptied his glass. He figured the more they drank the heavier they would sleep. That would make it easier for him to get at the safe.

Round about midnight the two Shanaghans staggered off to their bed. Brett packed his bag and checked the room to make sure he had left nothing lying around. Around three he crept downstairs. His descent was not entirely silent. He hadn't noticed it during the day but every second goddamned stair creaked. He waited at the bottom to see if there was any reaction from the Shanaghans' bedroom. There appeared to be none, so he continued towards the study.

He stuck the small torch in his mouth, focused the light on the safe and kept tapping out the code, all the time varying the last number. It wasn't as easy as he had thought. He had to get the numbers in immediate sequence. If he didn't, the thing locked which meant he had to start from scratch. While Georgie had been a good mentor it still took him time before he got it open. He was not disappointed. It was full of money and jewellery. He stuck his hand in and grabbed some of the boxes. That was when all hell broke loose. An alarm bell started to ring.

'Christ that was not on Georgie's list,' muttered Brett to himself. Then he heard a roar from upstairs. It was Jack, with Kathy urging him not to go downstairs.

'For God's sake Jack ring the guards,' Brett heard her cry.

Jack had already started for the stairs. Brett had just time to grab one of the brass fire irons and step behind the door before Jack charged into the room. He didn't know what hit him. He just crumpled down to the floor. There was another rush of feet and creaks on the stairs before Kathy came running into the study after her husband. She nearly fell over him in the dark. If anything Brett's blow with the fire iron was harder. He waited a few moments. The sound of the alarm was confined to the house. Brett wondered if it was linked to the cops.

He examined the safe again, found the lead and disconnected the current. The alarm stopped. The silence was deafening. Brett carried out another examination of the safe's alarm. It was an older type which was not connected to the outside. Satisfied that the sound was more or less confined to the house he moved over to the two Shanaghans sprawled on the floor and looked for a pulse. There were none because they were both dead. *Pity,* thought Brett, *but it will make things simpler.*

He dragged the bodies, one by one, down to the basement where they stored their peat. He then cleared a space in the middle of the pile of peat, put the bodies there and threw the bits of peat over them, taking care to have it look the same as when he had started. Satisfied they would not be seen he went upstairs and cleaned out the safe. He calculated there was maybe thirty thousand dollars equivalent in cash. *Add the value of the sparklers and I'm winning – so far*, thought Brett.

He then went through the house to make sure there was nothing whatsoever left which would break his cover. He picked up all the photos the Shanaghans had of Ryder. Prison had made him a good bedmaker so he made them up, hoping to give the impression they had not been slept in, leading people to think they had gone somewhere else for the night. He needed time, just a couple of days, before the bodies were discovered.

Kathy's car was in the garage. He put his cases, which now included the safe's contents, in the boot, drove out of the yard on to the drive and over the bridge. In the States the gates would have been locked in a spread like this, here they were open. That was a lucky break as he had overlooked that little item. The sun had not risen but he thought it prudent to drive the car, without lights, along the little road until he came to the main highway. There he put on his side lights. Later on with still no traffic he switched on his dipped headlights. When he saw the lights of a car coming against him in the distance he put on his full headlights and kept them on to the annoyance of the other driver. At least he was not going to recognise his car or himself, thought Brett grimly.

Soon he got to the airport, parked the car and proceeded to the terminal building where he bought a ticket for Hamburg in Craig's name at one airline desk. Then he purchased a return ticket for London from another airline desk, around the corner from the first, under an assumed name. He could do that because there was no passport control between Ireland and England.

Brett was glad the plane to London was almost full which meant he would blend in with the crowd. In London Airport he went from Terminal One to Terminal Three. He went to the departure point and noted the ticket was checked for destination but the passport was not examined. Satisfied, he went to the ticket desk where he purchased a standby seat under an assumed name. He then went into the departure lounge and on to the passport control where his portrait was compared. This he figured was the only weakness in his plan. He had to use Ryder's passport who by now could be wanted by the Irish cops. He could only hope he had bought enough time. The key was the maid, and she had the day off. The half bored clerk waved him through.

He managed to get a couple of empty seats on the plane which allowed him to stretch out and go to sleep. Before he did so he went over everything. For once he felt luck was on his side. At New York he took a standby to the first city that became available giving a false name. It was Albuquerque. When he got there he got another ticket, under another assumed name, to LA. That he figured covered his tracks. His contacts there told him they had heard nothing about his demise nor about any car crash in Highland Peak. Later he learned the area had suffered snow storms. He had made it.

Dublin, Ireland – Three Weeks Later

Inspector Pat Donovan was pissed off. Murder cases were always troublesome. High profile affairs with the public, meaning the media, looking for instant results. When the victims were wealthy, and politically well connected, then the pressure for results became intense. They were now three unsatisfactory weeks into this one.

Pat had never come across a case quite like it. They had a good suspect, a cast iron one according to the media, who had disappeared. A check with the Sacramento police revealed a profile of anything but a robber or murderer. Craig Ryder had left San Francisco for Ireland to visit the Shanaghans and by all accounts was a very nice guy. The maid had said he was a lovely man. Superintendent Paul King, Donovan's boss, had gone over the evidence again and again. Paul was as good a guard as you could get but it was tiresome repeatedly going over the same details without getting any nearer to a conviction. Essentially the guy had been in the house the night of the killings and had booked a flight to Hamburg that morning and disappeared.

'Look Pat I am in trouble if we do not find the killer. It may be an Interpol case now but the Minister for Justice wants us to come up with something. An American cannot disappear just like that. People keep telling me that it was too professional, even down to hiding the bodies in the coal.'

'Turf,' corrected Pat. 'But Super, the FBI are under pressure too.'

'Can you think of anything we have overlooked, or should look into, Pat?'

Pat was flattered, but Paul King knew his man.

'I really can't Paul. I have, like yourself, gone over this ad infinitum. I am convinced, no matter what the Americans say, this guy was a professional. No one kills two people, cold bloodedly, in those circumstances without being a hardened criminal. Then there is the question of psoriasis and no fingerprints. We have nothing tangible to go on. I have a gut feeling that somewhere there are two guys involved in this. The Shanaghans knew Ryder. We have got that photograph of him with Jack Shanaghan near that tree in Sacramento, you know the one we got from Jack's brother. There is mention made of that photograph in a letter, one with Jack Shanaghan and Ryder looking at a plant, similar to the one in the greenhouse. Everyone in that golf club says Ryder was a lovely man, a workaholic. The manager of the club even went so far as to say he wouldn't hurt a fly. It doesn't add up Paul.

'By the way, I did come across a small camera on top of a wardrobe in the bedroom overlooking the greenhouse. There were ten photographs taken, with sixteen to go. I sent them off to be developed. You never know what they will bring out.' He then looked over and saw his assistant Joe Tully striding towards them. 'That's quick, I see Joe coming over with the prints in his hand.'

'It would be a godsend if we can get a lead from them,' said Paul King feelingly.

Pat took the photos from the outstretched hand of a panting Garda Joe Tully.

'Good man Joe, you have made enlarged prints.'

He knew from the look on Tully's face they had got something at last. It was the last photo taken on the half finished roll that mattered. It had been described in one of the letters except that now Ryder and Jack Shanaghan were looking at the bougainvillea in the greenhouse in Dublin. Obviously Mrs Shanaghan had taken it from above when the greenhouse roof had been withdrawn and placed the camera on top of the wardrobe. Whilst her husband's face was fully visible Craig Ryder was standing sideways with most of his back to the photographer. It was well taken with perfect depth of focus. However, only a little over half Ryder's face was visible.

'Take a look at that, Super, while I go and get the other one,' said Pat taking off.

When he returned he held out the other to Paul who put them side by side.

'Looks like the same guy all right. He has gained a few pounds. Here, you compare them Pat.'

Pat held up the two photos and examined them very slowly, so much so that Paul King was forced to ask, 'Well?'

'It's difficult to compare them, I mean with Ryder side-faced in the second one. I wonder if it is possible to recreate that picture of Ryder so as to see him front-faced? That is my first point. The second is that in the earlier photograph Ryder was definitely a guy who played a lot of golf. Are you a golfer Paul?' and when he saw Tully, still within hearing, he said, 'er, I mean Super.'

'No, why?'

'We know from the police in Sacramento that Ryder was a keen golfer. He was amateur champion of the State or something like that. Look at his right shoulder in the first photo. The muscle on the right hand side of his back is larger than on the left, a sort of pronounced bulge. That comes from playing an awful lot of golf, whereas in the latest picture both his shoulders look the same, slimmer if anything.'

'So?'

'Ryder in the second photograph was not playing much, if any, golf.'

'The psoriasis prevented him.'

'Not quite. Remember they had no knowledge of that in the Sacramento. He did play in a big competition a few weeks before he left.'

'Are you saying this is not Ryder?'

'I don't know, Paul,' Tully was gone, 'but it's about all we can go on.'

'I'll get a friend of mine to see what he can do. If he can give us a reconstructed head-on picture with, and without, the moustache we can send it to the FBI and see what they come up with.'

'Pat, you have made my day. At least now we have something to go on.' He took off at a rate of knots with a definite spring in his step. Pat looked after him thinking that his promotional prospects could rest on Joe Tully's photographs. At least it's preferable to being knifed or shot by some criminal or other.

Superintendent Paul King came back a few minutes later looking pleased. 'I spoke to Frank, he says it will be very difficult, though not impossible. He said I must have seen *Gorki Park*, you know that film where they recreated a face from a skull.'

'I hope they succeed Paul, as I have a feeling my hunch is right.'

It took two days before Frank came back to Superintendent Paul King.

'If you weren't a good friend Paul you would not have got these,' he said as he placed six photos on his desk. 'It was quite a challenge, but at least we know it is possible; only after working over twenty hours in the last forty-eight. You will see how we got from about two-thirds to about nine-tenths, which should be enough.'

Paul called Pat into his office. They both scrutinised the photos carefully. Pat was the first to speak.

'Pat, if this bastard is caught you will be the one responsible. Clearly they are two different people; very alike, yes with moustaches.'

'The guy who committed the murders, he must have a record, I'm sure of that,' said Paul triumphantly.

'Assuming he has, the FBI will identify him. After that it's only a question of time.'

'He doesn't know it yet but I have a feeling he will learn to hate bougainvilleas.'

'That's where the credit should go, Paul,' said Pat smiling, 'to Detective Bougainvilleas.'

Cajun Country

Maison Du Cajun Boucherie

HIWAY 96 WEST OF ST. MARTINVILLE

ST. MARTINVILLE, LOUISIANA

French political influence in the United States may have ended with the Louisiana Purchase, but their traditions, language and cooking continued with the Acacias, or Cajuns, who, in 1775, were exiled by the British from their homes in Nova Scotia. They eventually settled in the swamps and bayous in the southern parts of the state.

A friendly native of Lafayette told us about the Cajun restaurant, warning that on a Friday night its popularity was such that it would fill up very quickly. He was right. The car park was almost full when we got there at a quarter past eight. The restaurant had been an old colonial-type house with low beamed ceilings, the original rough cut wooden beams carefully preserved. Two large original ground floor rooms had been opened up giving an impression of spaciousness. A portion of the dividing wall between the rooms had been retained which lent a degree of privacy to both. In a word, the place had character.

In spite of its size there only four tables left; one, set for two, was allotted to us. A quarter of an hour after our arrival there was a small queue at the receptionist's desk. An empty table to our right, set for nine persons, stuck out like a sore thumb. Sited in the centre, between the two rooms it caused the scurrying waiters to steer around it with toreador adroitness. After all New Iberia was just down the road.

The queue was growing, its original members staring grimly at the empty table with its inviting white linen tablecloth topped by sparkling cut glass and silver. It was evident their patience was being stretched to the full. Gradually mutual deprivation generated *bonhomie* amongst those in the queue who, up to then, had been complete strangers, to such a degree that they began gesticulating in unison at the empty table and pointing to the grandfather clock against wall. The counter gestures of the head waiter made it clear he was not releasing it. We figured the table must have been reserved by a very important customer to engender such loyalty.

We were well into our prawn and chicken gumbos for one and crawfish etouffée for the other, our hearts hardened against hurrying the consumption of such splendid food, when they came through in single file, closely observed by disappointed queuers and curious diners.

The unusual procession was headed by a thin man of low stature, in his late thirties, carrying, rather clutching, a black bricfcase to his chest, as if his life depended on it. After him came a native American Indian woman of dark good looks, marginally overweight, whose expression of serenity elevated her description to beautiful.

The man behind her, also a native American and obviously her husband, looked like a plump Charlie Chaplin. He seemed especially pleased with himself, and perfectly relaxed. There followed a woman in her mid-thirties, a brunette who looked as if she was anorexic, and decidedly unrelaxed. The next, a lady was a total contrast. A ravishing blonde in her thirties who walked in the sure knowledge most eyes were fixed on her. Her yellow and black silk frock looked as if she had been poured into it, forgetting to call 'halt'. The combination of figure and dress held every eye in the restaurant, for different Gallic reasons. After her came the quintessential salesman, or at least he looked the part, dressed in a too-blue suit with a cream shirt and a courageously, well foolhardy by some standards, red and purple tie.

The three men who brought up the rear were impressive, each in their own way. The first in his early forties was arrestingly handsome. He sported a tanned face, a head of fair hair slightly tinged with grey. He walked with an almost imperceptible stoop which marred an air of quiet authority. A patrician perhaps? The next, in his early fifties, tall and detached was an intellectual lookalike for the playwright Arthur Miller. Somehow he looked out of place. Last came the oldest of the group. In his early sixties, he was a throwback to the old pioneering days, dressed in a dark suit with a fancy waistcoat and a stetson over his leathery face.

The patrician stopped behind the seat at the head of the table which immediately established the pecking order. He then unobtrusively arranged the seating order, placing the native American to his left, his wife to his right. He motioned the salesman, the blonde and the Miller lookalike to his right. On his left there was briefcase, the anorexic and the rancher type.

When they were all seated hovering waiters took orders for drinks which, when they arrived, displayed a diversity of choices, running through wine, beer, gin and tonic, bourbon, and iced water for the native American and the patrician.

The salesman appeared to be the warm-up act. He amused the rest to outright laughter with his patter, while they chose from the menu. He failed with two, briefcase who was absorbed in extracting documents whilst anorexic's jerky body movements betrayed her dissociation with the rest. We could feel the tension emanating from them.

The non-native Americans were noticeably deferential to the patrician who, when he interrupted their conversation, broke off and gave him their full attention, especially when he said, in a voice loud enough for us to hear, 'Let's hear that proposition of yours, Jake.' He was addressing briefcase, the name 'Jake' certainly didn't fit him, while he looked at the native American with a broad smile.

Briefcase pulled out one of his documents and began reading in a monotone which was inaudible to us. Most of the others listened attentively and it struck us that the meal was built around whatever he was saying.

When he finished, the patrician again in his booming tone said to the native American, 'There you are, sir, you all can check what's on offer.'

The latter casually took up the paper, read it and then, all the while smiling, appeared to ask some questions. We heard him say something about his 'ancestors' and 'right of passage' causing the patrician's expression to alter, with a faint tightening of the lips, before he boomed out again, as if the other was deaf, 'Payment is guaranteed over twenty years, more than its projected life; with built-in provision for inflation.'

The native American looked dubious, saying something about 'Indian law' and 'trust'. Briefcase and the patrician locked eyes for an instant, with a mixture of fear and contempt in the former's expression. Both began to speak at once. We could only hear the patrician, whose comment drowned the others as he stated, 'No, it's not like that at all.'

Anorexic, looking even more unhappy, was furtively twining her fingers whilst whispering to briefcase. She ignored, or chose not to see, the patrician's look of disapproval. Briefcase was shuffling his papers like a demented three card trickster. Patrician, like the true professional he now appeared to us, was nodding his head for the waiter to serve the food. He knew when to withdraw.

We were spinning out our dessert, still trying to figure what exactly was going on. Immediately the dishes arrived, prawn and chicken gumbos, stewed greens with ham soup, crawfish etouffée, prawn jambalaya, trout acacia and the distinctive blackened cajun fish. The wines we had heard the patrician ordering earlier were a 1988 Meursault Montaine and a Robert Modavi Reserve Cabernet

Sauvignon. The pioneer opted for a Bud. Polite conversation seemed to flow right through the meal, until the dessert, which was confined to pecan pie and cajun bread pudding.

A more interesting scenario was unfolding further down the table. Arthur Miller, who had been most attentive during the serious conversation, was now quietly hitting it off with the blonde. Glances lingered that much longer, as did hand contact when passing condiments up or down. From our angle, his left hand appeared to stray fleetingly in the direction of her knee, giving rise to no noticeable objection. The others were too preoccupied with the trivia of polite conversation to notice anything. The salesman was doing his best, but the native Americans were the only two who seemed to be enjoying his jokes. In reality, the dinner had gone flat for the hosts. The patrician was as polished as ever, but, for us as onlookers, a brittleness had crept into his demeanour. Briefcase had shot all his bolts with his strained face beginning to match his wife's. The rancher was exuding uncertain joviality, leading us to conclude he was getting only the vibes, but not the substance of the discussion. At least we could relate to him on that.

By the time their coffee came, we were nurturing our third. The disjointed conversation heralded an end to their session. The patrician gave the invisible signal and they rose in unison, apart from the two native Americans who continued to look as urbane as ever, but noticeably taken by surprise at the sudden end to their evening. They walked towards the reception and the exit, talking softly to one another. Except for the patrician who, having regained his composure, was the personification of graciousness to his guests. A true professional who, we figured, would live to fight another day. We were left frustrated, as clearly a drama had taken place before our very eyes, about what though ?

Just as the native American's wife reached the cashier she stopped, turned and pointed back at their table. As they made their way back we could see a handbag under her chair. As they came level with us he glanced over in our direction; there was a distinct twinkle in his eye as he said to his wife, 'Those guys think we can still trade our heritage for glass beads an' fish hooks. That all died at Wounded Knee.' He knew we had been eavesdropping, that was for sure.

By then the restaurant was almost empty. The last of the queue to be seated were determined to take their time. I guess by the management's standards we had far outstayed our stay. Yet we would argue it was far more interesting than anything the motel TV could have thrown up.

It was clear the cashier was not going to tolerate the procrastinations of the rest of the diners for much longer. His day had probably been a lot worse day than theirs. He rattled money and drawers in his desk as a clear signal to all concerned that closing time was nigh.

Maybe he could help. So we enquired.

'Whall,' he drawled, 'that thar Indian fella is chief of one of the tribes hereabouts, the Tunica I guess they are called. They are sittin' on a mighty pile o' natural gas – is that what you'all call it in Europe?' He had done his homework on my Visa.

I nodded, 'Gas, not gasoline?' I enquired.

'Yep gas. Anyways their reservation goes clear round some land those others purchased. Their land is full o' gas but there is no way they can git it out if tha' there injun doesn't give his say so.'

'There was a right o' way under the old agreement with the tribe, but it only applied to cattle an' agriculture produce. It went to law but that did no good, seein' as the court upheld the injun's rights. You'all heard o' a right o' way?'

We nodded, not wishing to interrupt, lest he stop.

'I guess they fouled up. Some folks do say it was their attorneys. You'all saw that skinny guy with the black briefcase, Jake Harvey he calls himself, and his wife. She's as skinny as a polecat. Whall they are the attorneys for Mr Deveraux's company an' folks say they boobed, an' Mr Deveraux is in danger o' goin' bust.'

Emboldened by his apparent desire to tell us all we asked, 'And who are the others there?'

'Whall, let me see now. The old guy is a partner o' Mr Deveraux's, a rancher who owns land that they are surveying beside the reservation. The joker in the pack, whall he was gonna sell the gas hereabouts. The purty one in the dress, she's Mrs Deveraux, that's to say the third. The other guy with the spectacles is a friend o' the injuns who is a Professor o' Law somewhere close by. He is, I'm told some sort o' an adviser to the injun. Though I fancy he was workin' hard for himself tonight,' he said with a leer.

Poor Deveraux, he got two arrows here tonight in exchange for an excellent meal.

Thanks for Nothing

The bitter cold from the slanting sleet, blown up the Liffey from the sea, caught Bob unawares as he stepped out of the warmth of the Clarence Hotel on to a whitening Wellington Quay. Turning up the collar of his crombie, he crossed the deserted road and made his way up river, thankful the icy wind was on his back.

Still, Bob reflected, the evening had gone well, in so far as he had left two very contented English customers behind him in the hotel. It was obvious they were impressed with the meal, particularly the lobster thermidor and the ballotine of duck. The managing director confessed the Sancerre Domaine Henri Bourgeois was the best Sancerre he had ever tasted, whilst Bob had to smile at his expression when Claud, good old reliable Claud, produced an eight-year-old bottle of red, a Chateau Margaux 1947.

'I've read about this wine, though I never thought I would actually get to taste it,' he had said, obviously impressed.

Their order for barley, at two hundred tons, was bigger than Bob had expected; moreover, they promised to return and explore the possibility of selling on his malting barley to a group of overseas companies in which they had a share.

'You'll put us up in the Clarence of course old boy. We might even make a weekend of it to see more of Dublin. We hardly saw anything this trip, excepting that fantastic Sancerre.'

If the truth were known Bob was not a great one on wine. He had buttonholed Claud, the head waiter, before the meal and told him to spare no expense on the wine. While seven pounds ten shillings wasn't cheap, Bob was glad it had helped to swing the deal.

God, it was a bloody cold night to have left the Minx as far down as Merchants Quay, he thought, pulling his overcoat closer around his body. His balled fists were plunged deep into his pockets, as if that would make him warmer. The '55 Hillman Minx was his pride and joy, so much so he had parked it up the street where the road was wider and there would be less chance of it being damaged.

The cobbled street glistened with half-melting sleet, uncertain whether to turn completely white or revert to all black. He looked over the wall into the Liffey. It looked dark, cold and unusually high. The latter probably due to a spring tide. Increasing volumes of pellets of white sleet dying in the surface of the river caused him to shiver violently. It was then he noticed the black hat floating on the surface of the river. *What's that pale thing behind it?* he asked himself, hoping his initial guess was wrong. *Christ Almighty it is a face. A face?* There it was again. This time it came within the outer limits of light from the nearby solitary wrought iron street lamp. The face appeared to have a pair of glasses which reflected the weak light from the lamp.

Bob felt a rush of adrenalin surge through him. Before he realised what he had done he had torn off his coat, jacket and shoes and dived into the freezing Liffey waters. He used his competitive swimming experience to dive far out from the granite wall into the river and near the silent face in the water. There he encountered two surprises; the first that he was actually in the icy water at all; the second when the figure in the water started struggling to get away from him all the while shouting 'No, no, no, leave me be.' This was accompanied by thrashing about and a blow to Bob's throat.

'Jesus fella, I'm only tryin' to save you from drownin',' gasped Bob, through a mouthful of vile river water.

While he wasn't as fit as in his lifeguarding days he was confident he could tackle him. The trained grips, coupled by a couple of immersions worked, after which he gradually dragged him to the nearest steel ladder attached to the quayside wall.

Aidan realised he wasn't going to free himself from his rescuer. An unfit fifty-one, a poor swimmer, half-drowned by this ignorant bastard, he knew struggle was useless. So, he merely brooded about what ill luck produced this interfering moron who was frustrating the work of Anna Livia.

There hadn't been a sinner around when he had left Mulligan's after a few pints. He had walked to Merchants Quay and lowered himself into the water, wearing his black crombie coat and a wide-brimmed black hat. He had even put some lead into his pockets. You would think at that hour on a Tuesday night in February, with near freezing sleet, no one would be about. Hadn't he made a reconnaissance two weeks ago to find the place was deserted? Why couldn't this meddling idiot leave him alone? Better for both of them, he thought grimly. Leaving this infernal world, with that crowd of over ambitious insurance creeps, was to be his last great pleasure. Now denied by this bollocks.

Bob reached the steel ladder and managed to get a fireman's grip on his by now semi-conscious man and, gasping with the effort, he levered him up the ladder, cold rung by cold rung. At least a high tide made for less rungs. His numb hands would never have made it to the top if the tide had been out.

Fortunately Aidan, now only half-conscious, had no resistance left. His tangled mind told him it would be useless anyway as this fellow would half drown him to complete his good deed. Bob just about managed to heave his burden, fortunately a person of slight build, over the parapet, without injury. His lungs were fit to burst and his hands were numb as he struggled over the granite parapet, toppling down beside the motionless figure on the white footpath.

Having got some air into his lungs, he gasped, 'Now matie, I'm gonna give you artificial respiration, so remember, take it easy.'

Bob staggered to his feet and turned the man over on to his back before he placed his lips against those of the unconscious man's. He blew as hard as he could. Nothing happened for a minute or so. Then a trickle of water came out of the side of the man's mouth before he began to cough and splutter. This was followed by another trickle of water.

Aidan's first feeling, as he regained consciousness, was one of total revulsion at this bastard's lips on his. Dear God, what did he do the deserve this?

'For Christ's sake stop it. You're making me ill,' eventually rasped Aidan. He realised he hadn't taken in that much water. With revulsion came sufficient energy to push Bob away.

'So you're as right as rain now, matie. That's a good sign. You'll live, but we'd better put something warm on you,' said Bob, picking up his overcoat from the ground. He passed it over to a recumbent Aidan whose face looked pinched with cold and frustration. Somehow the toothbrush moustache seemed to add to his misery, thought Bob.

'Here, let me give you a hand up, matie, you're shiverin'.'

Before Aidan could respond he had grabbed his right hand, pulled him upright and had placed coat around his unreceptive shoulders.

'My name by the way is Bob, Bob Ryan, what's yours, matie?'

'It's certainly not matie,' said Aidan, in as cold a tone as he could muster through the chatter of his teeth. 'Aidan McCann to you. I would like to remind you I was not in distress. Did you hear me call? You did not.' He answered his own question before Bob could reply.

'From your perch, life maybe fine for you, but it's up to me, me alone, to decide what it is for me; to act accordingly without interference from the likes of you. Why couldn't you mind your own damn business?' Aidan asked with uncontrolled malevolence in his expression, his words emerging as cold as the surrounding pellets of sleet.

Bob found it hard to believe his ears.

'You can't be serious, ma... er, Aidan. After all life isn't that bad. Sure, we all have our ups and downs, but that doesn't mean we throw ourselves off the nearest river bank to end it all. Think of all the poverty and misery there is a stone's throw away from here, over in the Coombe for instance. Should they be filling the Liffey? Let's skip all that for the minute, if we don't get dry clothes neither of us will survive. My car is down the quay.'

'You are living in another world,' Aidan said dismissively.

Aidan's plans did not include spending any more money, so he had no money for a taxi. This left him with little alternative but to allow himself be led to the car whilst he brooded on his bad luck; without this interference he would be gone by now. If only that bastard hadn't seen him in the river.

When they got to the car, a red Minx, Bob unlocked it on the driver's side. He leant across the driver's seat and pulled back the door handle on the other side. He then led Aidan around to the passenger door and locked the door as soon as Aidan was seated. This was noted by Aidan, who had no intention of making a dash for the Liffey.

As soon as he seated himself behind the steering wheel Bob opened the little locker in front of the passenger seat and extracted a stainless steel hip flask.

'Here Aidan, take a swig of this. It'll warm the cockles of your heart.' Aidan took it gratefully. He felt the Paddy go down to his stomach like a hot electric current. It didn't stop him reflecting that this fellow should be drowned in his own clichés.

He passed the flask back to Bob with a grudging, 'Thanks.' Bob then took a liberal swig.

'Nectar, that's what that was,' he said licking his lips.

He then pulled out the choke and started the car. It gave a cough before it fired into life. Even the engine wanted to live, thought Bob philosophically as he swung the car around into the driving sleet. It had become a hard powdery snow by now, thus winning the colour battle with the black cobblestones.

'I have a heater in this car,' Bob said proudly, 'it will warm us up in a few minutes.'

Aidan said nothing since he had no interest in cars. Bob's pride in his heater went over his head. They drove in silence through the whiteness, down a deserted Westmoreland Street, round the Bank of Ireland and turned right up Dame Street, left into George's Street and on towards the canal.

The heater was by then warming the car. Bob, feeling better, decided to have another go at conversation.

'I know you didn't want to be rescued. Sure I had to go in after you. I couldn't just leave another human being die when I could save him. Look Aidan, it can't be that bad. I really do want to help. At the very least a problem shared is a problem halved. Maybe you are looking up the wrong end of the glass, maybe if you look down the other way you will see things differently, even better.'

Aidan didn't reply at first. *Stuff his glass up his ass*, he thought. *Better sound grateful though, if only to get this bastard out of my hair.*

'You think I should be grateful to you for saving my life, yet do you not appreciate that, for some at least, death can be a welcome alternative to life. There can be worse things than death. If for example I was imprisoned for the rest of my life it would be a living hell for me, locked up with my thoughts. I assure you what I was doing was in my own best interests. No one else really cares, or I suppose matters.'

'That's where you are wrong. People do care. I care. Have you got any relatives?'

'Not any more. I had an older brother. We never got on. He died of TB some years ago. My mother died last year, at the age of seventy-six.'

'Never got hitched then?'

This is becoming tiresome, thought Aidan, aware he had little alternative but to humour him, for the present at any rate.

'No, I was going out with one girl for some years, when I was younger. She met someone else, with better prospects than me. She married him. Later I met another girl, but lost interest in her after a while. That's not to say,' he added quickly, lest he be thought a Howth Man, 'that I haven't got friends of the opposite sex; I have several in fact, especially in the art world. I felt there was little point in getting married. An added factor was that I had to look after my mother until she died.'

'Sorry about your mother, her death must have been a big blow. Now that she's gone should you not be thinkin' about a wife?'

'You sound as if you are married?' Aidan asked, deflecting the conversation while scarcely able to keep the irritation out of his voice.

'Yeah, Noreen and I are very happily married, but I suppose we were lucky.'

I don't want to rub it in, thought Bob.

'We've five kids. Not that we didn't have some minor problems from time to time. We first met at a rugby hop in Bective.'

They had reached red-bricked Rathmines, and Aidan was again lost in thought. What could he say to a self-satisfied prig whose view on life was conditioned by total self-satisfaction? Before he could decide Bob broke the silence once more, adopting a different tack.

'By the way I am sales director for a company selling malting barley, mostly for export. What do you do?'

Now we are bartering, you tell me and I will tell you, thought Aidan.

'Assistant manager,' muttered Aidan.

'In what?'

'Regal Insurance.'

'Ah, I guessed you had a good job,' Bob noted with satisfaction.

Good job my ass, thought Aidan, *just because I wore a crombie and a black hat he regards those as signs of wealth.* He recalled the lines, by whom? Thomas Dekkers maybe:

Canst drink the waters of the crisped spring?
Oh sweet content!
Swim'st thou in wealth, yet sink'st in thine own tears?
Oh punishment!

He could neither sink or drink in the Liffey, he thought sardonically. Ryan didn't look like a man to whom he should quote poetry. A bullshitter likely, but not a poet. Neither was smug Mr Larkin with his rimless glasses, unless it was 'Ode to the bottom line' or 'to the Balance Sheet', or even 'My own lovely Regal'.

Why didn't he persist in getting his final accountancy exam from the Institute of Chartered Accountants of Ireland? He seemed to lose interest after getting immersed in the Arts Club. It had certainly made it difficult for him to get back into serious study. Paradoxically, when he was sailing through his earlier exams he was seen by the others as a real competitor. When he failed the final for the fourth time he was just pitied as a casualty in the promotion stakes. Larkin always complained about his examination leave, until his first failure. After that he kept on suggesting he keep trying, secure in the knowledge he was never going to get it. What a hypocritical bastard! Oozing sincerity at every syllable he would say, 'I am sorry to interfere with your studies, but this work is urgent.' Whilst overtly encouraging staff to improve their educational qualifications the hypocrite covertly blocked them. Crises always occurred near exam times, necessitating overtime, much to the 'concern' of Larkin. Being a diploma man himself, degrees were anathema to him. David Mackey it was who nicknamed Larkin 'Egghead'.

It was David too who gave him the lifeline of the Arts Club, which opened up new vistas, including Joyce's *Ulysses*. Only philistines could have banned such a masterpiece. Thinking of such reminded him of the time Larkin had seen it in his drawer. Full of curiosity, he asked to borrow it, later to announce he had heard tell of Molly Bloom's soliloquy. Heard was about all he knew about Joyce's *Ulysses*. The ignorant bastard wouldn't understand a word of it.

He knew he had never reached the level of management once forecast for him. That was why his engagement to Angela ran aground. He simply could not afford her. 'Was he a team man ?' was the question frequently asked of him

at Regal interviews. 'What exactly do you mean by that?'
That response caused the interview panel to exchange
knowing looks. The outcome was that they lost interest in
him. He remembered blurting out, 'But an insurance
company is not a bloody football team.' He realised, too
late, how that remark had affected his future career in the
Regal. Thanks to Larkin it became part of company
folklore.

'Are you all right?' Ryan's query interrupted his
recollections, 'you seem deaf to my question matie, I'm
sorry, Aidan.'

'Can you repeat it?'

'Is there anyone in your house?'

'No, but that does not present a problem.'

'Okay, I can leave you home after we have had a change
and a bite to eat in my house.'

'I would prefer it if you just got a taxi for me.'

'Aidan, that wouldn't be right, besides which where
would we get a taxi on a night like this? I'll leave you home.
It's not a problem.'

They were now headed for Terenure when Bob turned
left into a road with two storey semi-detached red-bricked
houses on either side. Edwardian most likely, thought
Aidan, with their small front gardens; all indistinguishable
from one another in the snow.

Bob drove the Minx quietly into a snow-carpeted
driveway, and cut off its engine. The top half of the large
front door, Aidan noted, had a lead glass panel with red and
blue glass flowers set into it. Hideous, thought Aidan, as
Bob unlocked the door. He motioned Aidan to follow him
into a hall which had a staircase to their left and a shiny
mahogany hall table on the right, with a black phone on it.
At the end of the hall there was a door which led into a

large square kitchen, whose warmth hit them as soon at they entered. The source was a mottled grey black Aga cooker to their left. It burnt coke, a half bucket of which was to its side. The large mahogany table on their right was neatly set for breakfast. On the wall in front was an old walnut grandmother clock.

The silence in the house was palpable; a silence of sleep broken only by the quiet tick tocking of the clock which, while obtruding upon the stillness, yet served to accentuate it with its hollow sounding tick, tock, tick, tock. The floor was covered with rough grey carpet tiles. These helped to absorb sound. Somehow Aidan felt reassured by the ticking clock.

'Here take this towel. Strip off and dry yourself while I nip upstairs and get some clothes. Don't worry, I'll get another one off the hot rail in the bathroom. I've put the kettle on the Aga for tea.'

He bounded out, leaving Aidan alone in the kitchen.

There was a wooden clothes horse beside the cooker with a variety of clothes, including a woollen dressing gown whose cord hung loosely down to the floor.

His clothes won't dry that quickly, thought Aidan. Slowly and thoughtfully he took off his damp clothes and hung them on the stainless steel rail in front of the Aga. Soon the river water caused the drying clothes to smell, the odour spreading all over the kitchen. His socks seemed to give off the worst smell. He would have to put on his shoes and socks very soon, so he placed them on top of the stainless steel lids covering the hot plates where it was hottest. This caused an even more pronounced evil odour of river in the kitchen.

Bob strode into the kitchen, making surprising little noise for such a big man. To Aidan he looked as fresh in his change of clothes as if he had stepped out of a band box.

'God what a pong, the family will be curious about this in the mornin'. Here Aidan try on these,' he said, throwing him a complete change of clothes. 'I don't think the shoes are big enough, but try them anyway.'

Muttering 'Thanks,' Aidan took the clothes and put them on. They were too big for him. At least they were dry. His body felt a lot better in dry clothes. His mind however was in torment. Can a man not die in peace without interference from farts like this? This blabbermouth will tell everybody about tonight.

'I wonder if I could borrow the cord off that dressing gown?'

'Sure, you can drop it back at your convenience.'

Bob had that self-satisfied, even condescending, look about him which infuriated Aidan. Worse was to follow.

'By the way I know a chap called Larkin, works in the Regal, nice fellow. Plays golf in my club. Used to play tennis with Noreen. You must know him?'

Aidan felt as if he had been coshed on the head with a piece of lead pipe. Tonight's events were going to get all round the Regal for sure. This no good do-gooder would talk to Larkin. He could visualise the conversation.

'Met one of your staff the other night.'

'Where?'

'Pulled him out of the river.'

Aidan moaned at the thought of it. This was it.

'Are you all right?' Bob asked with concern, the cup of tea poised in mid-air.

'I'm fine, but I just thought of something. I left a file case at the quay wall with a note in it, a suicide note you might call it. I need to get it back now. Can you call a taxi for me?'

'You won't get a taxi at this hour of the night. I'll drive you in, and leave you home. Now,' said Bob as Aidan demurred, 'it's settled.'

'Look, you feel I should be grateful. I'm not. I really would prefer to get a taxi and be done with you.'

'Now don't be like that. You're slipping back, just when I thought you were relaxed. I really want to help you, Aidan.'

'Why? So you can stroke your image down at the golf club at my expense, leaving me to face the voyeuristic pity of others.'

'Don't be so hard, Aidan, I did it because you are a fellow human being. I would do it again. You are being unfair to say I would talk about tonight at the golf club. You speak as if I've taken something from you.'

'Precisely. My right to take my own life, ending this misery.'

'Shush, keep your voice down or we'll wake the whole house. What they don't know about won't hurt them. Let's go back to the quay if we're to get your letter. When we have done that we can talk some more about the future. I have some friends in the medical profession who could be of help.'

Aidan decided further dialogue on the topic was a waste of time. He changed tack.

'I'm sorry, but you really don't understand my situation. How can you?' said Aidan bitterly, indicating he did not want a response.

'All right, let's go and get that note. Given the night that's in it, it's not likely to have been seen by anyone.'

They crept out of the house and into the car. Bob started the still warm engine at the first pull of the starter. He reversed slowly down the short driveway and drove out on to the main road, leaving tracks on the white snow-covered sleet.

Aidan was silent, thinking of Alexander Pope's words in 'The Dying Christian to his Soul':

> Quit, oh quit this mortal frame:
> Trembling, hoping, lingering, flying,
> Oh the pain, the bliss of dying!

'The bliss of dying,' he said out loud, 'you would not understand that?'

'Bliss my ass. I don't have a mind to die yet,' Bob said with feeling. 'The book of life is short enough without dwelling on the last chapter.'

Silence now descended between them. Bob could see Aidan had gone into one of his reveries. Strange fellow. He'd never met anyone quite so peculiar. Intelligent, no, highly intelligent, but a bit arty and very melancholic. He seemed to have a good job, an accountant of some sort working under Stephen Larkin, who was a decent sort of fella, so far as he could judge. Aidan, as a single man, must be reasonably well off. Sure nowadays wasn't a decent job half the battle? Something had gone seriously wrong along the way. Still there must be a cure.

The car was now approaching a deserted Westmoreland Street, if the odd bits of the previous night's *Evening Herald* and *Mail* blowing about in the wind were excluded.

He turned left down Aston Quay which, in this weather and at this hour, Bob thought, had lost all its charm. They soon passed along Wood Quay, with the grey keep of Christ's Church to their left.

'You see the wall over there near the river. There should be a black document case lying against it somewhere. The note is in it. Just pull up, anywhere here. I will get it,' said Aidan.

'I'm nearer,' said Bob, alert to the possibility of another wetting for the two of them. He jumped out of the car before Aidan could reply and made for the wall.

Aidan had a quick look around the car before he removed the pyjama cord from his waist. He then tied it to his left foot. He tied the other end to the tubing forming the under part of the passenger seat.

'Here it is, half-covered in snow. It wasn't disturbed,' said Bob triumphantly, as he passed the case over to Aidan who quickly opened it and extracted a single sheet of paper with uniform writing on it. He rolled down his window, tore the paper into tiny pieces and cast them into the air. The wind swept them up to mingle with the snow which had replaced the sleet, some disappearing into the night whilst other bits were blown into the icy water.

'At least we have a role reversal. If I could not end up in the Liffey part of my suicide note can. Now, if you turn around you can drop me off at Sandymount. The best way to go is straight down City Quay, on to Sir John Rogerson's, turning right into Cardiff Lane for Macken Street and on through Ringsend.'

Bob was surprised at the detailed directions given by Aidan, who had expressed no interest in their earlier routes. It didn't sound as if he was thinking of jumping into the water again. Maybe he had influenced him to change his mind.

'How good is your job?' asked Aidan unexpectedly.

'Well, the basic salary is small enough. With commission it is very high and, with last night's work, I expect to have my best year yet. We are in the malting trade, with a growing export business.'

'I suppose you have a good pension to boot?'

'Yeah, Noreen would be well looked after if I were to go now. I would even have a modest pension if I were to retire next year.'

The Minx was on Sir John Rogerson's Quay with the windscreen wipers finding it difficult to clear the powdery snow when Aidan shouted, 'Watch that thing on the road.'

Bob, whose mind was on the conversation, instinctively swerved to the right whereupon Aidan pulled the wheel sharp left. Coincidentally he pushed his right foot on top of Bob's two feet causing the already sliding car to accelerate and the car to jerk forward at speed. It headed straight for the Liffey.

'Jesus Christ are ye mad? We are going for the river,' roared Bob.

Bob pushed Aidan away from him and released his foot sufficiently for him to apply the brakes. This caused the car to skid even more on the snow and sleet, thereby losing all control. Its own momentum carried the car well out into the lowering tidal waters, its front dipped down with the weight of the engine. The car managed to land front down but on all four wheels. There was a huge splash. It slowly sank in the river. As it did so the sideways current turned the front of the car down river. The two occupants were badly shaken, though not seriously injured.

'This is murderous. You'll kill us both,' roared Bob in the darkness.

'No, only me – I have some unfinished business and your intervention has made it more urgent.'

'Don't be a fool. I can rescue you. There is more to life than this. Look, the car is settling on the bottom. We still have time.'

There was an uncanny sound in the darkness, no engine noise just the gurgle of the water coming through the pedal holes, the instrument panel and the other small apertures.

Aidan said in a composed tone, 'I am staying here. You save yourself.'

'For God's sake, Aidan, there's very little time. As soon as the water reaches our necks I'll open the door, take a deep breath and pull you out,' Bob shouted, urgency competing with hysteria.

'Save yourself, if you will. I am tied to the seat with your pyjama cord. I am not leaving. If you try to rescue me I will take you with me.'

In the darkness they could feel the icy water was now chest high, rising faster as the area to be filled decreased. It was numbingly cold in the darkness of the car with an almost overpoweringly putrid stench.

Bob couldn't understand Aidan's attitude. One thing he was certain of though, the uselessness in trying to reason with this lunatic. Aidan's silence denoted their relationship was at an end.

Bob now felt his priority was to think of his family, and save himself.

He wound down the window and let the water into the remaining space, simultaneously taking as deep a breath as he could. He then pushed at the door. Once it was ajar the current flung it fully open. Bob floated to the roof of the car where he got a grip on its outer edge. He then began to lever himself out of the Minx by placing his left foot on the steering wheel with the intention of using it as a fulcrum for the final heave out of the car.

Unfortunately his foot slipped into the centre of the steering wheel's chromed spokes, which bent under the pressure. His foot was now jammed. Try as he might, he could not get it free from the steering wheel. The water restricted his ability to pull his foot free.

His lungs screamed for more air. He had one last chance. To lever himself back into the car and use his hands to get his foot out from the steering wheel. It would have been a simple enough manoeuvre if he had enough air in his lungs. But he hadn't. He got back and felt for his foot. It was jammed fast in the twisted spokes of the wheel. By now mere willpower was keeping his mouth shut. He couldn't hold out any longer. As if prised by a giant hand his mouth snapped open to admit the evil tasting water. Bob knew he was finished. All he could think of was, *Oh God, what did I do to deserve meeting this ungrateful bastard?* It was to be his last thought on this earth.

Volcano

'Gee Shirley, don't tell me that view wasn't worth the climb? Doesn't it take your breath away?'

They were climbing, or trekking, up to Villaricca's smoking rim under a clear blue sky. Their view of the surrounding countryside spread out beneath them was, by any standards, spectacular. Right below was the resort town of Pucon, to their left the town of Villaricca and dominating all was Villaricca lake with its surrounding necklace of mountains mirrored in the its placid surface. In the distance they could make out the other volcano whose name, mentioned by their guide Carlos, they had forgotten.

'Sure Doug it's spectacular,' said Shirley, gasping in the thin air, 'but I still don't like the thought of the Morris' being able to afford the airplane trip. It's just that Biff—' she started to say when Doug interrupted.

'No, in fairness it's Miriam who was behind that decision.'

'Okay it's mainly Miriam, flaunting their wealth. You still can't ignore Biff. Goddammit Doug, he's her husband who made the pile of dough in the first place,' said Shirley vehemently. 'I wonder if they have been an' gone. I'd sure hate to be here with them flyin' over us. You know very well I woulda liked to go over this here volcano in a plane.'

'Sure I do pet,' said Doug soothingly, 'but look yonder. The kids're knockin' a great time coming outa that snow.' The two girls, Linda and Chris, shrieking with delight, were giving a protesting brother Joe a roll in the icy snow, all three oblivious of the striking scenery.

'I've never seen a snow line end three quarters way up a mountain,' said Shirley trying to take her mind off Biff and Miriam's good luck.

'The crater is heating the ground under our feet, more so as we get closer to the top. Not too far into the mountain it's all boiling lava,' said Doug, who was glad of the change of topic from that which questioned his friendship with Biff.

'Si, signora,' said Carlos, who was standing nearby, 'you will see the red lava when we get to the top, and haf the heat from eet.'

'Yeah, we tend to forget this is an active volcano. Come on kiddoes,' he yelled to the three.

The combination of thin air and the steepness of the last stage slowed them all down. Doug pretended to be slowing for the children, who in fact showed no sign of tiredness, when in reality he didn't want to rush Shirley who might return to the plane trip topic.

As they trekked up the final stage Doug began to reflect on his friendship with Biff. It went back to their college days, to third level when they attended university. Both qualified in business administration. They decided to remain in touch agreeing to go on vacation once every three years if they didn't see one another much in the interim. That arrangement had worked out very well for the first few years. Then they drifted apart with he taking the corporate route and Biff branching out on his own into importing and exporting. Biff's business had grown, particularly so prior to the Gulf War, when he bought forward a lot of oil. From then on the dough simply rolled in until he was now a very rich man.

By corporate standards Doug knew he was well paid but marriage, a mortgage and three kids meant he was in a different league from Biff. Not that Biff had flaunted his wealth. When they went on vacation he took care to stay within Doug's limits. But then came along the wives, specifically Miriam. It wasn't that Doug disliked her, it was just her attitude towards money and the tensions it created between the four of them. It particularly affected Shirley whose Bostonian upbringing clashed with Miriam's New Yorker brashness and 'crass display of wealth', as Shirley put it.

Biff had hinted to him that Miriam wanted to go to Hawaii for this vacation, to a luxury hotel way above Doug's budget. Biff had a tough job persuading her to come here to Chile. Then nothing would do her but to rent the small single-engined plane to fly over Villaricca.

'We can all go,' she said.

'Sorry,' Doug had said, 'we would need two planes if we are to take the three kids. That'd mean Shirley going up in one and me in the other.' He knew it would cost too much and that Shirley would not want to go up without him.

Miriam countered this by saying to Biff, 'Couldn't you get a bigger plane pet and we all go up together?' To which Biff had the tact to reply, 'They don't have one that big. Anyway I don't think a bigger plane could go that close to the top.'

Shirley later claimed that Miriam was just being her selfish self with no thought to the embarrassment she was causing. 'I had said to her the plane ride must be a great way of seeing the volcano,' Shirley had told him later. 'She knows very well that it was outside our budget and we wouldn't want Biff to pay for it. That woman is a mischief-maker, Doug.'

He could see Biff was uneasy and whilst neither he nor Biff wanted this to be their last vacation together it was shaping up that way. He kicked the mountainside in disgust. *Damn Miriam*, he thought to himself.

'*Señor*, we are near the top. Pleeze hold the children. It can be dangerous up at the reem. Hot lava, eet is just below us,' said Carlos, conscious of the three children's capacity for high jinks.

'Now Shirley, isn't that something. We must be up nine thousand feet. Look at that molten lava down there below. You can even smell the sulphur and look behind you where we have half the lake district spread out below us. This view is far better than from a plane,' said Doug enthusiastically, and tactlessly.

'I guess you're right. I didn't realise we would have the chair lift up into snow.' That made it easier and the children certainly loved it. It didn't take a feather out of them. It's just Miriam's attitude. I think she wants to...' she was interrupted by cries from Linda, Chris and Joe who were shouting and pointing below them. 'Look, look Da, a plane down there.'

They all looked down and saw a small plane circling below them, gradually gaining height.

'It's Pepe,' said Carlos, 'he goes around in, how do you say it?'

'In circles,' offered Doug.

'Si, si Señor, in circles, to come up to reem,' said Carlos.

Sure enough the small plane was gradually gaining height by going around in circles. It seemed a funny way to come up thought Doug, unless of course it was underpowered.

'Da, do you think it's uncle Biff?' asked Linda.

'Si Señorita,' replied Carlos when Doug hesitated. 'Eet is Pepe's old plane.'

'Not too old I hope,' said Shirley, 'Miriam would only want the best.'

'Now pet, don't be sarcastic. I guess they will be here in a few minutes. What say we wait and wave to them guys?' said Doug.

'Now wouldn't that be nice,' said Shirley.

Doug figured it better to ignore the sarcasm, especially in the presence of the children.

The little single-engined plane continued its tortuous climb as they watched in silence from the rim of the volcano. When it got near them, Linda screamed, 'Uncle Biff, he's waving at us.'

No one else could identify who was in the plane but their mood was such they wanted to believe it was Miriam and Biff. So they all waved their arms and jumped up and down.

Suddenly the plane, when it had almost reached the rim, took off in the direction of the lake. They stopped waving and watched in silence at this unexpected manoeuvre. It then did a U-turn and flew straight up towards the rim as if it was going to sweep over where they were standing. They could clearly hear the roar of its engine, which to Doug seemed to be going flat out.

The little plane flew over their heads so close it forced them to duck, the children shrieking with a mixture of terror and delight.

'It's them, it's Biff and Miriam,' exclaimed Shirley, forgetting her antipathy.

The plane roared right over the bubbling lava and waggled its wings before climbing almost vertically up into the sky right over the lava. Then it happened, just as the pilot appeared to be levelling out. The right wing dipped to the right followed by the rest of the plane, and what followed appeared to be in slow motion. The pilot seemed unable to regain control as the plane went into a dive, straight for the burning centre of the volcano. The two girls' shrill shrieks cut the thin air whilst Shirley simply covered her face with her hands crying, 'Oh no, oh no.'

Doug hardly recognised the roar of terror which came from the horror unfolding before his eyes. All of them could clearly see Miriam's screaming mouth through the side window of the plane. Just when they thought the little plane had reached the point of no return, where the passengers must be feeling the heat from the lava, the pilot miraculously gained control and managed to drag the plane over the rim to their right. It roared off and began to descend.

They watched it in stunned silence, their mouths opening and closing like those of beached cod.

Doug was the first to speak, 'Jeeze I have ta hand it to that pilot.'

His children started jumping up and down clapping their hands in excitement. Joe in particular. 'It was like a film Da.'

'Thank goodness it was them and not us who were in that plane. They will never be closer to death than that. I wonder what price Miriam would have paid for her life,' said Shirley slowly, as if speaking to herself.

'They certainly owe the pilot one for that. He must have got caught in a downdraft of hot and cold air,' Doug said, turning to look at Carlos who had remained unperturbed throughout the incident. 'Carlos, you took all of that very calmly.'

'I haf seen it before, Señor.'

'What?'

'Señor Doug, that is not the prim... first time I have seen Pepe's airplane do a dive. Pepe's a very good, how you say it?'

'Pilot,' interjected Doug.

'Si, señor. Pilot.'

'But it was going to crash?' said Doug, puzzled at Carlos's answer.

'Señor Doug, the people in Pepe's plane will be very happy not to haf fallen into the lava so they will give him money. His car is no good. You savy señor?' replied Carlos with what Doug regarded as an old-fashioned grin.

'Sure,' said Doug, not really certain that he did.

'Pepe, he's a very good pilot. I haf seen him come up the side of Villaricca an do a loop de loop. Up and turn over to go to the ground. He can stop it just before the end an, how do you say it, go straight.'

'Straighten or level out,' offered Doug.

'Si señor, level out. He was in a circus,' said Carlos proudly.

Doug didn't ask Carlos what Pepe did in the circus, a trapeze artist most likely.

The little plane was now a speck gradually becoming smaller as it slowly flew inland and then out of their sight.

'Gee Shirley, aren't we lucky to be up here. Can you imagine the fright they musta got?' said Doug secure in the knowledge that his wife was relieved to be on the rim and not on the brink of a crash.

Shirley started to giggle and then began to shake with uncontrollable laughter, her sound echoing around in the still air at the top of the volcano. Doug, their children and Carlos at first just goggled at her, then began to laugh too, their laughter more a reaction to the tension of a few moments earlier.

Shirley was the first to stop. Smiling broadly she turned to a still laughing Doug and said, 'I can't help laughing when I think of Miriam's reaction when I tell her what Carlos has told us.'

The Whipping Boy

'I will swing for that bastard yet.'

The words, expelled with venom, were incompatible with the surroundings, a rosewood panelled office with a deep-piled, biscuit-coloured carpet. Three post-impressionist paintings hung on the end wall with four watercolours, one a Paul Henry. The furniture all had a matching rosewood veneer, and the desk was large enough to be imposing.

Perhaps the expletive was not so incompatible with the thick-set speaker, whose ample frame filled the large black

Managing Director's chair. Andrew Roystone pushed the fingers of his right hand reflectively through his curly red hair as he looked at the man seated at the other side of his desk. An excellent financial director, let down unfortunately by his appearance. Too bloody thin of face and prematurely bald of head. Those stainless steel glasses make him look like a baddie from *The Spy who came in from the Cold*. Unlike Baldwin, Dempsey had not got the face, or personality, to front an organisation such as this, thought Roystone with satisfaction. Michael Dempsey, the said financial director of Natures Products PLC, was not one to chide his Managing Director for his crudeness. He had too healthy a respect for him. There was an expression there, possibly due to his combination of short neck, full lips and heavy-lidded cold eyes, which signalled handle with care. At least he was not Roystone's current whipping boy. He had to admit though that he was a little taken aback at the person against whom the expletive was directed. Justin Baldwin, the marketing development director, had had a very successful career with the company, up to now that is.

Michael prided himself on knowing exactly what was going on, well ahead of anyone else. That way he could ingratiate himself with Roystone by feeding him selected information and gossip. Yet he could hardly imagine Roystone was up to date on Justin's project. Even Justin himself was not fully aware of the brewing storm. *Ipso facto* Justin was headed for real trouble when all was revealed. He decided to play along, just to see how much Roystone knew.

'Andrew, I understand how you feel,' he didn't, but it sounded good, 'but why not let him hang himself? He is headed that way anyway, with this Luxor joint venture in Lyon.'

'Go on Michael,' said Roystone softly.

'Well, you know he is very committed to Luxor. It further internationalises our activities, as he so aptly put it, whilst omitting to mention its success will be a considerable feather in his own cap. It so happens that it's not going as well as he thinks.' Michael thought he had injected just about the appropriate gravitas behind his words.

'Tell me something I don't know.' Andrew's tone was sharp.

Michael refixed his glasses with his thumb and forefinger before responding.

'With due respect, as you *think* you know, Andrew,' said Michael maintaining, not without difficulty, his gravitas. 'We had agreed with Sommalier to increase our original investment in Luxor from three million to three and a half million, with grudging board approval, whereas I expect it is already heading for four million plus.'

'Okay, stop talking in riddles. I know about that. What more are we facing?' Andrew remained unimpressed.

'First, a ten per cent devaluation of the punt will cost us at least another three hundred thousand. This will ultimately have a knock on effect on our own raw material costs.'

'Second, there will be an overrun of about half a million pounds, because the French municipality are making Sommalier upgrade the Luxor plant's waste disposal facilities. Our clever partners, Sommalier, thought a less costly plant would suffice.'

'Third, remember the carrot we dangled? The use of our Greenlands brand name? Well, Justin has signed an agreement with Luxor permitting them to use it.'

Michael got the expected reaction to the third point when Andrew began drumming his fingers on his desk before saying, 'For Chris' sake, we only suggested to Baldwin he dangle that in front of them as a possibility when the plant was actually operational.'

Andrew's tone was unexpectedly measured; not fitting the exasperation present in the words. His eyes too, Michael could see, were cold, stone cold. He chose his words carefully.

'I know, Andrew, I was there when we discussed it. I have learned that Luxor can now use our Greenlands brand name on their products once we have granted them the franchise. Moreover,' he was tempted to wring the most from his information, until he saw the scowl on his boss's face, 'under some recent European Court decisions they are entitled to use that brand name, not alone for their products in France but also in any country in the European Community.'

'What!' Michael got more than his expected reaction. Andrew had sat up straight in his chair, his hands gripping the desk so hard his fingers were turning white.

'That's the legal situation.' Michael snapped out the words, his eyes shining behind their steel rims. 'And I am told Luxor are well aware of what they have got. My guess is that if we get stroppy over the increase in costs they will carefully examine how they can best use our Greenlands brand within the Community. Any good lawyer, versed in European law, will tell them they can use it anywhere within the Community.'

Michael closed his thin lips tighter than usual, giving added emphasis to the seriousness of the situation, adding, 'Moreover there is a possibility the product from our plant here in Ireland, as a result of the devaluation, will, in the short term, be more competitive in export markets, even in France. In effect the new plant in Lyon will not be competitive. This of course undermines the basic rationale behind the whole project. Essentially if Luxor uses our brand name they could end up competing successfully with our own brand in mainland Europe. As you know, the Luxor deal was intended to help us break into France, and her spheres of influence in North Africa; not to have them take us out of our existing European markets. The parity of our relationship with Sommalier is now gone if they have our franchise to use as they like, not to put a tooth in it.'

Michael paused, his face assuming his chief mourner's expression.

Good, he noticed Andrew's face had gone white with rage. He sat deep in thought, his right hand fingers again drumming the desk. When he spoke his tone was deadly cold. 'It will make us look like idiots. Have you spoken to Baldwin about this?'

'Not directly. He had asked one of my staff to produce some projections for him. I told him to put it on hold for the present.'

'Well don't, without checking with me.'

He was being dismissed. Michael made for the heavy rosewood door hearing a tuneless humming coming from behind him. He thought it sounded a bit like *Poor Judd is Dead* from Oklahoma, then again that may have been wishful thinking on his part.

Andrew, still humming, looked after Dempsey's departing back, dwelling on what he had just heard. He now knew Baldwin could be in difficulties with the board, but corporate responsibility was also a factor to take into account here. He could be burnt too if he wasn't careful. Dempsey was not telling tales for nothing. If he could tell tales to one he could tell them to others, always supposing he saw them as higher bidders in the corporate advancement stakes. He resolved to remain the highest bidder, at least until this was over. Luxor's position was not quite as bad as that ass-licker Dempsey made out. He had been involved in the first meeting with the Managing Director of Sommalier, Albert Poussance, when Baldwin had signed the heads of agreement. They had both gone to Lyon to wrap up the deal, he only going at the insistence of Poussance. He had got Baldwin to sign the final agreement at the dinner that evening, largely because Justin had received a message to go home to his sick wife.

It was not unusual for a joint venture, such as this, to exceed its budget, otherwise why have a contingency provision? True, a board could get nervous if management was unable to reassure them of a projects viability. Most boards, including his own, were bottom line merchants. Generally as long as management created acceptable profits they would be happy. The joint venture, as originally proposed by Baldwin, was a sound one, giving them a unique combination of transfer of technology and market penetration. If Natural Foods tried to get into the French market from scratch it would cost them far more. Morocco and Tunisia would be out altogether, not to mention the high risk of failure. Here they were linking into a successful French firm. Baldwin could get a lot of brownie points out of this if it was a success. *If*, he thought grimly. This business about the brand name being usable in all countries in the EU, if it was granted for one, put the cat among the pigeons though.

Justin Baldwin got the internal phone call he didn't want. Curt and to the point. It cut into the call he was having with the Frenchman.

'Justin, come to my office and bring me up to date on Luxor.'

'Sure Andrew, as soon as I can finish this call.'

He finished his discussion with Pierre Dupois, with whom he had established a very friendly relationship. He then leaned back on his green, leather-covered chair, deep in thought, with his hands behind his head. He was totally oblivious of his impressive surroundings, not as luxurious as his Managing Director's though. The furniture was modern Danish. He had chosen the decor himself, mainly green with some reds to add life, together with several original oil and water colour paintings, a framed first class marketing degree with an attendant Harvard postgraduate certificate, plus a couple of sports trophies with a large photograph of his wife and three children over the bureau. He liked the result, better than that terrible dark brown of his predecessor.

He stretched his tall frame in the chair wondering what next. He and Roystone had got on well when they were both executive directors. He would go so far as to think he had been extremely helpful to Andrew when, through inexperience of company politics, he had guided him through some, particularly one, nasty pitfalls. Some time after his appointment as MD his attitude seemed to change, more than one might expect in these circumstances. Not because he had been a candidate for the Managing Directorship; all the directors had applied as well. He never learned how he had done. At least he had not made a fool out of himself. The change had come, subtly at first but still tangible enough for him to feel it. Superficially they still appeared to get on okay yet Justin had an uneasy feeling about Andrew's sincerity. He also knew he and Dempsey were soulmates in ambition and power. Andrew, to be fair, had more flair, and he had been supportive of the Luxor project.

Trouble was Dempsey wanted to crunch numbers for one person only. Therein lay his perspective of power. His request for up to date figures on the Luxor job was met with a blank wall. He needed to know what had been spent to date, a forward projection, along with the full effects of inflation and the impact of the French cock-up over waste disposal. The Luxor people said they had given, in his absence, all his requested information to Mr Dempsey, the financial director, and expressed surprise that he was looking for it again. He guessed Dempsey got it from Sommalier's financial director, with whom he had struck up a good working relationship. It doesn't do for the Sommalier people to think Natural were having a breakdown in internal communications. He badly needed up to date figures, but Alec Gunn, the chief accountant, was complaining he was too busy just now. He sighed; the trouble with the corporate scene was that one had to get along with some of nature's bastards as colleagues, even to the point of seeing more of them than his own family.

He rose and grabbed the papers from his desk which contained the latest figures he had put together.

'Sit down Justin.' Andrew grimaced as he waved him to the vacant chair in front. He was on the telephone talking into his pride and joy, the large rosewood veneered phone consul on his desk, which gave instant access to everyone, and everywhere, in his empire. He switched over to the hand phone when Justin entered his office, not before Justin heard the word 'Luxor' from a voice that sounded like the chairman's. Andrew quickly finished the conversation, promising to call back.

'The last progress report you made to the directors' meeting on Luxor indicated a further overrun. I gather some of the directors are uneasy about costs. Where are we now?'

Justin gave him a brief résumé, bringing him up to their last meeting. 'Since then we have run into some further problems due to devaluation, extra costs on waste disposal and higher interest rates. I am waiting for up to date figures and projections from the finance division. I need to know the projected end cost for the finished product over the first three years of the new plant's life. Luxor's accountant sent the relevant figures on to Michael's people.'

'Surely, Justin, you can calculate those yourself? Or if you can't, your staff can do it.'

'Not so easy Andrew, some are generated here and others are theirs. In my absence Luxor liaised directly with our accounts people. I have done some calculations which show a current overrun of about a quarter of a million punts. That figure will be exceeded which is why I am trying to get Luxor's figures from Michael's people.'

'How much more?'

Justin hesitated, sensing there was more to the question than was apparent.

'Well, I am awaiting the figure for devaluation, which was unforeseen, together with some extra costs on waste disposal, some of which should be covered by the contingency provision.'

'You need to be careful with this project. It has got a high profile from the financial press. Our board, as you well know, are very interested in it. You will recall the difficulty I had in getting you approval for your extra half million. Let me have an in-depth report tomorrow morning. We will have an executive directors' meeting the day after to morrow at,' and he picked up his gold-lettered, leather desk diary, 'eight a.m. Depending on what comes up

I will decide if it should be raised at Friday's board meeting.'

Their discussion was ended. Justin made his way through the lush carpet to the door. Outside, at the secretary's desk he remembered he had forgotten his notes. He turned the gold-plated handle to re-enter. Andrew was at his desk, telephone in hand, reflectively humming a tuneless song. Justin nodded towards his papers, still on the desk, picked them up and departed again, thinking, *That man hasn't got a note in his head.*

'I really am sorry, Justin, but we have a board meeting Friday and we are trying to get out the quarterly accounts for it. I'll tell you what, I will ask Alec to assign Bill Smyth full time to your work.' Justin could visualise Dempsey trying, and failing, to look sympathetic.

'He's only been in the place a wet week, Michael, and will not be familiar with the detail.' Justin knew he was getting the run around.

'It's the best I can do.'

Justin put his phone down hard on the cradle. He never liked that smart-assed bastard, just now he hated him. If he had more time he would teach him a lesson, but Roystone was not giving him any. He could not go back to Pierre Dupois without losing face. Damn, he'd better get on with it. Try as he might, young Smyth could not get the required data from Gunn, who was said to be out of the office with the auditors. No one else appeared to have any knowledge of the account. Even the access code was confined to Gunn.

All the directors were in the Managing Director's office for the 8 o'clock meeting which, having dealt with a couple of routine matters, concentrated on the Luxor joint venture.

Andrew opened the discussion by explaining that 'the project had suffered from some recent outside factors which necessitated a review by all of us. Bear in mind this is a project which has a great deal to offer to our company. I have asked Justin to give us an up to date report. Please accept my apologies, Justin, for not being able to go through your report before this meeting.'

'Due to the accounts department's concentration on the quarterly accounts for the board meeting I encountered some difficulty in producing as up to date a report as I would like. However, you can read this,' Justin said, circulating copies around the table, 'which I will then take you through.'

He gave a decent interval for its examination by his fellow directors before elaborating.

'As you see, our original investment was for £3m which was subsequently increased to £3.5m, until devaluation added another £0.35m. I now must add an estimated £.8m for a more elaborate waste disposal plant. There have been other increases which have eaten up our contingency sum of £0. 25m. There may be other small increases but I cannot get a fix on everything until I get the figures from our accounts people. Devaluation will mean, in the short term at any rate, our Irish plant will be more competitive. Medium to long term this will be largely reversed as costs increase due to rising costs of imported materials. Add to this the likelihood that our interest rates must be set to rise in this new scenario. All in all our original projections are not going to be met.'

'How will this affect the eventual market price of the product?' It was Frank Dunlop, the marketing director.

'Difficult to give an exact projection until I have got all the details. It is fair to say that it may cause an immediate dilemma for our home manufactured products, which may be able to compete favourably with those coming from Luxor.'

'What do you mean about waiting for final figures from the accounts?' Dempsey's tone betrayed his scorn. 'You should have them yourself. Besides, haven't I given you one of our best young accountants to help you compile this report? By the way, did you cover forward our exposure on the contract price, Justin?'

Justin chose his words carefully, lest he betray his real feelings. 'I discovered from Pierre Dupois that he had given all the up to date information on additional costs to Alec Gunn, who was not available to give them either to me or young Smyth. It didn't seem proper for me to ring Dupois to ask him to let me have a copy of figures he had just sent. As regards covering forward, is that not your job?' he asked smiling.

'My people have their own pressures just now, with a board meeting at the end of the week and all the financial reporting which that entails. Normally we get a specific request to cover forward. None was made for your project.' Dempsey was looking at Andrew as he finished speaking.

'Yes it was. I asked Gunn to keep an eye on our requirements,' said Justin, with a hint of irritation in his voice.

'Justin, how could we act on something as vague as that? We need a specific request in writing before we can act on covering forward any expenditure. You realise, with devaluation, we have incurred an additional, and unnecessary, cost of £350,000,' said Michael twisting the knife.

'It so happens I did send a written request to Gunn. Here is a copy,' said Justin, passing over a copy.

'I am not interested in recriminations just now. All I want to know is where we are in this project, Justin,' said Andrew interrupting Michael's baiting, 'You're responsible for this project, not Michael. If you have a problem in getting figures why did you not go to him or failing that, me?'

Justin hesitated before replying knowing he was facing a catch-22 situation. Going to Andrew was a sign of weakness, whilst not forcing Dempsey to co-operate would also make him appear to be weak. *Aw to hell*, he thought.

'I don't think I was getting the co-operation the situation demanded,' he said with feeling.

Frank Dunlop, the marketing director, conscious of the trenches being dug around him, tried to offset the conflict by saying, 'Can we now determine how the project stands? After all, we all know the figures are now in the building. When the up to date figures are on the table we can have a more meaningful discussion leading to a decision.'

'Okay by me,' volunteered Michael. 'But there are some things I would like clarified now. Luxor have hinted they may have to include a further £1m for a more sophisticated waste disposal plant. On my estimation the project could run out at a final cost of over £4m. Secondly, they have said they had been granted a franchise for our 'Greenlands' brand name. If that is so they will be entitled to use it in any country of the European Union. It seems as if we have some very careful thinking to do.'

His words left their intended silence of unease. The others studied their reflections in the shiny table, apart from Joe Fortune, the company secretary, who concentrated on recording what was being said. Andrew watched the faces from under his heavy-lidded eyes, waiting to see if anyone would come to Justin's defence.

Apart from a clearing of throats, the silence continued until Justin could contain himself no longer.

'Michael, you have been sitting on this information without discussing it with me. I think it is most unethical to raise this here. The up to date figures were denied to Bill Smyth and me up to now.'

'Look Justin,' Dempsey's words were exiting through near clenched teeth, 'I resent the implication in your remark. You have run this project like it was your own fiefdom, until now, when it is a balls up, and likely to bring the whole company into bad odour.'

'Michael, I don't know what all those goddamn people are doing in your department. Aren't they supposed to be servicing the rest of us? Power without responsibility...'

Andrew interrupted Justin's outburst, 'We could be here until doomsday and still not have a clear-cut idea where we are. Justin and Michael, get together and produce a position report which we will look at tomorrow at eight. Meanwhile I had better alert the chairman that this may have to be considered at the board meeting. Any objections?' It was a rhetorical question. The meeting broke up with everyone, for varying reasons, glad to get away.

Justin knew he was being stalked. The smell of executive cordite was not unfamiliar to him. But he felt he was being outmanoeuvred because, unless he could get an accurate state of project report, he was in trouble. He'd better look into the franchise position. There was a reference to it in the contract. Andrew had the version he signed that night in Lyon after he had to get home to June. Andrew had looked at it while he was on the phone and said to him it appeared all right to him but he could run his expert eye over it anyway. Truth to tell, he had taken too much wine to read it carefully. The odd thing was he had no recollection of drinking much at all that evening. However, if he attempted to report to the board with the details he had now he would be torn asunder, then or later. Dempsey was simply setting him up.

Michael got a phone call from Andrew. 'Michael, ring Baldwin and arrange to give him whatever information you have got. Tease out the implications of that franchise thing.'

'Give him everything?'

'Yes. Produce a worst and best scenario for tomorrow's meeting. That's a good fellow.' The phone was put down.

Andrew asked Mary, his secretary, to get the chairman, John Kelly, on the telephone. As soon as he came through, and had exchanged the usual pleasantries, he outlined the position on the Luxor joint venture.

'Andrew, I thought Baldwin was doing a good job there. I know you expressed some reservations about him in the past. But it seems he has walked us into it here.'

'Well, John, I am as taken aback as you. The overrun is not Justin's fault. I accept the use of our franchise is very serious. It hands all the initiative over to the other side. Do you think we should report this to the board?'

'What else can we do? You are telling me we have two major problems on our hands. The Luxor project's viability and, worse, one of our main assets, our brand name, is now going to be devalued. No Andrew, these must be raised at next Friday's meeting. Is there no way that franchise agreement can be upended?'

'I could have Baldwin go into that, seeing as he signed it.'

'Okay. Try it then. And Andrew, do not underestimate the trouble some of your detractors on the board can create for you if this goes wrong.' The chairman then hung up.

'The worst is that we will over run by approximately thirty-seven per cent, or £1.3m.' It was the following morning and Justin was making his report to the executive directors' meeting.

'Add to that an anticipated loss of £200,000 per annum for the first couple of years instead of a projected profit at the end of the third year. We, Michael and I that is, cannot say for sure how many years it will take to turn around, two or at most five. I cannot quantify the effects of the franchise agreement until I get counsel's opinion.'

There was silence around the table; the others waited to take their lead from Andrew. Justin was more at ease, though still worried, after his meetings with Dempsey whose demeanour had altered. He had given him all the help he could and seemed to think the project had good long term prospects. That blasted franchise arrangement, they both admitted, was the real cruncher. Dempsey had ignored his remark that Roystone had read the contract before him.

'Justin, you will have to fly to Lyon immediately to ascertain precisely what is the situation with that waste disposal problem. More importantly, we need to get out of that franchise concession. You are the only one they might listen to.' Andrew was sounding conciliatory. One or two others expressed their agreement with his suggestion.

'Let you and I, Justin, meet later in my office where we can decide how you might approach them.'

Now the decision had been made Andrew was positively benign. The meeting ended with the other directors saying very little, lest they got drawn into the mess.

'Justin, I must update the board on Luxor.' Andrew was lolling back on one of the four easy chairs surrounding the brass and glass-topped coffee table in his office. He looked relaxed. 'It's not going to be easy. We must have all the facts and projections. I will have to tell them precisely what will be our overall exposure. Some will get excited, the usual directors who are always gunning for us. I am sure we can carry it off if we have done our homework. After all, Justin, you did not devalue, neither did you make up the cost of the waste disposal plant. At any rate stay in Lyon until you are satisfied you have got all the necessary information.'

'But should I not be at the meeting, Andrew?' Justin did not want to be absent. He had seen how easily things could go wrong at a board meeting. Besides, he was in the best position to answer any difficult questions.

'But of course, Justin. It should not take you long to get what we want. I have to emphasise how urgent it is for those two items to be cleared up. Otherwise the meeting is going to be a difficult one.'

He then turned to Dempsey, 'You will liaise closely with Justin on the financial report. It will be your report Justin, so, before I get it, you must be satisfied it is okay.'

'Fine. I'll go to Lyon now,' Justin said, feeling relieved that Dempsey was prevented from submitting a doomsday report to the board.

'By the way, Justin, don't leave Lyon before checking with me. There may be something in your report which might require further discussion with the French while you are there. See you on Friday morning before the meeting.'

Justin and Michael got up to leave. 'Michael, you left those draft quarterly accounts with me. I want to you to go through them with me now.'

They did not talk about the accounts though.

Afterwards Andrew rang his chairman.

'John, I'm afraid the Luxor thing is going to give trouble at tomorrow's board meeting. Justin has simply not been able to persuade them to give up on the franchise issue. We cannot agree to cover up their mistake on the waste disposal overrun. At over £1m it's just too much. I have told Baldwin to stay in Lyon until the board meeting starts on Friday morning, just in case a solution pops up.'

'Look here, Andrew, the board is not going to stomach a balls-up. That is what you are telling me it is.' Roystone knew from his tone the chairman was worried. *Good*, he thought.

'What will they do?' he asked.

'They will look for a head to roll. It has been leaked to some of them that Luxor has run into difficulties. Problem is, what do they know? Brady and Doyle have asked me if the Luxor project was sound. What could I say other than a progress report was due at the next meeting. That, Andrew, is what you and I agreed I should say.'

Kelly's tone was getting reproachful. Andrew was hunched over the console, his eyes fixed on the watercolour in front of him, seeing nothing. He chose his words carefully, picking up the fawn hand piece for greater intimacy.

'John, I appreciate your concern. The situation is quite worrying. It was only the other day that Baldwin updated me on what we are now facing us. I had told him at the outset that this project had got such a high profile that I required constant briefing. But for Michael Dempsey I might not have been alerted to its full ramifications. Fortunately I was aware of it, without knowing its parameters, when Doyle rang me. Baldwin is in Lyon without having reached any agreement with Sommalier on the two substantive issues – the waste disposal plant and the franchise. The others are uncontrollable cost increases, except Justin might have covered forward our foreign exchange exposure. While he is still in Lyon he wants to come back for tomorrow's board meeting. I have told him to stay and keep up the pressure on them until our meeting ends at lunch time tomorrow, just in case they make a concession. We can deal with the matter under "Any other Business", with your agreement, that is. Justin, of course, is still strongly resisting my request for him to stay in Lyon.'

'Good God, Andrew, is he crazy? He has got us into this mess and now wants to disobey your reasonable request, which is after all geared to save his neck. His behaviour is irrational. So much so I wonder at your bothering trying to help him. In the circumstances better make it the second last item on the agenda.' The chairman knew, if it were included in the rag bag of items under 'Any other Business', the members would think the item was being downgraded to suit the executive. That would only infuriate them to a point where they would demand a special meeting. He did not want that.

'Good thinking, John. I will do that. As regards Baldwin, he did a good job in the past though,' proffered Andrew. This remark merely increased the passion at the other end of the phone.

'Past is past. We have to deal with the present. To think he nearly got the post of Managing Director. He would, you know, if it wasn't for my casting vote and I had to take some stick for that from one of the board when I voted for you. Andrew. I question if a man like that has any future with the company?' John was in full flight.

'It could come to that tomorrow, John,' said Andrew quietly.

'Andrew, if he appears at the board meeting tomorrow against your wishes, with no solution to the problem, then he will have to go.' The chairman was not in a mood for objections. Andrew was not finished.

'John, I appreciate your concern. Nevertheless, let us not rush into anything until we see how things pan out.'

'Andrew, I appreciate your loyalty to Baldwin, I really do, but business must go on. When the brown stuff hits the fan in this high profile exercise someone is going to get hit. Justin Baldwin deserves to be that someone. I will speak to you tomorrow before the meeting.' John Kelly put down his phone thinking Andrew was unusually soft-hearted on this one.

Andrew, for his part, put down the receiver carefully, noticing the sun coming through the vertical blinds straight into his eyes. Humming through his closed mouth, he wondered, as he pushed back his chair and walked around the large desk, if a blind could be invented which would shift around with the sunlight. Sunlight, he felt, couldn't be good for those paintings facing the window.

Pierre Dupois, director for business expansion, with Sommalier PLC looked after Justin Baldwin's retreating back. He could clearly see the metaphorical knife in its middle. He liked Justin. They had become good friends out of their negotiations on the Luxor venture. The question was, did he know the truth? Seeing as he had been head-hunted out of Sommalier by a Parisian firm, he would be gone next month, maybe he should wise Justin up on what was going on? Justin, for his part was puzzled and concerned. He had cleared his report with a surprisingly co-operative Dempsey. The figures were not good. Yet if they kept their head it could work out okay in the long term. He had met a brick wall on the franchise arrangement. He couldn't understand how they had got such a complicated provision through Roystone. That much he had managed to prise out of them. Roystone had carefully examined the contract that night. The combination of drink and worry about June had blunted his critical faculties. What puzzled him was their sense of smugness about the whole thing and Pierre Dupois whom he sensed was embarrassed. Nor did they appear too concerned about the waste disposal plant costs. Roystone had insisted he stay in Lyon to see if he could achieve any change of mind. He had said, 'I have your report for the meeting. There is little you can add to it, Andrew. Ring me again at ten in the morning, just before the meeting.'

'But Andrew I will be of more use in Dublin at the meeting,' offered Justin, 'after all it is my head the board are likely to be after.'

'I hardly think it will come to that, Justin. Do as I say and look, take the weekend in Paris. We could even send June over,' Andrew said solicitously.

Justin smelt a rat. 'Thanks all the same Andrew. I really appreciate your offer but June has commitments this weekend,' and thinking on his feet, 'in fact I had promised her I would be home for Friday afternoon.'

'I will ring her and tell her you are delayed.'

'All right, Andrew, if you insist I will stay,' said Justin, unwilling to make him an enemy at the meeting.

He immediately picked up the phone and got his wife in Dublin. He explained she could expect a call from Andrew when she was to tell him it was extremely important for he, Justin, to be home on Friday.

He then rang his friend Joe Fortune to find out where Luxor was on the agenda, and at what time it was likely to arise. He then, as requested, went to Pierre's office.

At the board meeting the chairman's unease was palpable. The thought of the forthcoming Luxor discussion disturbed his normal smooth chairing of the meeting, so much so that when asked by Doyle about Luxor, under matters arising from the minutes, he said, 'Can you not see it is item seven on the agenda?'

An item that far down the agenda, with a meeting scheduled to end at one o'clock, merely alerted those members in the know to ensure it was reached in good time. Any attempt by Roystone to procrastinate on other matters generated acute restlessness amongst those members. Thus when item seven was eventually reached, Andrew had lost any element of surprise among those who mattered.

The chairman introduced the item by saying Andrew had brought it to his attention just recently.

'As you are all aware gentlemen, the director in charge is Justin Baldwin. He had been at the last two meetings when you approved of the project, and later when you approved an extra £0.5m. Since then the project has encountered some problems, but let the MD give his report.'

Andrew apologised for the absence of Justin saying, 'For reasons he would explain later, he was in Lyon. However I have his report which I shall have the secretary read out to you.'

At the conclusion, Andrew said, 'If there are any queries I shall be glad to answer them.'

There was a stunned silence. The only sound was the hum of the motor overhead in the plant room. Some members found their hazy reflections on the table in front of them totally absorbing. Others just kept staring into space. No one was prepared to open the batting. The silence continued.

Eventually Dave Doyle opened the discussion, setting the tone, by asking, 'Who, Managing Director, is responsible for this mess? Who authorised the granting of the franchise? How could a water treatment plant be undercosted to such a degree? Would we have approved of this project if we realised where we are now? Both we and Sommalier have milked the maximum publicity from this Luxor project. How are we going to explain away this to the media, our shareholders and the public at large?'

Andrew, amidst the murmuring of assent, got in first, 'As Managing Director I must accept responsibility. There are however extenuating circumstances...' He hesitated for a second when his chairman interrupted him.

'Gentlemen, gentlemen, the Managing Director's defence of his director is highly commendable, but the reality is that the marketing development director is the director responsible. That is perfectly obvious from the report, and also from my knowledge of events. I know Justin Baldwin has served this company well in the past, but regrettably not in this case.'

'Are you telling us chairman,' it was Tim Russell, a confidant of the Chairman's, 'in a round about way that Baldwin should go? If so, I agree. If not, tell us what you think.'

'It is really up to you as directors. The MD feels the venture could be viable in the future and is reluctant to dismiss Baldwin. He has accepted my view that the granting of the franchise is a disaster. Hence the reason he has ordered Baldwin to stay in Lyon to see if that problem can be rescued before this meeting. Unfortunately he has not succeeded.'

The chairman then said each member should be given an opportunity to express their views.

This they did after which Jim Brady and Dave Doyle proposed and seconded a motion that 'The chairman and

Managing Director negotiate a severance settlement with Mr Justin Baldwin, following which the Managing Director personally takes responsibility for negotiating with Sommalier on the future of the project, and the withdrawal of the franchise.'

It was put to the meeting and carried.

Just then the door of the boardroom opened. Justin Baldwin walked into the room. Again the silence was deafening. He walked round the table to a vacant seat opposite an astonished chairman. He sat down and pulled a tape recorder out of his black briefcase, plus a sheaf of notes.

Recovering his composure John Kelly, with as much dignity as his unpreparedness allowed, said, 'Mr Baldwin, it is not usual for directors to barge into a meeting like that.'

'Chairman and directors,' Justin was careful to address all, 'I know you are discussing Luxor at this meeting and I have some information relevant to your discussion on this tape. Just in case the tape is not enough I have here a sworn affidavit of what is on the tape, it's in this briefcase. No pun intended,' he added hastily, tapping the case and lowering the hostility somewhat, 'I can assure you that I was not on holiday in Lyon, but I did get a nice souvenir.'

'Mr Baldwin, how dare you come in here and speak in this manner?' The chairman was nearly apoplectic.

'Gentlemen, I take it you are dealing with my career. I have some information vital to your discussion which will be of great interest to you. If you do not want to hear me out then I can leave right now and I'll take it to my legal advisers.'

This statement created even more surprise than his sudden appearance. There was a shuffling of papers with members looking at one another wondering what to say.

He had got their attention. Tim Ryan, one of the two who had voted against the motion, and who had a suspicion that Baldwin was being made the whipping boy, said, 'We had better listen to what Mr Baldwin has to say. It will cost us nothing, I presume.'

'It may be to your advantage,' said Justin.

'Oh all right,' said the chairman, wondering if he was in a catch-22 situation, 'go on.'

'The voice you are about to hear is that of Pierre Dupois, a director of Sommalier.' He then switched on the tape.

After the preliminary hissing which caused at least one listener to hope it had been wiped out, a voice with a French accent said, 'Can I commence?' This was followed by a statement: 'I, Pierre Dupois, wish to swear that what I am about to relate is wholly the truth relating to the events which took place on the 19th and 20th June last in Lyon, France. The substance of what I shall say here has been sworn before an attorney and the original given to Mr Justin Baldwin on this day, 16th September.'

'In the Hotel Royal in Lyon, France after the heads of agreement in principle had been agreed and annotated by Mr Albert Poussance, president of Sommalier PLC and Mr Andrew Roystone, Managing Director, Natural Foods, for the production and marketing of alcohol-flavoured pizzas, a dinner party was held, hosted by Mr Poussance. As one would expect on occasions such as this there was a plentiful supply of good French wine and Cognac. So much so that Mr Poussance got ill. Naturally he did not admit his *maladie*, I mean indisposition, merely excusing himself on the grounds of urgent business. He did expressly ask his wife to stay. She too apparently made her farewells to Mr

Roystone. I say 'apparently' because she was seen to return, and accompany Mr Roystone to his room.

'Someone, unknown, telephoned Mr Poussance at his house and informed him as to what had happened. He returned with the company's security guard who went with him to the hotel bedroom where Mr Roystone's presence was recorded on an instamatic camera. The security guard has given a written report of the... incident. Mr Roystone at first attempted to brazen it out. When Mr Poussance threatened to forward proof to his chairman and board he offered compensation. I need not go into the settlement terms in detail here. It is sufficient to say that he offered *inter alia* to let Mr Poussance have a franchise of your "Greenlands" brand name. The franchise agreement covered use by both Luxor and Sommalier, not just a promise of use as he subsequently maintained to his fellow directors.'

'On the evening of 20th July, when the agreement was to be signed, Mr Baldwin was given specially strengthened wine to dull his perceptive powers to a degree that he would accede to Mr Roystone's urgings to sign the contract without examining it. If he had done so he would have seen that the franchise proposal had been altered, in a convoluted legal fashion, to a commitment. I believe Mr Baldwin left for home immediately afterwards having received a message his wife was ill.'

'I must add that it is my opinion the Luxor project is a good one. The extra costs are unfortunate, but not unusual in an undertaking of this nature. In the long run the joint enterprise will, in my opinion be very successful. That is all I have to say now. I am available to answer any questions on what I have said.'

'In conclusion, I have been asked to join another company in Paris, where I lived in the past, effective from next week. I leave Sommalier on good terms. It had not been my intention to get involved in this regrettable affair. My conscience however forbids me to leave, knowing the precarious position in which Mr Baldwin has been placed. In my estimation he has handled this project with great skill. He should not be made a casualty of another man's er... mischief...'

For the third time that morning not one word was spoken by the board members as Justin wound back the tape in the little grey Sony tape recorder. Justin was the first to speak. 'There are copies of the notarised sworn statement here, for anyone who wants to see it, together with a copy of the photo.' He added dryly, 'I hardly think anyone wants to view that photo.'

Dave Doyle spoke first, clearing his throat as he did so. 'Chairman, we are all devastated by these revelations. It is damnable and needs careful consideration by us, immediately I should think. Now, I suggest the board ask the executive to leave the boardroom and await our call in their offices, if we should need them. They should talk to no one about this, not even talk to one another.'

John Kelly was still in a state of shock. Doyle's initiative was a direct assumption of the role of chairman, his role. This roused him to take control of proceedings.

'Mr Roystone, very serious allegations have been made in that tape. They could be defamatory if they are not true. We will need our lawyer here immediately.' Turning to Joe Fortune he said, 'Mr. Fortune, will you please do that straight away.'

Then turning to the Managing Director, he asked, 'Managing Director, have you anything to say at this stage?'

Andrew, ashen-faced, tried to make the best of the situation, 'Chairman, it would be imprudent for me to say anything until I have spoken to my lawyer.' He knew he was ruined by those two bastards. The board would run miles from a scandal. He knew there lay the route for him to get the best settlement possible. Added to that was the statement the project was still viable. All in all, there was something to be rescued out of the mess. Goddammit he had had Baldwin cold; the decision to fire had even been taken at the meeting. That creep Dupois; he could swing for that lousy French bastard.

He rose from his seat and followed the rest of the executive as they trooped out of the boardroom.

Everyone does not Surf

If it was not for the strong wind off the Mediterranean the heat from the early June sun would have been unbearable. The more cautious newcomers from the United Kingdom hugged what shade they could squeeze from their Canvas Holiday tents or inadequate campsite trees. Their shade was sufficient to enable them to scoff at the degrees of redness of the foolish returning from the nearby beach. Not that it was entirely ideal for the onlookers either, with a gusting wind that threatened to take their tents into the sky. They didn't, of course, but the strong gusts did give them vicarious pleasures. That and a common language engendered a type of camaraderie among the viewers. Besides, their voluntary imprisonment by the blazing sun gave them an excuse to observe the comings and goings of their fellow campers, old and new.

The noon arrival of a French couple, with their ageing Renault 21TD pulling an even older Caravelair caravan, at first did not attract much attention. That is until it was observed how skilfully they manoeuvred their caravan sideways into the apparently too small emplacement. The size of the emplacements caused every other caravanner to park their caravans with their fronts facing the sea and their cars squeezed in parallel. One whole side, the one with the door, of this couple's Caravelair faced out to sea with hardly a foot to spare from the stanchions marking out the limits of their site. The viewers watched fascinated, fully expecting a stanchion to be smashed by the caravan.

The couple, however, displayed total confidence in their co-ordinated approach to the manoeuvring of the caravan. He drove, while she gave hand signals and precise instructions in a low tone. The siting was performed with the minimum of fuss. The onlookers had only a rudimentary grasp of French yet they were in no doubt as to the clarity of her directions to her husband in the car. One of the observers had decided to time the manoeuvre. To everyone's surprise, it took a mere four minutes and twenty seconds whereas those observers who had towed a caravan agreed they could not have done it without knocking down one at least of the two stanchions which provided light or water.

Once the Caravelair was sited to their satisfaction the man, there was a difference of opinion whether he should be called partner or husband, parked the Renault in an adjoining vacant emplacement. He then took a sailboard and mast from the roof of their car, checked it out and then returned to help his partner erect an open-type awning on the sea side of their caravan. Once up, they laid down a plastic floor to cover the sand on which they placed a table and two chairs. Finally she covered the table with a check-coloured cloth before placing a vase of flowers on it. Those of the viewers who were behind the Caravelair heard a *sotto voce* account of events by one of their group. She, for it was a she, gave a graphic account of the furnishing and, more particularly, the kiss he gave her when she had arranged the flowers. The lady observers, or rather listeners, gave a smile of approval at this expression of true romance from what was after all a middle-aged couple.

There was some argument amongst the viewers as to whether the awning would hold in the wind. A surreptitious inspection by one couple, self-confessed experts in these things, gave a thumbs up sign. It would not blow down. Another discussion, started by the men, centred on whether the flowers were artificial or fresh. The fresh argument prevailed as over the next few days the flowers changed every second day.

When they had finished with the caravan he again checked out the sailboard by erecting its mast and sail. Satisfied, he went back to the caravan. Neither at any stage gave any indication of being observed, nor of understanding English.

Later she strolled over to the tap and filled their water container, not before greeting the observers in French. Her greeting was neither friendly nor unfriendly, perhaps best described as matter of fact, though with a ghost of a smile. Whilst the tap filled the container it gave them an opportunity to observe her at close quarters. Her left hand had a wedding ring so they presumed with pleasure she was his wife, not a just a companion. They figured she was in her mid-forties. At first glance not a great beauty, however further consideration brought out the suggestion that she had an indefinable magnetism. The Welsh lady in the last tent put her finger on it. She suggested she could have been the Mona Lisa thirty years after de Vinci had finished his painting. 'Fifteen thirty three, now that ages her,' offered one wit. They all agreed she had that same air of repose, even the same knowing look but the years had given her a more thickset body.

He, it was agreed, was very French. A macho type who still looked superbly fit, even in middle age. A London lady observer said he had 'the look of a middle-aged Jean Gabin, still carrying a reminder of a marvellously good-looking youth.' The others chose not to dispute that as they had no idea what she was talking about. Those who might have known were not going to offer a clue as to their age. The more perceptive ladies noted that the silver-streaked hair, cut suitably short, together with a muscular frame produced some concealed envy among their spouses.

The couple soon settled into a routine over the next six days. He went out sailboarding every morning, and most afternoons. Those who began to brave the beach reported he was totally at home on his sailboard, even outclassing most others in the strongest winds.

She went to the shop every morning and returned with a baguette under her arm and a bag of groceries. Her greeting, on passing, was always polite and inscrutably reserved. There was no conversation because neither side knew the other's language. While he was surfing she read, either sitting under the awning or in the sun. Each morning she accompanied her husband to the beach where she had a swim and he windsurfed. Invariably she returned alone while he continued his windsurfing.

On his return, morning and evening, they exchanged kisses and he would then help her with the preparation of a meal. Most evenings he would carefully check his board and equipment before they went for a stroll, either to the village or along the beach. The observers accepted them as a very self-contained, if not devoted, couple who kept themselves to themselves. As a result they soon lost interest in them concentrating instead on the Russian family who had, incredibly, reached the Languedoc in their Lada.

Then one morning the awning was down. Apparently taken down by Mrs Lisa as she became known. The surfboard was not on view; in the caravan they figured. She reversed the car out of the emplacement and began pulling at the caravan's tow bar to get it out on to the pathway behind the Renault, not an easy task for a woman. The male observers fell over themselves to help her. They received that composed smile, coupled with a *'merci beaucoup'*. Together they got the caravan attached to the Renault and, after a final check on the lights and attachments, she carefully drove it down the narrow path towards the entrance and the office, probably to pick up her husband at the cashier's office.

One viewer remarked that their departure did not fit the husband's macho image, but no one thought any more about them. The Russians were far more interesting. That is until just before noon when the husband came up from the beach in his wet suit with his sailboard under his arm. He looked around the empty emplacements in undisguised perplexity. He looked at where the Renault had been parked. He turned around in a complete circle with his sailboard under his arm, and stopped before firing his precious sailboard equipment to the ground. At least it explained to the viewers the whereabouts of the sailboard.

He strode over to the nearest viewers' tents and let loose a flood of French. They looked blank so he waved his arms up and down before going next door and repeating the process. It was all to no avail. The observers could only make signs to indicate his wife had gone off with the car and caravan an hour earlier. To communicate that information was in itself an achievement.

One husband reaching into the recesses of his memory whispered to his wife, too loud as it transpired, '*Cherchez la femme*'. The Frenchman turned and glared at him. For a second it looked as if he would hit him. Instead he strode off, without another word. He never returned, nor did his wife, not even to collect the sailboard which lay on the ground as a plaintive reminder, of what? Incompatibility, or even infidelity? Who knows?

Some Flowed over the Chinese Carpet

It wasn't as if Gerry didn't know the dog. Of course he did. He could hardly miss Bill and the Great Dane taking their daily walk down the West Pier. Besides, Bill was a neighbour of long standing and Gerry had stopped to pass the time of day with him on innumerable occasions. Funny thing though, Zinger always ignored him. Mutual antipathy maybe, because while Gerry couldn't speak for the dog he was not keen on big dogs himself, and Zinger was a one hundred and fifty pound monster.

To further complicate things, Bill did not even own the dog. He just volunteered to bring it for a walk each day. Gerry had been curious about the arrangement, though not to the point where he would ask a specific question; it was unusual for a man to be so devoted to a dog, especially a dog that size, and not his own. After all what did the owner mean having an animal that size and not be prepared to look after it?

All was revealed, by sheer chance, one day when he met Bill with Zinger at the end of the West Pier, just as the HSS was between the two piers on its way to Holyhead.

'You know Gerry, never in my life did I think I would see a ship as big as that. Isn't it a magnificent vessel?'

'It's supposed to be as big as a football pitch,' volunteered Gerry.

'Size always impressed me Gerry, that's why I walk Zinger.'

Hardly had he mentioned his name than Zinger started to jump around the pier to the consternation of the other people who were marvelling at the giant vessel. He was like a bucking brown bronco, thought Gerry. When he had calmed the dog down Bill continued, 'All my life I wanted to own a Great Dane but I could never afford to keep one because of cost and lack of space. They would eat you out of house and home. That's why when Jack asked me to take him for a walk while he was away, I jumped at the chance. We got on so well we sort of drifted together. It suited Jack too as he is away a lot. I suppose it appears odd to you, Gerry?'

'Oh not at all, he is a magnificent creature. Obviously he is very fond of you, Bill,' offered Gerry, not in all sincerity.

A few weeks later Gerry answered a ring at his door to find Bill there, thankfully without Zinger.

'Gerry, sorry for bothering you, but I wonder if you could do me a favour?'

'Sure Bill, what is it?'

'Gerry, I have to go down the country tomorrow to an uncle's funeral and I need someone to take Zinger for a walk. Unfortunately Jack O'Reilly is away too. I wouldn't put Zinger in everyone's care, at least he knows you from our walks on the pier.'

Gerry hesitated for a second. It's amazing what thoughts can pass through one's mind in a split second: *that animal terrifies me, I don't think he cares for me, never saw him wagging his tail when he saw me, how can I control him if he wants to go his own way? I read they originated in China, bred to take on bears, Jesus how can I really refuse Bill when he wants to go to his uncle's funeral?*

'Of course I will Bill. What do I have to do?'

'Just call in about eleven and take him out for a walk, the lead will be on the table. I'll have fed him before I leave. I would not like to have you feed him all those cows' heads.'

Gerry's stomach nearly turned at the thought of what he might have been in for. At least it would give him a chance to see Jack's antique furniture and Chinese silk carpets. He had heard they were worth a fortune.

On the morning, the closer it got to eleven, the more apprehensive Gerry became. He called in at ten minutes to the hour. The stories about the furniture were correct, so far as the downstairs was concerned at any rate. It was shown off to its best effect in the big old house. The Chinese handmade silk carpets in the living room and the blue vases really took Gerry's fancy, so much so he almost missed Zinger lying on the biggest beanbag he had ever seen. It was in the far corner of the room.

Zinger with the minimum movement of his head viewed Gerry's entrance impassively. He showed no sign of recognition, nor was there any movement in his tail. Gerry interpreted his look as baleful, which did nothing for his peace of mind. Gerry waved the heavy lead in Zinger's general direction. For one ridiculous moment he felt like a clergyman waving the incense in the thurible at the faithful, or even an Egyptian priest waving it at the Sphinx. He hoped he was not going to be the sacrificial victim. It was useless; if the dog had an expression it was now one of disdain.

He tried another tactic. He made for the door shaking the lead and calling 'Zinger'. The great Dane slowly, imperiously it seemed to Gerry, turned his head away from him. It was an impasse. He was not going for a walk with a stranger. He would wait for Bill.

Gerry was conscious about Bill's detailing of the sequence of events. Walk, interrupted by a pee and later maybe a turd. Time was running out, he had better get the damned dog out. He repeated the lead rattling and name calling.

This time he got a response, or it seemed that way. Zinger slowly turned his massive head in Gerry's direction, never mind his look of utter disdain, and slowly pushed his forepaws up until he was sitting upright. Then he got up on all four legs, stretched, and looked directly at Gerry who began to wonder how he would get the lead clipped on to an unfriendly Great Dane.

Zinger ambled across the room, stopped at one of the mahogany antique stands which had a Chinese Ming vase on it. Foolish, thought Gerry, positioning it in a room where there is a dog that size.

He was right of course. Zinger lifted his right hind leg and let loose with the power of a fireman's hose. Gerry watched, appalled at the flood. The Chinese vase began to rock on the stand before it slowly fell over and landed on the wet carpet. The flood of dog's urine appeared to be never ending, Gradually the fine silk carpet was submerged. Gerry stood petrified until he realised the floods were coming his way. He leaped back towards the door just as Zinger lowered his leg and casually made his way back towards the beanbag, taking great care to avoid placing his paws in his own urine.

Gerry gave a feeble and unconvincing wave of the lead while calling 'now Zinger.' It was really only a gesture. Zinger ignored him as he lowered himself into the beanbag and closed his eyes. The interview was ended.

Gerry looked at all his options, all one of them. He gently closed the door of the living room and locked the front door behind him. At least Bill would be home in the evening. He would leave a note for him on the hall table to the effect that Zinger had refused to go for a walk.

The Perfect Trek

Liz was mature beyond her twenty-six years which, when combined with exceptional beauty, gave her a head start on most mortals, especially male mortals.

John, before he laid eyes on Liz, figured, over his fifty years, he had seen the perfect woman several times over. Liz destroyed, rather pulverised, that belief. Her face was derived from a classical bone structure which was shown off, to an exhilarating degree, by her natural golden-brown hair. To which could be added a simply flawless figure and, later when they met, a compatible personality. He was not permitted to pick up a certain detachment in her character. John, for his part, in daylight at least, looked ten years younger whilst in artificial light, with his still black hair, could even be taken by a stranger for a thirty odd year old. He could even act that younger age sometimes in social circles, not so well in business circles. Close examination revealed a slight tendency to put on weight, too thin a mouth behind the *bonhomie* and one tell-tale brown liver mark on the back of his left hand.

Surprisingly the millions of dollars he had accumulated had not left their mark, in spite of a lifestyle of excessive working hours, playing hard, a reputation for never taking prisoners and of course a wonderful accumulator of enemies. He liked to think he was fit because he trekked and played tennis, both somewhat episodically though. Business tended to limit his trekking to a couple of times a year in the Rockies.

John believed he was born to be wealthy. Dollars were attracted to him. He responded by accumulating millions of them, as if it was his God-given right, though he did admit privately it had more to do with Mammon. A merchant banking colleague was told-off once with 'Time is money and he who wastes mine has his hand in my wallet.' That story did the rounds to the extent that he was occasionally asked if he had any time in his wallet. The medics would have labelled him a fairly typical Type A.

Liz, Liz Christiensen, to give her full name, was a nurse, a good one at that, having won the gold medal in her final year, after two silver medals earlier for obstetrics and medicine, from one of the most prestigious hospitals in the country. She charted her career with care, gaining experience in a couple of well known clinics before being head-hunted by Dr Swartz. Some of her colleagues saw it as a step backwards but Liz knew where she was going. Dr Swartz had about the most upmarket clientele in the State and Liz knew she was not married to nursing. Definitely not. Like John, she adored money, lots of it. It did not reciprocate her affections so she had to look to her other talents, one of which, the obvious apart, was an ability to act.

Her prowess at tennis delayed her entry into nursing. That is until an elbow injury prevented her from ever learning just how good a professional tennis player she might have been. In retrospect she was not that sorry, finding the budding professional players tiresome, with no conversational horizon beyond their base lines.

John was not a true romantic but when he saw Liz he was smitten, telling Swartzie that his first sighting was 'of a rare specimen of perfection in a nurse's uniform'. Liz, he added, 'to put it in the vernacular, was an arresting sight for sore male eyes'. A market-led product, for males at any rate, if ever there was one. Dr Swartz knew how to please his patients.

John wanted Liz, he could afford her and he was going to get her. For John it was as simple as that.

No percentage though in rushing in mindlessly. He needed about a week to check out the merchandise. Swartzie first, since he employed her, and having made a few bucks from his friendship with John he was more than accommodating. Liz passed that test, particularly as there was an absence of any current romantic, or marital, entanglements.

Liz allowed herself to be swept off her feet. A few 'Oh Johns' now and again for the sake of credibility.

She too had done her homework, even before she first encountered John in Dr Swartz's clinic, having read about him – who hadn't – and his financial wheeler dealings; plus his messy divorce from his childhood sweetheart. More factually, his childhood conduit to his first million, whose father just happened to be a multi-million dollar property tycoon. Their marriage, initially successful while he was struggling then, with wealth, then meandering along for the next twenty years. Apparently with Ruby was myopic to John's preoccupation with his favourite sport on a six by five foot soft pitch. His animal magnetism and easy charm helped cloud her judgement.

The drawn out break-up, with its inevitable tensions, coupled with his 'A' type temperament and a macho lifestyle had begun to take their internal toll by the time he acquired Liz.

Some two years into the marriage there was a week of unusually intensive business negotiations, ending with a celebrity dinner on the Saturday and a game of corporate softball on the Sunday. This was followed by continued celebrations with his younger colleagues into early Monday morning, all of which took its toll.

John was still exhausted when he got up, much more than Liz had ever seen him. The mug of black coffee didn't do the trick. Well, maybe it did since it produced the first sign of bodily rebellion. Liz, sitting opposite, noticed his pallor, sweatbeads on his forehead, and a slightly crumpled expression on his normally firm face.

John felt terrible. His heart was pounding with fast irregular beats striving to break its way out of its ribcage. Energy seemed to be draining from his body as if through a sump hole. His left arm was going numb.

'Darling are you all right?'

'Honey, I could feel better,' was all John could get out.

'Tell me, darling, exactly how you feel? You don't look at all well.' It was the clinical nurse speaking.

It wasn't in John's nature to admit to pain, but this was different and so, with some difficulty, he described his symptoms.

'My darling John, you appear to be having a tachycardia attack.' Liz tried to speak calmly.

'Press your two forefingers on to your closed eyes.' John did so.

'Now keep them there, and try to relax.'

'Feel any better?' she said after a few minutes' silence, making for the phone on the kitchen wall.

'I'd better give Dr Swartz a ring and get him over here.'

'Liz honey, don't ring Swartzie, I think I feel better already.' John's instinctive dislike of doctors and hospitals almost overcame his condition. Surprisingly he did feel a little better, but Liz knew that could be the dentist and the toothache syndrome.

'Darling you must be checked out immediately. I could be quite wrong but at the very least you'll have to have an electrocardiogram. Please John, for my sake, I know you are probably okay but I will not rest until we get a medical opinion. Please.'

Even in his misery John was flattered by Liz's concern. 'Okay, if you must honey, give him a ring.'

Liz was a qualified nurse whose judgement Swartz could not ignore so he was there in a record ten minutes, by which time John felt in better shape.

To an outsider Swartz was his normally suave self. Liz however detected a look of anxiety in his eyes as she outlined the symptoms.

He felt John's pulse, listened to his heart, took his blood pressure and got samples of blood. 'It looks like Liz was right, you need a full check-up now John.' Swartz was not taking no for an answer. 'Assuming it is a tachycardia it didn't come out of the blue. I reckon John you are going to have to change your lifestyle if you are not to have another, or worse.'

John had known Swartz a long time. He would not bring him in for a check-up unless he felt it absolutely necessary.

The tests confirmed Liz's diagnosis – a tachycardia attack.

'John, you now must change your approach to work, if you don't want to be in here again. Pace yourself, recognise that at fifty-three you cannot do what you did at twenty-three. It's not a big deal. Your body is just as anxious to stay alive as you. It just doesn't want the candle burning at fingers and toes.'

John realised Swartzie was trying to be helpful but really... He wondered what he was getting at about fingers and toes, then he remembered about burning the candle at both ends. Maybe he knew about Marge? or at least guessed. A wily old bird was Swartzie.

If it hadn't been for this he had intended to sound out Liz on a divorce. Marge was getting impatient about his reluctance to divest himself of her. Mind you, he was glad he hadn't said anything to her the other day, even if he had promised Marge, given Liz's concern about his illness. She had been good. God (as if He cared) what a mess. He hoped Liz knew nothing of Marge. She certainly gave no indication, quite the opposite if anything.

He was glad to get out of the clinic and away from Swartzie's warnings about moderate exercise, less alcohol and a one-ended candle.

John did slow down his pace, not as much as Swartzie would have liked, and, over the following months, the incident became of less consequence, except for the smarmy business associates who enquired about his health, as if they gave a shit.

Liz did know all about John's affair with Marge and she had no intention of losing out to that child fashion harlot. None at all. The stakes were too high.

The situation was getting to John. Marge was giving him ultimatums, which he knew were going to be acted upon sooner than later. He could not live without her but after one long drawn out bust up in the past he could do without another. It wasn't that he disliked Liz. While she had many good points there was another, impenetrable, Liz under the goods on display; an air of detachment, aloofness maybe, leaving a faint feeling of unease. With Marge there was total empathy and warmth; all the barriers were down and he simply felt he could not live without her. Maybe a trek was the answer. He needed time to think. A trek in the Colorado plateau seemed like a good idea.

'Oh my darling is that not a bit risky after your illness? Do you really feel up to it?'

'Pet, I have just spoken to Swartzie. He tells me I am fit for my age and a trek would be a good idea so long as I don't run up the mountain.'

'Did he do a stress test on you?'

'Yeah, an' I walked that stupid treadmill for ages.'

'But John they can set it at different speeds, depending on your age and fitness.'

'Liz sweetheart, Swartzie said I came out so good the Rockies would be a cake walk,' John said with conviction and a large degree of poetic licence. He needed to get away from these two women.

'Of course, you have been there before, and know the terrain. Thank goodness you have gone off the Himalayas, which you wished to trek last winter. I'll always remember your telling me they were the youngest and highest mountains in the world.'

'The Himalayas would take too much time, which I couldn't afford just now.'

'You're dead right darling, stick to the good ole Rockies. No sense in taking risks after what you have been through. You are not getting any younger. I'm glad you are taking the sensible decision. When you first mentioned the Himalayas I looked up the statistics and was amazed to find they are twice as high as the Rockies. Mount Elbert is only 14,431 feet whereas Everest is 29,028 feet. Can you imagine that? Besides, Nepal is too far away for a trek, a day's air travel, and the risk of Montezuma's revenge, or whatever they call it there.'

John did not reply, nor did he raise the subject of the trek again for a few days.

'Liz, I know you are not going to agree with me but I have been thinking about that trek. First the Speedwell deal is going to come to a head sooner than anticipated. Second if I did the Himalayan trek it would mean I would no longer have to listen to those mealy-mouthed bastards enquiring about my health, and at the same time hoping I am on the way out. Thirdly I am fit enough now, according to Swartzie the other day, provided I take my time.'

'You're not serious, darling. I was talking to Dr Swartz yesterday when he told me you had this plan in your mind.

John, I should go to the Rockies if I were you. I would be worried stiff about your going so far away. You know these places are quite remote. It's too dangerous for you.'

'Mervin Sudds told me a couple of sixty year old friends of his did the Annapurna trek last November, over 12,000 feet, which is higher than our Mount Taylor.'

'Kathmandu is no Phoenix John. Please darling, stick to the Rockies.'

John said nothing. He was fed up with pious platitudes about his health; at least a climb like the Himalayas would shut them up for good. He could become something of a celebrity amongst his associates. He didn't say Swartzie had suggested he take Liz with him, at least as far as the last village, where her nursing experience could be an asset if there were any difficulties. Then there was Marge. She would go mad if he told her he was going trekking with Liz unless...

The following day Dr Swartz rang Liz, who then spoke to John.

'John dearest, I wasn't going to mention this to you but Dr Swartz suggested I go with you, if you decide to go to the Himalayas. Naturally I agreed but the decision would be yours.'

She didn't tell him that Dr Swartz urged her to dissuade him from going trekking anywhere.

This piece of information was coming a bit too soon for John where the germ of a solution was beginning to form in his head. If it could finish his relationship with Liz, Marge just might agree to his taking her with him. The present impasse was driving him crazy and he needed time to think his idea through.

'Liz honey, I'll give the whole question of going to Nepal some thought. I don't disagree with you about the

Rockies being easier, yet the Himalayas are very tempting. There's still plenty of time as November is best for the Himalayas, which gives me about ten weeks to set it up. Let me talk to Dr Swartz first to see what he has to say.'

Dr Swartz was anxious not to lose his favourite patient and strongly advised John to take Liz, not to the Himalayas but to the Rockies, leading John to believe Swartzie knew nothing about Marge.

'John, whichever trek you decide on the maximum height should not exceed 12,000 feet, and John, please take it easy. You are too good a friend to lose.'

When he came home that evening he spoke to his wife, 'Liz pet, I have cleared it with Swartzie to go to the Himalayas with you. It suits fine as Foster Reynolds can't go to the Rockies with me, or anywhere else for that matter. He has got an offer for one of his companies which is going to tie him up for the rest of the year. I can go for fourteen days, commencing 10th November, if that's okay with you.'

Liz was delighted. Things were looking up so she immediately went into serious training, even to trekking up the Ramapo Mountains.

Marge was unenthusiastic at first but then anything which terminated the sharing arrangement was attractive to her. John guaranteed he would arrange the break with Liz before he returned. The flights to Kathmandu were tediously uneventful and after nearly twenty-four hours journeying the haze surrounding the city was a welcome sight. The Indian Air airbus landed smoothly on a landing strip surrounded by the nearby Himalayan range, giving John his first sight of Everest. The airbus disgorged its weary passengers into a new world of smog, dust, noise, bustle and sacred cows. The Nepalese officials were disarmingly polite about stamping every piece of baggage and documentation which could take an imprint of their rubber stamps. Once through the crowded customs area the travel agent placed a garland round their necks and whisked them to the Soaltee Oberoi, reputedly the best in town.

Dr Swartz had done his homework on the area and, apart from injections for hepatitis, yellow fever, typhoid, polio and malaria he advised them not to take uncooked vegetables, drink bottled water only, keep their mouth shut in a shower, and take malaria tablets. The trek guide warned them not on any account to drink water from the rivers or streams in the mountains, no matter how high up they got. Apparently there were always people higher up using dry, or no, lavatories. The trekking agency insisted on a deposit of $6,000 worth of unsigned American Express traveller's cheques in case any one had to be evacuated by helicopter. Liz was not impressed with this requirement. Still less about being warned that sleeping tablets were dangerous above 14,000 feet.

'Gee John, we couldn't be gettin' more medical advice if we were going to the moon. Are you sure you really want to go on this trek?'

'Well honey, this is the big one, and precautions are necessary. We are going on the toughest trek around to a country that doesn't have our facilities. That's what I like about it – higher, tougher and more primitive than the Rockies. You know I'm sure glad I took this trek and not one of the walkabouts. No, we will stick to the plan. I hope those bottles of scotch aren't broken on the way up.'

'And the brandy that you also brought, clever darling.'

The small Tata bus was waiting for them in the early morning sunshine packed with luggage, provisions, porters, cook, cook boys, sherpas, the sirdar and the group leader.

They were told the Everest trek was off due to heavy fog at the Lukla landing strip. John was advised the Langtang trek was in fact better as it involved a higher climb – from about 6,000 to over 11,000 feet. Liz was not unhappy with this change of plan. It would be less crowded and there was no landing strip. To compensate for missing the trek to Everest arrangements were made for them to hire a small plane on their return to Nepal to take an early morning flight around Everest. John had no intention of going back without having been close to Everest – bad enough the trek there was off. Each had their small knapsacks for daily needs, especially water to prevent dehydration, and John checked his camera and video equipment. He was determined to have visual evidence of this trek. 'It will shut up those punks who think I am past it,' he said. He could already feel the adrenalin coursing through his veins.

The other passengers in the bus comprised a fit-looking Australian sheep farmer and his wife, a New Zealand professor and her husband, a middle-aged German couple and an Austrian writer. The bus made its way through the Kathmandu streets peopled with overloaded three-wheeler motorcycle taxis, ancient battered small Japanese cars used as taxis, lorries and buses, all belching out black fumes. People, cows, dogs and world-beating potholes got in the way, making progress slow, but interesting, for the trekkers. Leaving Kathmandu required patience which was wearing thin for Liz.

Outside the city they soon ran out of surfaced road with the commencement of the ascent around the foothills of the Himalayas. The drops to the off-side became more spectacular and the road surface likening to a stony river bed, except where monsoon waters had washed away entire outside sections, causing the driver to crawl over the precarious surface remaining alongside the mountain. When a lorry or bus, crowded with people, inside and outside, came from the opposite direction the porters jumped out of their bus to bang on its sides and back, signalling to the driver on how much road was left for him to back on to, the space was never apparent to the passengers who with varying levels of failure did their best to look nonchalant.

'I wonder if we should have stayed with the Rockies after all, John.'

'Don't worry your beautiful head, Liz pet, I have been in situations like this before, these guys know what they are doing,' John assured her, thinking to himself that the journey was crazy.

When they safely passed three buses coming in the opposite direction he began to think they might after all get to the trekking point in one piece.

The creaking and groaning of the tortured bus as it shuddered its way around the mountainside lasted about eight hours, apart from a stop at Trishuli where the trekking staff piled out on to the dusty street and into a 'restaurant'. Discretion left the passengers eating their bananas and bottled drinking water in the bus after the sheep farmer and his wife gave a thumbs down on the café. The next, and last, stop was Dhunche at 5,800 feet from whence their trek began.

'Liz, I ain't seen anything like this before, not stateside nor anywhere else; that's for sure. A village taken straight out of a Wild West film with one unpaved dirty street, several so called hotels and the snow-covered Himalayan mountains as a spectacular backdrop. Now aren't you glad you came?'

'Gee John. It's wonderful. What a place to die in,' she laughingly replied.

'Don't be silly Liz,' said John testily, 'nobody is going to die here. It's only a walk.'

Liz fell silent, conscious she had made a slip. She had better be more careful.

They walked through the village before they left the road for a narrow track up the side of a steep hill. The cook and his helpers set off in advance so they would have refreshments ready when they stopped for lunch. The guide, sirdar and two sherpas stayed with the trekkers. The two Australians were brimful of energy compared to the New Zealanders who, as they later explained, were conserving oxygen for the tougher trekking to come. Their narrow stony track meandered its way across the side of the mountain, with some stiff climbs, before descending to a small river foaming its way down the steep mountains. The bridge consisted of several small tree trunks tied together, and no sides. The sherpa was on hand to assist the ladies across, ignoring the men. Liz was amused at John's expression when he first saw the bridge and his studied concentration in crossing.

They could only do a couple of hours' trekking before stopping for the night. Just as well as they were quite tired. None more than John, Liz noted, who was putting on a brave face.

'That goddamn German seems to want to race the sheep farmers to the top. I hope this is not too much for you, Liz honey?'

'Not so far, John darling. I really was concerned for you though.'

'I am fine, Liz. I can handle these guys. They have never trekked before and if they are not careful will suffer burn-out. Can you imagine me, the most experienced trekker of the group pushing myself too far?'

After a meal prepared by the cook on a three-burner paraffin stove it was too dark to do anything else but to go to bed in their tents. Before retiring John regaled the others with his experiences in the Rockies, and Kilimanjaro. Liz detected a slight note of boredom amongst his listeners.

'Now John you are the oldest here, and after your illness you must not try to do too much.' She sounded just like the concerned spouse.

'Liz pet, I'm as fit as a fiddle – fitter that a man half my age.'

They broke up and made off in the darkness for their tents. Like most first nights in a strange bed sleep did not come easily, more so on the hard ground insufficiently protected by a thin rubber mattress.

When one of the porters handed in tea to their tents at 6 a.m. John had only just begun a deep sleep and would have preferred a later starting time. Maybe he had too much brandy the evening before. They were on the trek by 7 a.m.

Soon they were leaving the shade of the pine forest for the mainly scrub oak forest, the path first going up from and, after lunch, down to the river before taking a long steep difficult climb over broken stones and gravel towards the little village of Chongong and the Lama Lodge Hotel, near which their tents were already erected by the porters. It had been a rough day for all.

Next day saw a steady pace being maintained by those who were now getting used to the trek, okay on the flat but chest heaving at the very steep incline that followed. John was finding it difficult enough, but covered it up by stopping to take photos.

Liz urged him to make his own pace and ignore the rest, but to no avail. Thankfully a pack of monkeys, with grey and black faces, led to a longer photo session. The temperature varied. If they were in the sunshine the heat was considerable, necessitating removal of heavier clothing, whilst in the shade the position was reversed. Climbing through the forest helped to block off the direct sun's rays, but when they got into the open again and up a steep track everyone found it tough. It was obvious who found it hardest but the others noted that it was Liz who generally halted to take some water from her knapsack for John.

'Here John, take some before you get dehydrated.'

'It's okay, Liz pet, I'm fine. This will sure get me into condition,' he said, drinking back the water.

They stopped in a tiered site above the few 'hotels', tired and happy with what they had achieved that day. After a superb meal John produced his brandy and offered it to the others. The Australians took a small amount, for politeness' sake Liz felt, but John, a hard trek behind him, took several measures. Unfortunately late night shenanigans by some locals kept some of the party awake. Liz slept poorly, but then her reason for doing so was not attributable to the hard ground.

The next morning the porters distributed boiled water for their water containers. Liz had given herself the task of filling both hers and John's. She knew that timing was important for success. She filled John's bottle from the nearby stream. A Swiss group leader the previous evening had warned his trekkers on no account to even wash their hands from that water.

They were now at around 8,000 feet and had to get to Langtang village, at over 11,000 feet, which meant going up more than 3,000 in one day; crossing the critical 10,000 feet where Acute Mountain Sickness (AMS) could begin to effect some trekkers.

'Despite what is claimed AMS does not really affect a person until 12,000 feet,' John observed loudly.

'Vell there is no reason to go so slow. Is that not so?' said the German daring a contradiction.

'Well, if that is the case we can spend more time at Kyangjiin Gompa when we get there,' said the New Zealander hopefully.

It was the highest point in the trek. Liz knew they would be all right if they walked slowly, but felt she should be recorded as being concerned on John's behalf, knowing full well John would disagree.

'That American woman looks after her husband very well,' she heard the New Zealander observe to the Austrian.

The trek was easy at first along the floor of the river valley, surrounded by the towering mountains on either side with tempting glimpses of Langtang Lirung's white top rising 23,000 feet in the distance. Herds of yaks and cattle were grazing in the sunny pastures to their right creating an idyllic setting. The sense of remoteness however was diminished when they had to check in at the National Park checkpoint in the Ghora Tabela valley. That was before the continuous steep climb to the village of Langtang.

'Gee look at those houses, ain't they quaint?' said John between gasps.

'Darling, I read they are said to be Tibetan style. You know we are not far from the Chinese–Tibet border,' offered Liz.

The climb was now getting very strenuous with the thinning air and the hot sun slowing down progress. John with diarrhoea and spasmodic pains in his stomach was forced to dart into the scrub and rocks every so often. Liz noted the strained look on his face, but in front of others he would not admit he was unable to continue.

Some particularly difficult sections of the climb tore at the lungs requiring short slow footsteps, frequent stops and good deep breathing. Even so John, weakened by the runs, had difficulty hiding his problem.

Urged by Liz he stopped more often than the others, but never for too long as that delayed the rest. She could see his energy was drained by the combination of stomach upset and thin air. He refused to accept that the air was having any effect.

'For God's sake Liz we are only at a little over 10,000 feet, I have not been affected at that height in the Rockies.'

The group leader was disinclined to let him have any medicine until the 'bug had passed through his intestine' although he noticeably slowed the group's pace.

Liz did not hide her disagreement about the medicine, 'I know you have more experience, backed by specialised training in this area, but I reckon he needs something to at least reduce the pain of the spasms.'

'I think it would be better to wait until he has got rid of most of the bug before we start anything. We will reconsider the matter this evening,' offered the group leader.

'I'll be okay Liz pet, we should go by the groupie, I can manage.'

So John struggled on, privately feeling terrible, but not prepared to be pitied. He carried on through the warm sun in the steep climb up over sandy slippy ground where any lack of care could have a trekker fall to serious injury, or over stony ground where a misjudged footing could have similar consequences.

The scenery was magnificent, if one was in that frame of mind, with the snow-clad mountains as a backdrop, the highest of which, Langtang Lirung, was just 23,750 feet high.

Even the two Australians were encountering some difficulty in walking at more than a snail's pace. One of them, to Liz's relief, admitted to having a 'dose of the trots'.

By now they had passed through Langtang Village and were well up a scenic valley of yak pastures and small villages widening out to the settlement of Kyangjiin Gompa at just under 12,000 feet with its nearby glacier, monastery and cheese factory. Despite his discomfort John was impressed.

'This is the highest I have been Liz. Isn't it great,' he said as he waved his hand weakly in the direction of his surroundings. 'Christ we must celebrate this tonight with their Nepalese wine. It might even do something for my guts.'

Darkness descended quickly accompanied by a penetrating cold. Liz hardly felt the cold. She had other things on her mind.

The cook had anticipated the need for hot food, and he quickly served it on a small folding table in the dining tent. They ate by an oil lamp which gave out as much heat as light. A last supper thought Liz grimly. Now that the last act was near she, to her surprise, felt more relaxed. The high altitude had affected her more than she had anticipated. She felt drained and breathless. Excusing herself she went to their sleeping tent, torch in hand to get the thyroxin tablets. They would have to be broken up to a powder for his drink. She had taken one of the tin mugs and returned with the powdered tablets in the mug.

'Let's have a good drink of wine to celebrate.'

To which John replied, 'I may have Delhi belly or Montezuma's revenge or even the trots but we have achieved one of my life's ambitions. Let's drink to that. Here we will have a drink of Napoleon brandy.'

For weeks Liz wondered how she would feel at this precise moment. In fact she had no feeling at all – nothing – zilch – except a little annoyed he could be so devious as to ditch her for that skinny scheming clothes hanger. She could handle occasional mini-gymnasium exercises but to dump her...

There was work to be done. 'John let's have a toast with your brandy.'

'Excellent idea if I may say so Liz honey,' said John in an imitation English accent. She poured out two brandies making sure John got the one with the powdered thyroxin in it.

They drank a toast to the Himalayas. When John had finished his she took his cup and filled hers which she gave back to him. She then carefully washed out his cup with some of the bottled water she had left in the darkened corner of the tent. She didn't want to get any of that stuff herself. On a high, John was the life and soul of the party, matching glass for glass of Nepalese wine with the Australian liberated from sobriety by a dead tired wife's snores in the corner. Liz was getting worried lest the dose was too small. Surely he must react to such a large dose?

He did. A little later John slumped sideways in the canvas chair. Elated, she made sure not to show it. She said as casually as she could, 'Must be the drink and exhaustion.'

When she was sure he had reached a point of no return she put on her worried look and went over to sit him up. When he slumped off the chair she exclaimed, 'I had better feel his pulse.'

When she could not feel any she looked alarmed and cried, 'I cannot feet his pulse. Oh my God, he must have had another attack of tachycardia. He had one before.' She then began to weep and shake uncontrollably.

The group leader hurried over and felt John's pulse. 'I'm afraid I can't feel any either,' he said.

'What can we do? Can we call the helicopter at once?'

'I am very sorry madam, it is impossible. Even if I can contact them it would be too dangerous for it to come up here in the dark.'

'We must do something. My husband is seriously ill. Why let us come here and take money for a helicopter if you cannot provide the rescue services? At least have the porters carry him to the lodge. There may be a doctor there.'

Liz knew John was dead but she kept up the pretence that something should be done. Everyone was very shocked. The others did their best to console her. She explained he had been under medical care and kept saying over and over again, 'If only he had listened to Dr Swartz. I should have done more to stop him coming.'

She knew she had done a good job. The thyroid tablets had done the trick. There should be no trace. From then on she gave a command performance – and why not? She was to be well paid for it. Did she not do John a favour? After all could there be anything less dramatic than dying in bed in New York?

A post-mortem took place in Kathmandu which gave a verdict of death from natural causes. All of the others, including the leader, gave evidence of John's signs of stress and his wife's extreme concern for her husband whom, she had said, had had some sort of a heart attack before. The coroner noted that John's doctor had given him a clean bill of health for the trek, but warned him to take things easy.

One of the Australians rang Dr Swartz and advised him of Liz's distress, warning she was close to a nervous breakdown. 'It would be better if the funeral took place in New York as soon as possible as she is in no state for any more trauma.'

The funeral in New York was huge and Liz in black presented a pathetic figure in the first snow of the winter. His business associates were lost in admiration at the manner of his going, 'in Kathmandu, the Himalayas, at twelve thousand feet. As soon as he reached his targeted height!'

Marge appeared at the funeral, in tears, which only engendered more sympathy for Liz amongst those who knew, and thought Liz didn't know who she was.

A few days after the funeral John's attorney called and gave her details of his will.

John had left the bulk of his property to Liz, the only real surprise was the $2m he left to his first wife. 'You know he was adamant that that would be recompense for the money his former father-in-law gave him to start off in business.'

Later, having nothing else to do she went through his elaborate bureau. One drawer was locked which when opened had some correspondence which indicated that John had not been faithful to his two wives. One letter in particular caught her eye, or rather the date did. It was dated 7th November, two days before they had left for Nepal. It was from Marge. Most of it was as she would expect, except the last page. After reading it she gave a faint moan and dropped the letter on to the floor. She made no attempt to pick it up.

The interesting piece went as follows:

> *John while I love you dearly and I know it has been difficult to break it off with Liz, nevertheless I have grave misgivings, on ethical grounds if nothing else, that you should even think about giving her the Aids virus. Why not just tell her? Surely you do not have to prove Aids to establish infidelity?*

Liz recalled the afternoon on the trek when John had accidentally, and rather clumsily she had thought, fallen over a canvas chair. He had had a knife in his hand and had accidentally cut her arm as he fell. He was so concerned he had insisted on the leader giving her an anti-tetanus injection from his medical bag. He then had insisted in bandaging the cut himself. She wondered...

'Damn, damn, damn you John Galliano,' she shouted at the empty study as she picked up the phone to ring her doctor.

The Chaffinch

Some of the bride's guests, an otherwise disparate group, had gravitated towards the alcove, more or less in self-defence against the other side, the invitees of the groom who had monopolised one end of the room.

'So you are a writer Jack?' asked Charlie with an air of condescension, as if writing was a pastime for layabouts.

'What do you write?'

'Anything, articles, reviews, biographies, short stories. I have just finished a short story,' replied Jack diffidently.

'A short story, like Damon Runyon?' asked Charlie knowledgeably, remembering *Guys and Dolls*.

'Well, not exactly, I am not in his class.'

'Then what is the story you have just written?' persisted Charlie. 'Can you tell us about it?'

'That would be difficult,' said Jack. 'It needs to be read. I have a copy here, you can read it when you get home.'

'Why don't you read it to us now? We would be the first to hear it. That would be something for us to say when you are famous, Jack,' said Charlie, who had forged a strong alliance with the champagne.

'Do Jack, let us be the first to hear your story.' It was Alicia, Charlie's wife, whom he liked, and could hardly refuse. The rest of the group joined in urging him to read his story. When they were quiet Jack pulled the typed sheets out of his breast pocket and began to read.

Michael felt drowsy. The combined effect of fresh air, morning sunlight and late night drinking distanced him from the newspaper's account of the latest bout of atrocities in Bosnia. A catalogue of barbarous killings of women and children by former neighbours, was not sufficient to hold his attention.

The newsprint became more blurred. How could they do that to one another, he reflected as unconsciousness began to take over? Brutal lot of bloody bastards, he muttered to himself. The sudden flurry of wings pulled him back to consciousness. Through a half open eye he saw he was under surveillance from the arm of the other chair, just six feet to his right. The bird was eyeing him querulously, first with the left eye from its cocked head; then, without visible movement, the head cocked to the left, fixing him with its right eye.

Now awake he noted the bird had a russet coloured breast, a bluish grey head and brown black and white on its wings and back.

Perky little bugger, thought Michael.

Apparently satisfied with its survey the bird hopped along the white plastic arm on its spindly legs until it got to the end. The jerky reconnoitre was repeated, left, right, left. Then the head tilted, the legs straightened with the left eye pointing towards the ground before coming back up to meet his gaze. *No point in taking chances*, he seemed to be signalling.

I suppose he can trust no one, thought Michael.

Its legs resumed their angular pose. The eye jerked in the direction of the ground again. Michael followed the line to Helen's plate on the grass where she had left it when she went into the caravan. It had a half slice of toast on it. Later he could swear to Helen the bird was clearly signalling for the bread to be thrown its way. It looked like a chaffinch.

Slowly and cautiously, watched by a bird ready for flight with its legs alternatively bent and straight, he directed his left hand to the blue plastic plate. He pulled off some tiny pieces of toast which he threw on to the grass about eight feet in front of him. At first the bird didn't move. Seemingly the situation had to be scrutinised first. Right eye on him, legs straightened as if for flight, then bent as if reassured the toast was for it. The grass where the crumbs lay was repeatedly examined with split second timing. A sudden flurry of wings and a piece of the toast was gone with the chaffinch. It flew, straight as an arrow, to the branch of a nearby sycamore tree where it was immediately attacked by a pair of grey birds of its own size. Fascinated, Michael, from his chair, could see the two attackers push forward the retreating chaffinch along the branch. They stopped only when he thrust his beak into their squawking beaks. From Michael's seat they appeared too big to be fledglings. Surely at that size their parents would abandon them?

The chaffinch broke away from his attackers and made for the ground in front of Michael, landing with a flurry of wings. The bird again eyed him speculatively. Michael was still preoccupied with the other two rowdies on the sycamore. *Fledglings would not be fed at their size*, he said to himself with increased conviction. The chaffinch gave a few chirrups clearly indicating more bread was the order of the day. He cast a few more crumbs in front of his chair, nearer this time. The chaffinch held its ground, all the while eyeing first him, then the toast. Even Michael was unprepared for the louder flurry of wings as the other two landed beside the first. Closer examination revealed they were not the same colour as the other. They had down, not feathers, on their heads. Presumably they were fully grown fledglings who had no manners, thought Michael. Immediately they began to jostle their parent, probably their mother he thought, as they screeched aggressively through their wide open beaks. Holding her ground she began to eat the bread, then regurgitated it before stuffing it into the insistent beaks of the two offspring. Michael threw more toast, about three feet in front of his chair. There was much hopping about on the part of the mother, then more chirrups before she was forced by the others to nip in and grab the rest of the crumbs. Once fed they all took off for the sycamore.

Michael resumed reading how the once friendly baker's boy ripped open the throats of his former neighbours in Bosnia. At once fascinated and disgusted he put the paper down on the grass and climbed the wooden steps into the caravan to tell his wife about the perky chaffinch.

'I know Michael. I saw the two ruffians bully the other. It was amazing. Don't expect it to come on to your hand, it's not that perky,' offered Helen over her shoulder as she finished tidying up after breakfast.

'Would you like to bet?' said Michael, not one to ignore a challenge.

'Sure, a pound.'

'You're on,' he said, thinking she should have put a time limit on the bet. He didn't intend to hurry the chaffinch.

Two mornings later when the bird had come no nearer than six inches from his hand Helen said, 'Do you give up?'

'Not yet,' he said cryptically. 'She's nearly there.'

'Okay, but remember we're going home in two days' time,' she said with an air of triumph.

The following morning the chaffinch landed as usual on the arm of Helen's chair, less time now on head-cocking inspection before flying down to the ground, a few feet from Michael.

Expectant little so and so, thought Michael, *but I'm going to ignore you for a while and see what happens.*

He buried himself behind the paper, ignoring the chirrups from the impatient bird. Then slowly bringing his arms down, so that the paper was on his knees with his face was fully visible to the chaffinch, they eyed one another for a while. The bird hopped around on the grass, every so often giving a few more chirrups as if to say what's keeping you?

Slowly Michael placed the paper on the grass to the left of his chair, revealing the plate on his lap with the piece of toast. Out from the far wall, there was a flurry of wings as the two fledglings landed, before bossily strutting and squawking for their food. Michael placed one crumb just in front of his hand. The chaffinch studied it, and Michael, with great care, seemingly oblivious of the continuing demands from behind. Then she hopped in and grabbed the crumb, backing away until jostled by the others, who seemed more beak than body. Pushed and pummelled she retreated backwards as she chewed the crumb and dropped the chewings into the two bottomless abysses.

Buns to bears, thought Michael, as he placed three more crumbs on the palm of his hand and, not without some strain, placed the back of his hand flat on the ground. The chaffinch edged closer, now eyeing him with the same intensity as on the first day. She didn't like it, but the racket behind urged her on. She finally darted in and took a crumb before Michael realised it had gone. The usual pantomime took place beyond his hand.

His right shoulder was aching; his arm was getting numb. The fact that he had won his bet did not stop him from keeping his right hand pressed to the ground. Logically he should have thrown the remainder of the crumbs to the birds, but he wanted it to come back for more.

She did, more purposefully this time, as if it felt safer. She hesitated just off his index finger. Then he could feel the bird on his hand. The tiny claws tickled his palm giving him a peculiar sense of elation.

'He closed his hand,' shouted Charlie, a wild look on his face. 'He killed it, didn't he?'

'Oh do shut up Charlie,' said Alicia, as if she was talking to a child. Jack continued, now glad he had agreed to read his story to Charlie.

Michael closed his hand. Not slowly, but fast. He surprised himself at the speed of its closure, given the pain in his wrist and shoulder, coupled with the numbness in his arm. The bird felt warm in his hand. He was conscious of a brief feathery struggle before she went still. Slowly Michael opened his right hand. The thumb first, followed by the index finger, then each of the others in turn, ending with the little finger. The body of the chaffinch lay inert on the palm of his hand. Her liveliness of a few seconds ago was gone. *Nothing perky about her now*, thought Michael. He raised his hand, slowly, feeling it was no longer part of him. The body of the dead chaffinch rolled across his fingers on to the dry grass. As if from a distance he heard Helen's scream.

When the World was Young

Denis abandoned his mother at the front door, his little legs moving like pistons as he tore through the hallway towards the sitting room. Fortunately the door was open, otherwise he would have gone smack into it. When he saw her sitting on the easy chair he stopped dead, unsure of his next move. A glass of orange, clasped in her two hands, was just about to reach her lips when his tumultuous arrival caused her to replace it on the stool in front of her on which there was a plate with two mikado biscuits.

Denis took a couple of hesitant paces towards her, giving a 'Hi,' whilst most of his attention was focused on the two biscuits. His mother breathlessly followed him into the room and suggested he give her a kiss. Shyly he approached to plant a quick kiss on her cheek. Looking demure she took it in good part, after all she was a distant relation. She then followed his glance to the biscuits, giggling she took one up and bit into it. Satisfied with the effect on Denis she gave him the other, much to his relief.

'Denis,' his mother cried reproachfully, 'what about the magic word?'

'Thanks,' muttered Denis looking as if butter would not melt in his mouth, a mouth stained from licking the jam on top of the mikado biscuit.

He dug his right hand into the pocket of his jeans and pulled out a small solid rubber ball which he threw in her direction. She just about managed to catch it and began to examine it very carefully, as if she had never seen one like it before. Satisfied she made a poor attempt to throw it back to him. It bounced all over the room, with Denis chasing it, just missing a Waterford vase before trickling under the sofa. Denis did his best to impress her by trying to push the sofa off the ball. It was no use, even a big grunting three year old made no impact on the heavy sofa. There was nothing for it but to let his mother push it out of the way while he grabbed the ball before she pushed it back. Once retrieved he decided not to risk throwing it to her again.

'Have you seen my new bed?' he asked, knowing she hadn't. 'It's on the floor. I fell out of the high one an' hurt my arm.'

He then proudly held up his elbow which had an impressive blue bruise.

She was drinking her orange. So, before there could be a response, he continued, 'Would you like to see it?' making an offer he felt no one could refuse.

'Yes,' she managed to say in the middle of downing the rest of the orange. When she had emptied the glass she followed him upstairs to his bedroom. Denis meanwhile had pounded up the stairs, thrown himself down upon his new bed and awaited her entrance with considerable excitement.

She entered the room, her face expressionless while she examined the bed, the room, a large white teddy bear and a brown lion. Apparently satisfied with her inspection she smiled approval and gingerly sat down on the bed near a Denis who was fit to burst with pride. Her seal, or rather seat, of approval made her, if not a friend for life, at least one for the time being.

He crawled over, grabbed the teddy bear and passed it over to her with as much ceremony as he could muster. She gave him a quick smile followed by the magic words, 'Thank you, Denis.' This only made him seek more approval so he went over to a wardrobe, opened the door and pulled out a large ball covered in Disney characters. He rolled it in her direction. This time she missed it, so laughing he ran over, picked it up and handed to her. He then stood back to share in her appreciation of the ball. He was not disappointed. Every time she recognised a Disney character on the ball she exclaimed with pleasure. They spent the next twenty minutes engrossed in things which attract children of an age.

They were interrupted by the voice of his mother from the stairwell, 'Denis, where are you? What are you doing with your gran?'

With that she came into the bedroom. 'Granny, what on earth are you doing sitting on that bed on the floor? Denis, your poor gran gran.'

'But Mam, we was playin,' said Denis aggrieved, as if playing with his ninety-year-old great-grandmother was the most natural thing in the world.

Her grandmother looked up at her grand daughter with an expression of great disappointment. 'Mary, I was in a magic world.'

The Silver March Brown

What lousy weather, thought Edward, as he pulled his car left, on to the wide untarmaced shoulder which overlooked the Caragh River. His body, stiff from the five hour drive, emerged slowly from the driver's seat. His back was damp with sweat. From his vantage point his eyes could follow the flow of the river, starting from his left, beyond the edge of the furzy field below him where it emerged, fast flowing, through the brownstone supports of the dismantled Victorian railway bridge. It raced into a large pool with a large black rock on its far bank, the top of which he could just see above the green and yellow of the furze bushes. The water hurried from the bottom of the rock pool through stones before making its way towards the granite arches of the road bridge from whence it disappeared from his sight. Further on he could just make out its estuary into Dingle Bay. The bay was mirror calm, right across to the white sands of Inch, behind which rose the subtle browns of the Brandon Mountains.

Looking up too suddenly, he was blinded by the intensity of the sun. He turned his gaze to the rest of the sky which was blue, interspersed with cumulus. The scene he conceded could be idyllic for some, but not for him. The combination of low water and bright sunshine made salmon fishing a joke. A few sea trout at night would not get him off the hook upon which he had impaled himself.

A simple phone call from Dublin would have alerted him to these conditions, which in truth he had suspected. Pride blinded his judgement when, at lunch with Robbie and Tess, he had boasted, in Mona's absence, that he would catch a salmon in the Caragh for her thirty-first birthday dinner, to which they were invited. That salmon had to be caught if he was not to lose face. He would now admit that he had had an uneasy feeling, from the very beginning about this trip. In a way he was glad Mona could not leave her job to accompany him. It would have destroyed the surprise element of a salmon caught by him for her birthday dinner. She was getting depressed about their not being able to produce a child and it was important he continued to demonstrate his love for her as she got older.

Hopefully JJ would have some ideas about catching a salmon. Admittedly, his reputation as the best gillie in the area would be put to the test in this bloody weather. He turned away from the river reflecting on his hatred for anticyclones.

A CIE touring bus slowly passed by his car, heads craning to get a better look at the scenery. It reached the end of the road, turned left to squeeze its way over the bridge before stopping at a thatched cottage beyond it. A depressed Edward followed down on foot, thinking he may as well find out just how low was the water below the bridge.

Standing on the granite bridge he could see right through the gin clear water below him; the stones, every single stone, visible in the river bed below as if there was no water there at all. Nearby, the bus passengers, mostly elderly Americans, were being served tea and griddle cake by two grey-haired ladies in traditional dresses. The visitors were noisily exclaiming at the beauty of their surroundings, enhanced by the uniquely pervasive smell of burning turf, or 'peat' as they called it.

'Imagine Sharon,' one exclaimed to the other, 'that hill over there is Carrauntoohil, the highest mountain in Ireland. The driver tells me that it is generally covered in cloud; ain't we lucky to see it to day?'

Edward looked over to his right where the top was indeed clear. Even he had to admit the mountains were attractive, mixing green, purple, maroon and grey. He could even see the absurd stone walls on the hill climbing up through the grass and mountain heather towards the bogland at the top, dividing one scrap of poor boggy land from another. The sheep grazing near the top looked like little white maggots. Under other circumstances it was idyllic.

Upriver the tall, tapering supports for the former Victorian railway bridge attracted his attention, not because they looked like giant headstones reaching up to the sky, but because of the anomalous white cloud suspended just over them. Lower than any other cumulous in the sky. Was he imagining it, or was it shaped like the face of a young girl? In spite of the warmth he shivered. Curious, but more to the point was his need to catch a salmon for Mona's birthday next Friday. He made his way back up the rising ground to the car, wondering if JJ would have any suggestions.

The Towers Hotel's appearance belied its reputation for food and comfort. The proprietor, an outstanding Swiss-trained chef, had an ever widening reputation that extended far beyond Ireland's shores. Edward's first sight of the converted shopfront facing him as he entered the village, now used as an office-cum-store, was, to say the least, unprepossessing, as was the entrance porch off the main Caherciveen road. Presumably designed before the motor car, it now appeared designed to catch all the carbon monoxide from every car taking the Ring of Kerry.

It only deceived to flatter, as once inside charm took over, personal and environmental. The former via the pretty red-haired receptionist who greeted him cheerfully.

'A great day sir, perhaps not too good for you, Mr Fuller. Never mind, JJ is in the lounge waiting for you. If a fish is to be caught JJ is your man.'

Smart girl, he thought, seeing as this was his first visit. The fine weather had left the reception area deserted in favour of the nearby beaches. The receptionist, he figured, had time for questions.

'Anyone else catching fish?' inquired Edward hopefully, realising, too late, the unjustified presumptuousness in his remark; he had not caught any yet, and was unlikely to do so he thought grimly.

'Some French fishermen were here last week. They caught two grilse and about eight white trout, or is it sea trout you call them?'

'Any young salmon, I mean grilse, caught lately?' he enquired hopefully, ignoring her query.

'I'm not up to date, better ask JJ, he's in the residents' bar,' she replied, parrying the query.

Sizing up the situation, Edward took the proffered key and made his way down a hallway the walls of which were covered with pictures of celebrities, and other mere mortals, surrounded by salmon; lots of them. He noted with satisfaction several were caught in summer, which made him feel a little more hopeful.

He decided to look at the bedroom first, leave his cases there, and have a wash before talking to JJ. The view of the bay from the bedroom was stunning. Satisfied, he made his way to the residents' lounge, and JJ.

The small bar, set into the right hand wall appeared too small for the hotel's clientele, but the lounge was cosy, despite being cluttered up with a grand piano and a large moquette drawing room suite. The walls on either side of the bar had even more pictures of celebrities, some performing, others with large, well generally, catches of salmon.

'Shure ye must be Mister Fuller, wouldn't I recognise a fisherman anywhere,' said a slight, sallow-complexioned man in his mid-fifties, with that crinkly black hair so common with Kerrymen. He spoke in a soft Kerry accent as he rose from the couch with outstretched hand.

'And you are JJ,' said Edward giving his hand, adding anxiously, 'is the fishing as bad as it looks?'

'The white trout are taking after dusk, even in the low water, but to tell the truth, sir, the river is bad for fish.

There's a share a dem out in the estuary waitin' for rain. How long have you got, sir?'

'Three days. I want to catch a fish for my wife's birthday. It's very special for me.'

He ordered a Powers for JJ and a Blackbush for himself, feeling he needed it. JJ then introduced him to two others who were sitting nearby; an older, spare, grey-haired woman and a curly black-haired man, a younger edition of himself. The woman it transpired later was his sister, the younger man his nephew. Edward felt if buying drinks improved his chances of a salmon then why not? Two more whiskeys, a Crested Ten and another Powers.

'Go on JJ, you must know where a fish is lying?' The dark-haired, sharp-featured nephew asked in a lilting high pitched Kerry accent, which almost made the sentence sound like one word.

'You are not so bad at sousing them out yourself, Patsy, except you don't believe in rod and line,' JJ parried.

'What about the pool beside the old railway bridge? Shure isn't this the time o' year for that?' the nephew asked.

JJ looked a little doubtful. 'Ye won't get a fish there in daylight now, an' it may not be the best place at night.'

Edward sensed they both knew there was a possibility of a fish there, but, since JJ did not appear to be forthcoming, he decided to press the initiative opened up by Patsy.

'I am used to fishing for white trout at night so why not salmon?'

JJ hesitated before replying, 'At this time a' year an occasional fish is known to get through the shallows at the end of the bridge pool, when there is a full tide at eleven or twelve o'clock at night. A big fish has been known to make it there. Though big ones have been seen, they have never been caught; hooked and lost maybe, but never caught.'

All three were silent, as if wanting to say something else, but could not, or would not. Edward broke the silence. 'I would like to have a try. After all what is there to lose ? Will you act as gillie JJ?'

The question hung in the air for a few seconds, maybe longer, before JJ replied.

'Meself, sir, I have to go to Tralee tonight. But if you are used to fishin' in the dark why not give it a try yourself?'

At this Patsy's mother, in an even more pronounced Kerry accent, interrupted in a too loud tone, a bit nervously too, thought Edward.

'Wouldn't ye be better off sending the gentleman somewhere else rather than that place tonight? The Laune is a bigger river, and will have more water.'

Patsy looked a little sheepish, but held his ground.

'Ma, we don't want the gentleman going home without a fish for his wife's birthday. The Laune is useless at the moment. Any that are in it are so long in the pools they are only teasing the fishermen. Auld wives tales have no part in fishing. Will ye let up now Ma.'

His mother pressed her lips together in a thin line, picked up her handbag saying, rather tartly, 'There's Jimmy Foley over there. I'd best go an' see how that heifer of his is doin'. I hope you two know what yer doing.'

'Don't mind her, she has too much imagination,' whispered Patsy, when she was safely out of earshot.

JJ hesitated no longer.

'To tell ye the truth sir, I'm not that optimistic about you're getting a grilse there, big or small. First ye should go for the white trout in the rock pool at about ten thirty, then move up to the bridge pool around eleven for the fish, grilse I mean,' he was now all business, 'ye will need a Jungle Cock, a Butcher and a Black and Silver. Ye need to look at the bank and the river in daylight, so as to familiarise yourself with the area in the dark. Also, the approach from the road can be tricky, with the soft ground in the middle and the furze bushes on the river side of the field. Ye can easily lose direction in the dark; that can be frustratin' sir, or worse, particularly if ye are in a hurry. Oh yes, bring a good torch and, in this water, put up small flies for the white trout. Now for the fish ye need a Silver March Brown. Any other fly appears to be no good in these conditions. Here I have one,' he said, turning back the left label of his tweed jacket revealing a host of multicoloured flies, 'it's a number eight size, here too is a size six, which you can use later if you don't get a take to the eight. Put it up at about half eleven.'

He then passed the two light brown hackled silver shanked flies over to Edward, who took them between his thumb and forefinger, examined them intently before saying, 'I have a few like those, but your tying is better. Strange, that's the first time I heard of a March Brown for salmon in the middle of summer.'

Visibly more relaxed, as some are after making a difficult decision, they quickly responded to Edward's offer of another drink when the discussion turned to tourism and the exceptional weather. Not long after they took their leave.

Edward's feeling of expectation was raised to a high pitch. He felt as if he could clasp his enthusiasm, it was that strong. Even a long walk along Rossbeigh beach did nothing to diminish the palpability of that expectation. He ordered a too early meal, having to hold himself back from pointlessly going down to the river before nine o'clock, which itself was too early. There would be no white or sea trout until ten thirty at the very earliest. Arguably, going down to the pool too early could scare off the trout, maybe even stop him getting his salmon. So sure was he now that he would get a fish that he began to subconsciously think of it as if it was his salmon. Something niggled him though. He had a feeling the two lads were not telling him something. Was it that the fish were diseased, or what?

By nine o'clock he had parked his car off the road above the river, though common sense, and the strong evening sun, was telling him it was far too early. He took his time assembling his rod, even exchanging views with another angler, who was going down to the more popular pool below the road bridge. He expressed surprise at Edward wasting his time at the bridge pool. Edward did not enlighten him. He just wished him well and slid through the barbed wire and down the rough earthen bank below the car, carefully walking making his way over the drying boggy surface, except for the middle where a drain still held the remnants of past rain. His right foot sank up to his knee before his other foot found the covered stepping stone. That could be tricky in the dark, he thought, if he wasn't careful.

He then made his way through the prickly furze bushes, carefully noting the narrow passage for his return. The faint path, made by sheep, led him to the rock pool below the bridge where JJ had said sea trout would rise at dusk. Better not to disturb the pool in this light, he figured, in case he put down the trout for later.

There was time to survey the river and to familiarise himself with the area before darkness. Starting at the end of the pool, carefully holding his rod in the air he pushed his way through the thick gorse, before going round a tree that had stretched itself out over the river. A small stone wall with rusty barbed wire on top was next, followed by some slippy rocks in muddy water, presumably taken from the railway bridge when it had been dismantled in 1960. The brown rock-faced stone supports were still perfectly jointed, a tribute to Victorian craftsmen, as they tapered towards the top. It gave the impression, looking up to the sky from its base, of vast height; even a feeling of dizziness, as he watched the swallows chasing flies sent up by the rising warm air. Strange, he thought, for some reason the air at the railway bridge pool was cold, despite the heat which should have been retained by the hot sun.

He moved to the top of the pool where gurgling water cascaded through some large rocks before losing its urgency to the tranquillity of an eighty yard long pool. At its end the water gathered speed again as it flowed around two of the three brownstone bridge supports only to be backed up by a line of rocks. That is where the salmon will lie, he thought.

There were no particularly dangerous hazards for a careful angler, even in the dark. Looking up he noticed the end of a truncated railway track sticking out over the river. He hoped it stayed there.

The plaintive four note cry of a curlew circling the mountain in front interrupted his study of the pool, causing him to look at his watch; time to make for the rock pool and the sea trout.

The water there, in the gathering gloom, appeared like a giant sheet of clear plastic with hundreds of sedges frantically engaged in birth, procreation and death above, under and on it. A widening circle here and there in the water denoted sedges taken by the small brown trout. To Edward it signified the imminent evening rise of the sea trout, one of which was rather noisily grabbing flies under the bushes at the far, inaccessible, bank.

The Jungle Cock was hardly in the water before he got a violent tug, followed by the swish of the line through the water and the rapid successive jumps of the silvery sea trout, giving him the impression it was dancing on its tail over the surface of the water. It was a good one, thought Edward full of excitement, needing careful playing before he managed to net it. Another followed a few minutes later before he suddenly realised it was eleven o'clock, time to go after his salmon.

He made his way carefully in the dusk to the bridge pool where, with the help of his torch, he changed his cast to one of 9 lb, putting up a Silver March Brown, JJ's, at the end. As he entered the river he was conscious of how different it was in the dark. The water in the rapids sounded louder in the cool night air, whilst distances were foreshortened compared to daylight. The bridge supports seemed monolithic. He could just about make out the bats darting around. Damn nuisance if he hooked one, he thought, could ruin his chance of catching his salmon.

He was prepared for a grilse, not the powerful splash he heard at the end of the pool. Over ten lbs, he guessed. It must have just come up with the tide as JJ had suggested, because it was certainly not there earlier. There it goes again. Edward was now almost shaking with excitement. Should he put up a stronger cast? That would waste time, maybe it would move upstream while he was out of the water, or even go back to sea on meeting the low water? He decided to stay with what he had, and to hell with it.

Just then he heard a sharp whistle above the gurgle of the water. Sounded like a train whistle. Probably one of those novelty motor car horns English visitors use, he thought, as he cast the fly diagonally across the pool towards the far bank. No take. There that idiot goes again with his noisy whistle. But there was another sound. Like a steam engine. Wonder if they are having a steam rally hereabouts? He cast again, a better one this time; he was getting used to casting in the dark.

God that sounds like a train, on rails at that. Jeasus, he thought he could hear the clickity clack on rail joinings, together with the rattle of carriages. Must be getting too exited about this salmon. His excitement was letting his imagination run riot. The rails have been gone since the Sixties, this is nonsense. But it wasn't, there was the definite roar of a train approaching sounding as if it had jammed on its brakes. What the hell is going on, he thought? Is it really his imagination?

His cast was at its extremity downstream when the rod was almost whipped out of his hand by a powerful tug. The salmon had followed it across and, Edward, in retrospect, thought the first drag was the fly going over a stone in the river. It wasn't; the salmon had gently taken the fly in his mouth before taking off with a surge up the far side of the pool making him reel as fast as he could to keep the strain on the fish, his fish, which he was determined he was not going to lose.

Whatever you do, he said to himself, don't panic, keep the top of the rod up, maintain a firm pressure, do not try to halt its run. He felt his mouth run dry. Why hadn't JJ told him to use a treble hook for a fish this size? The salmon stopped, sticking to the middle of the river.

The noise was now deafening, and probably had been for the last few minutes, whilst he was distracted by the fish. The train and carriages were now visible on what – the bridge! It was coming straight in his direction from Glenbeigh, the engine and carriages screeching to a halt over his head covered in steam and smoke with sparks falling into the river in front of him. Edward knew it was ridiculous as he stood in the water, rod in hand, open mouthed, at the sight above him. The noise was deafening and terrorising.

His only contact with reality now was the feel of the rod and the pull from the salmon. That was real. But what about that train? Was he going mad? He shivered, as he clearly heard the hiss of steam overhead from the now stationary engine, whose smoke was rising into the sky. It looked real enough. So was the salmon which made a sudden move down the pool, accelerating before leaping into the air, a mass of silvery power, creating a large splash as it hit the water.

The size of the fish nearly caused Edward's heart to burst with excitement, and God knows he was having enough of that. Again the fish stopped, as if it had run into the base of the bridge, where it lay quiescent. He didn't know what to do? Run? And leave the rod and fish? He was trembling with a mixture of fear and excitement. His tongue was transformed into a dry sponge. Try as he might, he could not swallow. For sure, there was a fish on the end of the line, whatever was above.

His attention was caught by the opening of a carriage door, the back of which hit the carriage with a thump. Next a white-faced young woman appeared at the door with what looked like a young baby in her arms. She was wearing a black shawl and a type of wide skirt. It looked red but in the moonlight he could not be sure. She stood there, hesitating, before throwing herself on to the rocks opposite him, landing with a sickening thud. Edward shuddered at the sight, appalled; he wanted to scream for her to get up, but his mouth was too dry. He could only raise a croak. Woman and child slowly slid into the water, and disappeared. They cannot disappear, his mind screamed, there isn't enough bloody water in the river for that. But they had. There was no sign of them. He could feel the hair rising on the back of his neck as the train started to puff. Puff, puff, puff. Puff, puff, puff, puff. Everything around was becoming obscured by steam and smoke as the train started off again. It moved off gradually towards Caragh Lake watched by a transfixed Edward standing up to his knees in the river whilst holding on to the only bit of reality that now existed for him – his rod and his salmon.

The gurgle of the water slowly began to be heard again as the noise of the train receded, until there was no other sound except for the swish of tyres and the lights of a car on the road as it sped towards the granite bridge below, slowing down before crossing it and then the headlights disappeared as the car continued towards Glenbeigh. The angry squawking of a water hen in the bull rushes opposite nearly caused his heart to stop. This and the stillness of the summer's night disoriented Edward to a point where he wondered if he had been hallucinating. The supports were pointing into the sky without any bridge. He was wading in the river and as further relief he felt the salmon moving again, fast, coming straight at him. Reeling furiously he kept a light strain on his fish when it shifted to the pool centre, as if it wanted Edward to be satisfied he was still there. Again it hesitated in the centre. He exerted more pressure, slowly reeling the salmon in his direction. While still trembling from his experiences, Edward, the fisherman, was reasserting himself. The movement of the fish then changed. It was unusual for a salmon. It felt more of a dead weight, slow and stodgy, heavy, like an old sack he had once hooked. Strange he could make out a shape in the current that looked white or pink. Difficult to be sure, even in the moonlight. Maybe his eyes were playing tricks. Not surprisingly, for when it got quite close to him he saw it was not the colour of a salmon. It was white and pink; shaped like a child. In the moonlight, as he drew it closer, he could make out a baby's head, legs and arms. The hook appeared to be in the baby, whose mouth was puckered as if it was crying. Edward let out a moan, feeling sick and faint with horror, but unable to move, simply keeping his right hand on the rod butt for want of something physical to hold. He could see the child's eyes were closed. It had no clothes.

Frozen with revulsion and terror he could only stare at what he had at the end of the line, unsure of his own sanity, yet clinging on to the absolute certainty that earlier there had been a 12lb salmon on his line. For sure, but could he really be sure of anything anymore?

As he looked in total disbelief there was suddenly a salmon swimming diagonally away from him. He could see its dorsal fin, in the shaft of light from the full moon hanging over the mountain opposite. Suddenly there was a change with his salmon off again across the pool, leaping out of the water barely giving Edward enough time to drop his rod top and give out more line. This was no baby.

If he was to get this fish, and prove to himself that it was only a fish, then he must get below it. He gradually moved sideways, and down river, playing the salmon all the while. Just as he got opposite it he could see again the whiteness of a child, a sight that sent a fresh chill of icy cold through his body. He began shivering so violently he found it difficult to hold his feet on the river bed. His determination, held as a lifebelt to sanity, caused him to grip the rod until the knuckles on his hand were white. Again the sudden powerful movements of a salmon, for that was what it was again, forced him to continue playing it, never conceding it might get away.

Soon the unmistakable flash of silver signified the fish was going over on its side, and tiring. He knew he was now winning the struggle.

It felt like all night, but in reality it was only about fifteen minutes. One sudden pull if he lost his concentration and the line was broken. The fish began shaking its head from side to side trying to release the hook from its mouth, but to no avail. It then took off again, not with the same vigour though, heading towards the rocks, where the young woman and her baby had fallen. It stopped, hesitating as if wondering what to do next, when Edward again felt a cold chill run through him as if his very being was frozen. He felt his eyes being pulled in the direction of the rocks upon which the girl and her baby had fallen. She was standing there in her black shawl topping a long red skirt with her left arm outstretched, her index finger pointing straight at him, a pitiful look of entreaty on her face. He wanted to drop everything and run but he was incapable of even doing that.

The heavy pull on the rod diverted his attention, making him look down for a second. When he looked up the girl was gone, with his defensive mechanism silently screaming at him that it was only his imagination.

The salmon was now tired. Edward took the net from his waist extending the handle to its maximum. Slowly and deliberately he positioned himself below the fish maintaining a steady strain on it, letting it drift towards him.

The ease with which he netted the fish surprised him, but there it was in the net. He carefully made for the shallows and the bank where, in the light of the full moon, he carefully placed the net with the fish on the grass. He put his thumb and index finger on to the line, running it down to the end of the nylon cast where the hook should have been, in the salmon's mouth. It wasn't there, the cast hung loose. There was not a Silver March Brown at the end of the cast either. He switched on the torch shining it on the salmon in the net. Despite its powerful movements it was clear there was no fly in the mouth of the fish, nor did his search reveal any sign of a fly in the net, or elsewhere for that matter. How can I catch a fish on a line with no hook? thought Edward.

He looked at the fish, conscious of his rising heartbeat. There was a pattern beginning to emerge in his mind. He was meant to catch this fish, but was he meant to keep it? It was all of 12 lbs, caught on a light grilse rod, the largest salmon he had ever landed. He was convinced there was only one course of action open to him. Placing the torch in his mouth he carefully lifted the net with the salmon still in it and, walking back into the river until the depth was adequate, he plunged the net in deep, watching the salmon begin to move its large tail, slowly at first. He was certain it looked in his direction before finally swimming downstream.

With the fish gone, the rod out of his hand, reality for Edward exited too. He began to shake uncontrollably, with apprehension and terror over the evening's happenings. Slipping and sliding over the submerged stones and weeds in the river bed, oblivious to the water slopping into his boots and over his trousers, he staggered out on to the bank casting his net away from him.

Ignoring his tackle on the ground he instinctively slithered to his left, disregarding the prickly furze and brambles until he came to the stone wall where he was forced to use the torch; but his terror was such he wasn't even conscious of the rusty barbed wire tearing through his waders and legs. Pushing his way past the branches of the tree he staggered straight into the rough furze almost screaming with panic. He had lost his way. Frantically retracing his steps towards the river he managed to pierce a gap with his torch through which he floundered, falling on the moist ground. His right foot plunged into the glue like peat of the drain, where his terrorised struggles to get out merely plunged the rubber waders further down into the substance. By now moaning in uncontrolled fear he threw his body forward towards the firmer ground on the far side of the drain, thanking God for his earlier survey. He still managed to leave his right boot in the soft mud. Somehow he scrambled to his feet, losing the torch in the process.

Lurching like a drunk he made his way in the general direction of the road above him. As he reached the bottom of the slope the headlights of a car passed overhead giving him some reassurance there was a real world up there.

Christ Almighty, he had forgotten the barbed wire. He slipped on the loose gravel on the steep slope leading to the road, grabbed out; his hand dug deep into the barbed wire tearing at the flesh of his fingers and palm. Somehow he managed to lever his aching body up on to the road level and his car. The keys were deep in his wet pocket, refusing to respond to his agitated searchings. Now overtaken by unrestrained terror, moaning and crying, he pulled and tugged at his pocket before releasing the keys. Despite his trembling he managed to locate the door lock, not before scoring the paintwork all round it. He flopped into the seat, slammed the door shut and, with a gasp of relief, locked the doors from the inside. It was a diesel and he had to wait for the glow plugs to warm up before starting the engine. It was only a few seconds but it seemed like weeks. Enough time for him to see, not admire, the bright river below in its tranquil surroundings. He asked himself again, could all this have really happened? The answer must be yes.

Jerking out the clutch the car skidded on the loose gravel before hurtling forward along the tarmac down towards the little bridge, almost hitting the parapet when the steering wheel slipped in his bloody hands. When he was well up the hill to the village he became conscious of the warm blood flowing down his leg and the pains in his body.

He managed to sneak into the hotel unnoticed with his motoring first aid box clutched under his arm.

In the bedroom his examination revealed no serious injuries. Just cuts from the barbed wire. Even his hands, to his relief, were not as bad as he had first thought. A bath, plus a few whiskeys, steadied his nerves. As he crawled into bed he resolved there was going to be some explaining by JJ in the morning.

★

After a restless sleep Edward sought out JJ. If he could not give him an explanation then he knew his nephew's mother certainly could, that was for sure. To his surprise JJ was waiting for him in the dining room, a look of concern on his face.

'Good morning sir, you looked a sore sight last night and, with no fish in the fridge, we guessed something was wrong. Are you all right then, sir?'

Putting aside his surprise at the effective village surveillance of his return to the hotel Edward came straight to the point. 'JJ for God's sake, why didn't you warn me about what might happen down there last night?'

'What did happen last night?' asked JJ in typical Kerry fashion; answering a question with one back.

Edward was still too pumped up to notice the subtlety and so, with words spilling over one another, gave a detailed account of events, imagined or not. JJ listened impassively, nodding occasionally as Edward recounted particular episodes.

'Jeasus sir, that bates everything.'

Edward did not expect that reaction. 'How do you mean JJ "beats everything"?'

'Sir, I'd best begin at the beginin'. Ye know the railway was built to Caherciveen in 1893. It was closed by some fella in Dublin in 1960; the bridge was taken down for safety's sake soon after. Back Caherciveen way in 1897 the young daughter of a local farmer got herself into trouble, by an English soldier it was said. She tried to keep it quiet for as long as possible, until the last few weeks when even the dresses they wore then couldn't hide her condition. Naturally the father was mad, stone mad, and told her she had brought dishonour to the family. He then fired her out of the cottage. After that her mother gave her the fare for England. On the 14th March 1898, the girl took the train from Caherciveen. By then she was just nine months pregnant. You can imagine the awful scene, sir, an' how that poor slip of a girl felt. She was only seventeen years of age. At any rate the train reached Mountain Stage when the baby was born, an' she threw herself an' the baby off the train at the railway bridge down below. That March, the river was in flood so the bodies were never found. Some say the father was on the train and he threw her off, but that is hardly true. On the other hand no one has explained what caused the train to stop on the bridge. I'm not sure if they had communication cords in those days. It does seem strange for a girl of that age to know about such a thing.'

'There have been stories about strange happenings down there. Indeed, sir, I have heard many versions of what happened, even in my own lifetime. But they were only stories. Nothing ever happened in my time. Let me tell you, sir, that fish have been caught there during daylight in high water without incident. I even heard, sir, tales of people hooking a big fish in the dark, but never of one being landed, nor of any woman standing on a rock. And no train.

'Sir, I feel terribly bad about what happened to you last night. You wanted a fish so badly. I honestly thought those stories were old wives' tales, an' there could be the chance of you catching a grilse.'

The pitiful story placed the events of the previous night into some kind of perspective. In a curious fashion Edward felt better. He couldn't help feeling empathy with that anguished face. A thought occurred to him, 'JJ, was she left-handed?'

JJ looked surprised at the question, 'I never heard, but why ever do you ask that, sir?'

'Oh, just curious.' He did not want to appear to trivialise a tragic death, but the expression on that girl's face, as she pointed her left hand at him, above all else, would haunt him for the rest of his life.

He continued, 'The baby could not have been baptised and it's unlikely either got the last rites. That is the message I think I was getting. Let's go and talk to the parish priest, who has probably heard by now that something happened to me last night.' The irony was not lost on JJ.

'Don't get us wrong, sir. It's important that all fishermen from the hotel return safely; we just keep an eye out, that's all. I know how bad you want a fish. Rain, heavy rain, is forecast for this evening, which will bring a share of fish up the river. Tomorrow you and I will kill, not one salmon, but several. Maybe even with a large Silver March Brown. Ye may not think so, sir, but it's a good all round fly hereabouts.'

Walking on Air

If the old style latticed wooden seats, with their curved backs, were in other cities they would most likely have been long since vandalised. In Santiago, Chile, vandalism had been successfully discouraged. The comfort and elegance of the seat was lost on Sam who should have been luxuriating in the warmth of the early March sunshine as he sat at the intersection of Avenido de 11th Sept. and Ricardo Lyon. Instead, for about the tenth time, he nervously checked the names of the streets. They hadn't changed.

For Sam it didn't seem right that he should be sitting here, at the intersection of the two major roads in the middle of Santiago, waiting for a bus to take him nearly seven hundred miles south. He had been assured by the travel agency that any taxi driver would deposit him at the intersection of 11th Sept. with Ricardo for the 17.45 Vermontt bus to Puerto Montt. He was very dubious about this, until the taxi driver told him the Central Station could be dangerous. 'You... picka poka,' he said, tapping his pocket.

He glanced at his Omega again, for the third time in six minutes, and calculated that the bus had twenty minutes to arrive. By now, he thought, there should be other passengers coming along to make sure they were in time; after all they had likely prepaid for a very long journey. One way or other he was now committed to waiting so he decided there was little alternative but to observe the passing pedestrians and the traffic with its continuous din of competing horns.

He had been uncertain about taking a trip to Chile when Jim first made the suggestion. If he could have visualised himself sitting at the side of the road waiting for this bus when he was in New York there would have been only one decision; no. *Blast Jim*, he muttered to himself. *No, that wasn't fair. What else could he do but defer his departure until after he had buried his father.* Jim was a decent guy, a good friend, and one doesn't make many real good friends from business contacts. Over the years he and Jim had taken a few short vacations together when they had got on very well. It had been Jim's idea to go to the Chilean lake district for its spectacular scenery and fishing.

'There's good salmon and trout fishing, Sam,' he had said. 'Besides, you need a good break to put the trauma of your divorce behind you. There's a couple of Americans down in Villarica who have a great little Hosteria. It's called La Colina. A friend of mine urged me to stay there.' Well, at least Jim said he would leave London so as to meet in Villarica in four days' time. Sam sighed, divorce was a rotten experience and he did need a good break to settle himself down after the long drawn-out haggling. Chile was going to be different, and as Jim advised, 'That's what you need Sam, a completely different environment. Go down to Puerto Montt and spend the four days working your way back up to Villarica.'

His thoughts were interrupted by a taxi pulling up in front of him. A woman, in her mid-thirties, with two young children, a boy aged about five and a younger girl, got out, the children rushing over to see which of them would first get to sit down on the other end of his seat. The woman hesitated and the taxi driver, sensing her wishes, motioned the children to the seat and, to Sam's relief, pulled her cases from the boot of the taxi and placed them on the sidewalk near where the children were seated. They were obviously passengers for a bus, so he didn't appear to be on a fool's errand after all. Before they arrived he was beginning to feel sorry for himself at the thought of travelling overnight in a bus to a remote part of Chile, to a small hotel where he would know no one; always assuming the bus even materialised.

Something else caught his attention. It wasn't just the good looks of the girl who was walking on the opposite sidewalk but, to Sam's astonishment she appeared to be walking on air, literally on air, an inch above the pavement. He wondered if he was hallucinating. Travel can sometimes play tricks on the mind. As if for reassurance he let his gaze move upwards. She had the figure of Venus, give a few less pounds. It was her face, and jet black hair, which impressed him: high cheekbones, wide eyes, a full mouth and a nose which should have spoiled the overall effect. Somehow her slightly wide nose seemed to make her more arresting.

Great, thought Sam, *she's crossing the road*. She was wearing designer black jeans topped by an off-white linen shirt and carried a small black case.

He found it difficult to shift his gaze from her face to her feet, yet he could hardly avoid staring at anyone who appeared to be walking on air. How did she do it? He fixed his eyes on her feet as she crossed the road, all the while convinced her feet were not touching the ground. Then he saw a pair of men's black shoes tracking her feet. Sam raised his eyes to disclose a smooth-looking man, in his early to mid-forties, wearing an expensive grey suit, steering her across the road, his hand on her left elbow. He was carrying a larger version of her small black case. As they stepped on to the sidewalk near him he realised why he thought she was walking on air. Her shoes were made of some type of clear plastic which, from a distance, was invisible. *Pity*, thought Sam. (He had been far more impressed thinking she was walking on air.)

She looked at the adjoining seat, which the mother and two children were monopolising, before choosing the far end of his. Her companion placed her case down by the end of the seat and nodded to Sam before asking, 'You're waiting for the five thirty-five also?'

'Five forty-five,' corrected Sam smiling.

'Don't worry, it will get here on time,' he said, ignoring the correction. 'You're safer here than at the bus station. It's dangerous there, particularly for strangers.'

'So I hear,' said Sam.

'You're a stranger I see?' It was a statement more than a question.

'Yeah, New York,' said Sam guardedly.

'My name is Hans Rickter,' he said, handing his card to a surprised Sam.

'Sam, Sam Boyce,' he proffered, without giving the other his card.

Hans busied himself in close conversation with the girl while Sam's attention was attracted to the mother on the other bench who was analysing the girl from head to toe, ignoring her son's persistent questioning. After a very thorough examination she frowned before transferring attention to her son. Three young men, locals who were waiting for the traffic lights to change, made no secret of their interest. They just stared at her boldly, almost missing the green.

The Vermontt bus drew up precisely at five forty-five and Hans gave the girl a casual peck on the cheek, waved to Sam and said, 'Sam, if I can do anything for you when you next come back to Santiago give me a call.'

Sam muttered his thanks and thought to himself, *A bit over friendly*, glad he wasn't accompanying the girl.

Each passenger had a pre-allocated seat. Sam's was on the outside of two, an aisle seat. The window seat to his left was occupied by a heavily built man who lowered his seat's back, covered his eyes with a black airline-type mask and fell asleep. Across the aisle to his right there was a single seat in which the girl was already ensconced. Sam wondered if there was any advantage in her being so near to him, given that few Chileans spoke English, whilst he had virtually no Spanish. It was almost a disadvantage in New York to be speaking it.

The travel agent had told him proudly that the bus seats tilted right back, like first class seats on a plane.

'You know, Mr Boyce, these buses are really luxurious.' The man beside him had got his seat right back so Sam decided he had better test his luxury seat. He looked around for the lever, found it and released it gradually whilst applying pressure with his back until the seat was nearly horizontal.

Good, that's that, he thought, as he released the lever to return the back of his seat to its original upright position. Before he realised what had happened the seat shot upright, cannoning him into the seat in front. He swore and the girl on the far side of the aisle laughed.

In spite of his shock and hurt, her laughter reminded him of nothing more than the tinkling of the glass drops in a Waterford cut glass chandelier shaken by a draught.

'I am sorry. Are you all right?' she asked, in an accent which, to Sam, was bewitchingly attractive.

Still a bit disorientated he looked at her dumbly, as much due to her accented English as to the bang on the head.

His recent divorce, followed by prolonged settlement negotiations, had left him scarred and cautious about getting entangled with any other women. This was the first time his self-imposed immunity to feminine charms had weakened. It wasn't just passing curiosity: he was smitten. Alarm bells began to ring in his head. His inner voice warned, *You don't know this girl. You have only seen the exquisite outer casing and heard the accent. Beware!*

'Are you all right?' she repeated, when he did not reply to her first question, a touch of solicitude apparent in her tone.

'Oh fine, fine. It was just the shock of the chair jumping forward and head hitting the seat in front, if you follow me,' said Sam, still unsure of her command of English.

'I follow you well. My English is not strong but, how shall I say, adequate,' she said shyly.

Sam's inner voice was again urging caution, *Easy Sam, calm down, after all a smile is only a smile. Yeah but that's some smile, showing teeth like pearls that would make tigers roll over to have their tummies rubbed. God, I'd better respond before she thinks there is something wrong with me.*

'More than adequate, far better than my Spanish. I've only a few words picked up from spi... Spanish-speaking people in New York,' said Sam, cursing himself for nearly using the word spics, and possibly ending their discussion.

Their conversation was interrupted by the crack of a stone on the window above the driver's head which spread into a spider's web of cracks. The bus then turned off to the right and into a narrow road.

'Maybe he is going to get it replaced in case it falls out later on, or get another bus?' said Sam, concerned in case they were not given the same seats.

'No, I do not theenk so. They call here for food,' she said as Sam concentrated on recalling the way she pronounced the word 'think'.

'Good,' he said. 'Anyway the driver's visibility is not impaired.'

She looked puzzled. 'Paired? What is that?'

'Impaired,' corrected Sam. 'It means not... interrupted... he can still see to drive.'

'I understand. You see my English is not so good,' she smilingly replied in that accent that had Sam mentally simpering.

There was a brief moment of silence before she spoke. *Yes*, shouted Sam to his inner voice, *she… yes, she spoke first.*

'We have many buses in Chile with bro… cracks in their windows… front.' Then she changed the topic. 'Is this your first visit to Chile?'

'Yes, first time south of Mexico,' replied Sam.

'And what do you theenk of Chile?' she asked.

'Anorexic,' he said spontaneously.

She looked puzzled, until he realised she couldn't possibly understand the word.

'You know the map of Chile, it is long and thin, just like a very thin girl who eats nothing. The maps of other countries are squat or fat.'

She said something which sounded like '*consumido*' and then she giggled before saying, 'You are correct. The map of Chile is thin, very thin. I have never thought about it like that.'

'By the way, my name's Sam.'

'I know that. I heard you tell Hans. Mine is Rosario.'

The attendant came with canapés. She took two but Sam, mindful of Montezuma's revenge, passed. Noting his hesitation she said, 'Do not worry, they are safe. You know, it's a long journey for the bus and they do not want people sick so they never serve bad food.' He took one which he thought might be the most innocuous.

'How far are you going?' asked Sam.

'Castro, that is where I come from. You know the island of Chiloe?' she asked.

'I've heard of it,' said Sam, trying to jog his memory as to its exact location.

'I thought this bus stopped at Puerto Montt?'

'It is, I have to go on some more. I am going to visit my mother who has been in hospital in Puerto Montt. She had an operation for gall bladder.'

'Oh, I am sorry to hear that,' said Sam, taking another canapé from the attendant. 'And how is she now?'

'Okay, I think,' she said.

'You live in Santiago?' he asked.

'Yes, I have an apartment there. And you live in New York?'

'Yeah, Manhattan, in a small apartment. Have you ever been there?'

'Yes, a few times. I have much travel in my work.'

'I see,' said Sam, not wanting to pry further unless it was volunteered. Anyway he had plenty of time.

The bus moved on with dusk staggering into a cosy darkness when the attendant drew the curtains. By then their conversation had become pretty generalised. The dinner and drinks, she took beer, helped to break down barriers. It became a kind of English lesson, as whenever Sam used an unusual word she sought its meaning and filed it away, repeating it under her breath.

For Sam it didn't much matter what they talked about, the inner mind had been stifled, her voice and smile were like music to Sam. Not just any old ordinary music. He thought about the comparison for some time, before coming down on the side of Mozart's twenty-first piano concerto. It would be appropriate, or even the Brahms' violin concerto, the slow movement of course. He settled back into his chair, more contented than he had been for a while, and reflected on what more could a man want than speeding through the night in a comfortable bus, having a meal and drinks with a beautiful girl. 'With' was debatable, so he settled for 'near'. Then he began to fret about journey's end. What then?

'When did you last see your mother?' he asked.

'Oh, it has been some time,' she said. Sam detected a trace of wistfulness. As if she regretted leaving her mother.

'As I say,' she said, 'she is recovering at home from a gall bladder operation. The doctors say she has made a very good recovery.'

Again there was a wistfulness in her demeanour. Behind the smiles and the vivacity Sam detected something else – a sadness perhaps. He then realised why he had chosen the two concertos. Both have that mixture of wistfulness and sadness. Once he had sorted that out, Sam's feelings for her strengthened; he felt more protective towards her.

The inner man wasn't finished. *Jeez Sam, you idiot, back off and just think of having a good holiday. This is ridiculous. You have been hurt once already; avoid the pitfalls.* That was the problem with Gloria. He never saw the pitfalls until she looked for a divorce. To this day he still couldn't understand what went wrong with their marriage. She claimed she was seeing someone else but he wasn't satisfied that this was really the case. At any rate his job didn't give him much time to find out for certain.

Rosario said something which interrupted his train of thought.

'Sam,' God how he loved to hear her say his name spoken so seductively.

'Yeah, Rosario.'

'Are you getting off at Puerto Montt?'

'Yeah, I'm staying overnight at the Hotel Burg. I had planned to go to a place called Puerto Varas on Lake Llanquihue. If Jim, my friend, had been with me we would have made for a place called Frutillar where he has a pal.'

'I know it. It's very pretty. The Germans came there about the middle of the last century.'

'Rosario, I have some days before Jim comes down here, why don't we get together in Castro seein' as it's only a few hours from Puerto Montt.'

'First I must see how my mother is. I have only a week here before I have to go back to Santiago. After that I go to New York.'

Sam's heart leaped at her mention of New York. 'We can see one another in New York, Rosario,' he said enthusiastically.

'Perhaps, we can talk about that later,' she replied.

'You sure do have a busy time, Rosario, with all that travelling. If you don't mind my asking what is your job?'

'Demonstrating beauty preparations. A bit like a mannequin,' she said, and then asked, 'Where is your friend Jim coming from, New York too?'

'No, London, England.'

'Oh, I was there last week,' she said.

By then dinner was over, the attendant had cleared the plates and cutlery and dimmed the lights. She turned up the television for the news, which was in Spanish. It killed off further conversation between them. The combination of food and heavy Chilean red wine, together with an effort to catch any of the news, caused Sam to feel sleepy. He dozed off. When he awoke the television was off, the lights were out and Rosario was curled up under her blanket fast asleep. 'Damn, damn,' he swore to himself, 'I should have stayed awake.'

As the rest of the passengers appeared to be fast asleep he had no alternative but to do likewise. Not surprisingly he dreamt of Rosario as the bus drove through the Chilean night. They were walking hand in hand in the sun along the seafront at Puerto Montt, discussing where and when they would get married. New York, Santiago and London were discarded. Then Rosario exclaimed, 'Rome, Rome that is it. I have never been there.' Sam agreed, as the venue was subsidiary to the deed. He could sense the envious glances he was getting from the other men on the promenade, their wives or girlfriends displaying annoyance at their lecherous glances. He was very proud to be escorting such a glorious girl. No, not glorious, that was too close to home, exquisite would be better. There was a sudden push from behind as if someone had run into them. The dream and reality had merged into the stopping of the bus at the Varmontt Puerto Montt terminal.

It took Sam a few seconds to realise there was no hand in his left hand. It was a grey morning and passengers were already standing up to leave the stationary bus. A man blocked his view of the adjoining seat. When he passed by Sam, the gap between him and the next passenger revealed there was no one sitting in Rosario's seat. He jumped up, ignored his luggage, pushed his way past annoyed fellow passengers and tore around both sides of the bus, where luggage was being unloaded, frantically searching for her. She was nowhere to be seen.

He ran back around to the door at the front where he grabbed the arm of the startled attendant.

'Rosario,' he croaked to a blank look. 'La señorita, where is she?'

The attendant at first looked puzzled, then he realised what was being asked of him, probably, thought Sam, because he too had admired her.

'Puerto Varas,' he said and indicated by signs and signals she had left the bus there. Sam goggled at him and tried to repeat the name. 'Puerto Varas,' he muttered several times.

The attendant looked sympathetic. He had been on too many buses not to recognise the chemistry between them last night. Sam felt as if he had been kicked in the stomach. *Why had she got off at Puerto Varas?* he thought. She had said she was going beyond Puerto Montt, to that island. She may have had a good reason and didn't want to disturb him. Still, she could have left a note for him. His thoughts were wandering around a mental maze – going nowhere. The answer was that he didn't know why she got off there. He didn't know what to do so he decided to make for his hotel which, as it happened, was only a ten minute taxi ride away.

When he got there and had registered with a receptionist who could speak English he went up to his bedroom to shave and think. Whatever the reason for her departure, good, bad or indifferent, he had to locate her. He simply couldn't get her out of his mind. Where to start with no Spanish? The girl at the desk, that's it.

Sam hurried down to the reception desk. The girl was still there. He knew from their first meeting she would be helpful and sympathetic. He explained how he had met Rosario on the bus, didn't know her second name, only that her mother lived in Castro, on the island of... 'Chiloe?' offered the girl.

'Yes,' he replied, 'and she has recently been in hospital at Puerto Montt for a gall bladder operation.'

The receptionist was both enthusiastic and smart. Smart enough to see she was helping to smooth the path of true love.

'I have a cousin who works at the hospital, maybe she can find out if a woman, not young, was operated for a gall bladder in the hospital. Give me a little time, señor, and I will ring you.'

Sam thanked her and said, 'I will be in my room taking a bath. If the phone is not answered at first let it ring. Oh, on second thoughts, I'll let the bath wait.'

The receptionist laughed, 'As you wish, señor.'

The phone rang a short time later. It was the receptionist. 'I have spoken to my cousin. Such information is... what to you call it... yes... restricted.' Sam's heart sank. 'However,' the girl continued, 'my cousin has made unofficial questions and she has learned the only recent gall bladders taken out were men. There was no bladder from Castro.'

Sam thanked her profusely and replaced the receiver, wondering what to do next. Go to Castro? No, he wouldn't get far there with zilch Spanish and no surname. He could hardly go to the police with such flimsy information, or even for such a reason. Then he remembered the card from Hans. Why hadn't he thought of that before? He must know where she can be contacted, either here or in Santiago.

He began to search feverishly through his belonging for that now precious card. He couldn't find it in all the usual places. He sat down and carefully went through all the places where he could possibly have put it. Then he remembered the breast pocket of his shirt. It was there. He practically threw himself at the phone and dialled the Santiago number.

'Hello,' a girl's voice said cheerfully.

'Is Hans there?' he asked, hardly able to contain his excitement.

'Yes, who is looking for him?' she asked.

'Sam, Sam Boyce,' he replied. 'Tell him I met him at the bus stop the other day.'

There was some muzak switched on before a man's voice said, 'Hans Rikter here.'

'Sam Boyce, you remember we met yesterday at the bus stop in Santiago.'

'Oh yes, of course, I remember you. I just didn't have your card, your name slipped my mind. Where are you?' he said, sounding as if he was interested.

'Puerto Montt, but I really wanted to find out where I can contact Rosario. She got off at Puerto Varas when I was still asleep. Apparently her mother had had an operation and she was going to see her,' said Sam, rushing his words.

'Her mother?' Hans sounded surprised. 'You want to meet her again?'

'I sure do,' said Sam.

'You know she has an international clientele,' Hand said as if she was too good for him.

'Yeah, she told me about her work,' said Sam, wishing he would come to the point and tell him where he could reach her.

'It'll cost you. She doesn't come cheap,' said Hans, sounding like a school teacher.

'For God's sake, Hans, I'm not interested in beauty preparations,' said Sam, getting fed up.

'I look after all her clients. It generally costs $2,500 per night, seeing as where you are that figure could be negotiable.'

'Negotiable?' said Sam, feeling weak after his second kick in the stomach in the same day.

'Are you all right, Sam? Surely she told you, or you even guessed?'

'No, she didn't. I guess that's why she got off the bus early. Hans, would you do me a favour?'

'Sure, Sam, what?'

'Tell her I tried to find her. Tell her I tried very hard.'

'Of course, Sam, and remember you have my number if I can do anything for you. Goodbye Sam.'

The phone went dead, no more dead than Sam. All he could think of was a piece of poetry which popped into his mind from his school days. Was it by Sir Walter Scott? He wasn't sure.

> Oh many a shaft, at random sent,
> Finds many a mark the archer little meant,
> And many a word, at random spoken,
> May soothe or wound a heart that's broken.

He couldn't be sure he had got it right but Hans's three words 'It'll cost you' had gone straight, like an arrow, through his heart.

Donana Dreams

There are snores and snores. Jack's was neither loud nor quiet. Heard out of bed, in the light of day, a listener need walk only a short distance to be out of earshot. It was another matter if he, or she in this case, was confined to the same bed. As snoring goes it could be argued that his was almost melodic, like the slow movement of a symphony. If he had a few drinks beforehand, his sound, in snoring terms, reached Beethoven standards with his ample frame generating the mellifluence necessary for the equivalent of say the slow movement of his ninth.

Molly, his wife, didn't mind his snoring; not that she liked it. She simply didn't hear him. Why? Because he generally started about three hours after he fell asleep, by which time he had adjusted his 220 lbs so that he was sleeping on his back. Not until then did the music begin. As far as sleep was concerned, Molly was a Jekyll and Hyde. For the first couple of hours she was a light sleeper, a Dr Jekyll who could be disturbed and still be in good humour. Thereafter, she slept very heavily and woe betide anyone who woke Mrs Hyde. Jack was sensible enough not to disturb Molly out of her deep sleep, terrified lest he might meet the demons which he had married.

Generally their sleeping patterns dovetailed perfectly. So far as Jack was concerned the only fly in their ointment was his tendency to wake himself up after about an hour's snoring. He was wide awake now reflecting on the day's events.

The nature of Jack's work, as owner of a souvenir shop, meant they had to take their holidays in the off-season. Not all that bad if they headed south. Even in the south of Spain there were cheap rates for January and February, if one knew where to go. By now they were expert at finding the best bargains and he had to admit this year Molly had struck oil, pricewise, in this hotel.

The mile-long desert of shuttered apartments, bungalows, villas and hotels was a little off-putting, more for Jack than Molly. She maintained some of the hotels were open whereas he was disenchanted by the sight of shuttered dwellings and the dearth of activity. There were a few residents and workmen about, insufficient to lift Jack's feeling of solitude which the place engendered for him. Molly told him he was being ridiculously impressionable.

The first hotel they came upon did not impress either of them. It was full of geriatrics, some stooped and crooked. All were bent, thought Jack smiling at his own wit, on having a good time with that jolly hockey sticks attitude which is singularly English. As Molly and Jack were originally from Ireland they were a little put off by their 'this is enjoyable' attitude. They welcomed spontaneous socialising, not programmed herding. To spend a week having their noses pressed up to pictures of what they were likely to look like in twenty or so years time was not their cup of tea. Admittedly the price was low, around fifteen pounds for bed and breakfast for both. Molly was tempted at first, but the age profile was wrong, so they went further afield. On to the very end of the development where Molly came upon a real bargain.

Jack was not too keen on staying there as it was the last building before the start of the Donana sand dunes, desert for several miles before the marshlands of the delta of the Guadalquiver River.

'Look Molly it's the last watering hole before the desert. Even the approach roads are unlit and potholed. It's a forbidding place,' he insisted.

Molly, however, had the bit between her teeth, evidenced in her purposeful, even exultant strides back to the car after she had gone into the hotel.

'Jack, this is it. They will give us a south-facing room overlooking the pool and the start of the Donana National Park. It will have its own secluded balcony for sunbathing, with the beach no more that a few hundred yards on our right. I have had a look at the room. It's a steal. I told them I would get my husband's approval before confirming. The price by the way is four thousand pesetas per day for full board.'

'Per person?' asked Jack thinking under twenty pounds wasn't that cheap.

'No silly, for the two of us,' said Molly proudly.

Jack knew when he was beaten. At that price he had to agree. 'Okay Molly, we'd better take it before they change their minds. It's too late to go anywhere else anyway.'

They got their luggage out of their hired car and climbed the marble steps to the impressive entrance hall. With no doorman in sight they carried their luggage to the reception desk, their shoes making hollow click clacks on the black and white marble floor. The only person in sight was a young girl dwarfed by the massive tiled reception desk. Jack shivered at the austerity of the partially lit vista before him. Even the souvenir shop was closed. There was a tiled Islamic style covered fountain in the middle of the foyer which would be impressive if the water was turned on. *A dead fountain, that's a good start*, brooded Jack. For such a large hotel the silence was uncanny. He supposed in the high season there would be a bit of a buzz about the place. But now? He consoled himself with the thought that it probably cost about seventy pounds per night for bed only in July.

The receptionist was helpful and welcoming, just as if they were full paying guests. The bedroom was as Molly had described. The swimming pool below their balcony was vast. It even had an island in the middle with two palm trees. Beyond that was the sand dunes of the Donana stretching as far as he could see, and miles beyond that, if the blurb was correct. To their left, the evening sun was slanting downwards into the Atlantic Ocean, the breakers of which were pounding incessantly on a wide beach.

'Well Jack what do you think?'

'I have to admit, Molly, it's magnificent, though I still think it's a bit eerie. Do you not think it's a bit odd that there is hardly anyone else in a four hundred room hotel?'

'Jack, can you imagine the alternative? Full of people queuing for everything. Germans leaving their towels on the poolside seats at five in the morning, bursting to defend their plots with unintelligible abuse. We can't have it every way dear, now can we?' she said, her tone brooking no argument.

'There must be a catch, Molly,' was all he could say.

Anyway, he thought, here they were, no point in his grumbling. He looked at the luminous dial on his watch. It was only two o'clock in the morning. They had gone to bed at eleven and he seldom woke up after only three hours' sleep. The stillness was episodically broken by the beating of the waves on the shore below. They seemed close by, possibly due to the high tide. The rays of the full moon knifed their way through a slit in the curtain into the bedroom illuminating the dressing table.

Then he heard another sound, a low moan. There it goes again. Was he just hearing things? There it goes again. Was it outside or inside the hotel? It was so faint he couldn't decide. It certainly didn't come from their room. Molly was fast asleep in the twin bed, breathing deeply. He was straining his ears to make sure he would trace it next time. He wasn't ready however, for the choked scream. It sent an icy shaft though his heart, which immediately began to beat faster and faster; *di dum, di dum, di dum, di dum.* He placed his hand over the middle of his chest as if that would slow it down. It didn't. It only raised the beat. What should he do? Wake Molly? No, that would be the worst thing to do. Mrs Hyde would accuse him of dreaming, if the sound did not reoccur. Think. Was it a man's or a woman's voice, or even a child's? He couldn't be sure.

Then there was another startled cry ending suddenly as if someone had placed their hand over a mouth. Yes, it was a woman's tone. Was she being murdered? It certainly sounded as if someone had put their hand over her mouth to stop the cry. What should he do? He couldn't be dreaming. He pinched himself to make sure, feeling a bit stupid as he did so. Should he ring the desk? What would he say? For God's sake, ask them if they heard anyone screaming. Not anyone, a girl. Why did he say girl? How did he know it was a girl and not a woman? Oh for goodness sake he had better ring. He didn't want to turn on the light for fear of rousing Mrs Hyde. If there were no further sounds she was certain to accuse him of dreaming, particularly after his earlier misgivings. Then there would be moaning, right here in this bedroom. They had rung somewhere downstairs before they went to sleep, zero something; nine that was it. He carefully dialled the number, feeling better as he did so. He now had a line to outside assistance. There was no reply. It simply rang and rang. Still no reply. He was reluctant to hang up as the phone made him feel he was doing something positive. Besides, hanging up would leave him isolated again. Christ Almighty, that bastard was asleep on duty. After a while he had to hang up. There was no one there.

Then it happened again, a moan leading to a thin scream followed by a shrill scream, not so loud this time; then silence. He lay on the bed, his heart beating like a kettle drum, his mind racked by indecision. No sound. He felt there should be a sound of running feet; even stealthy steps. Nothing.

He couldn't just lie there. Well, maybe he could. Just to see if there were any other sounds. After all there must be other people about. They would hardly separate the few who were staying overnight in the hotel. That would be uneconomic. Their cost accountant would see to that. More than likely they would be all together on this floor, all five or six of them that is.

He could hear a tap being turned on in one of the bedrooms beside him. He could not make out which. Then the sound of a toilet being flushed. It was a reassuring sound, at first. Then he thought the sequence was wrong. The toilet should have been flushed first and then the hands washed. Even schoolboys knew that. But why the incongruity? Surely he or she heard the cries too. Why did he or she not do something? Because he was the attacker. That is the only explanation. Maybe he had cut her throat and was washing his hands before going to the loo? On the other hand, he could have washed them before and again after the murder. He just did not hear the first tap being turned on. He could hardly waltz into the next room in the middle of the night accusing some stranger of murder. Whether he was or wasn't he would be in difficulties with him. No, that option was out.

Everyone knows that in the middle of the night harmless sounds can sound menacing. No one is bothered about things that go bump in the day, whereas they can be dead scared if things go bump in the night. If he was lying in the sun on the balcony and he heard a cry or scream from the beach what would he do? Nothing. Even if he was having an after-dinner drink in the dusk what would he do? Again nothing. Of course there would be lights on and people around. There was no one about or even awake now, except himself. Even the bloody staff weren't there. His thoughts were interrupted by Molly turning in the bed and muttering something unintelligible. Except for the last word, spoken sharply, ' Jack.' Maybe that is what first woke him up. His name being called out like that by Molly. Anyone would wake up with someone shouting out their name. *Shall I try it out with Molly?* Better not, she would wake up in a rage. He heard the other sounds because he was awake, not woken by them. After all if he was fast asleep he would have heard nothing, and wouldn't be lying here worrying.

Molly had said he was being ridiculous about the place. But was there nothing spooky about an empty hotel with poor street lighting and, what's more, potholed roads and pavements? Then there was that Donana, full of wild boar and other animals. Molly just laughed, 'Jack they are trying to keep their key staff over the winter. If it was the middle of the summer you would be complaining of the heat and the crowds, not to mention the price.' She had a point. Jack knew that cost accountants ruled today and he was sure there was some tax advantage to them in their off-season price. Those fellows would sell their souls for a good tax credit scheme.

Molly was still breathing deeply in the adjoining twin bed. Regular breathing in, and out; in and out. The only other sound was the Atlantic rollers pounding the beach. It sounded like the spouting of a giant sperm whale. Regular as clockwork. Then he noticed a strange thing. Every so often the waves and Molly's exhalations would synchronise. She breathing out and the waves hitting the shore. Both together in the stillness of the night and the full moon. He listened as they synchronised, then deviated, then rejoined. Then he fell fast asleep.

He was having a dream that he was walking along the beach, along the golden sands under a blazing blue sky, past the upright rods of the amateur shore fishermen. He came to a part of the beach where the shell fishermen were out in the sea, up to their thighs, dragging a square metal contraption like a large bird cage, open at the front, along the bottom. They pulled their contraptions from a strap around their shoulders. He likened them to the dray horses of his childhood. It was hard work, he thought.

One of the fishermen dragged his cage out of the water and up the beach to where he was standing beside the fisherman's equipment and catch. He tilted the cage at an angle to allow the contents to pour out from the open end on to a brown sack in the hot sand. A young girl's head rolled out, eyes blinking in the sunlight followed by about fifty clams. Jack jumped back with a cry of horror knowing in his heart it was the girl he heard screaming. The Spanish fisherman moved in his direction, pushing him out of his way.

'Jack, Jack, what are you going on about? It's only a bad dream.'

He opened his eyes into the glare of the morning sun, Molly's hands vigorously shaking his shoulder. He rubbed his eyes with the knuckles of his right hand whilst pushing the fingers of his left through his hair, what little hair he had left, that is.

'Molly, I had a dream that turned into a nightmare, about walking along the beach and seeing the head of the girl who was murdered. Here in the hotel. And I could do nothing for her. I must have fallen asleep.'

'Jack what are you saying? You are rambling. It's only a bad dream. I'm not surprised after all your imaginings of last night. Sure, you've always had too vivid an imagination.'

'But, Molly, it's true about the girl screaming in the middle of the night in this hotel. I heard her. You're wrong, it wasn't a dream.' He gave her a detailed account of what he heard.

'Jack why didn't you wake me up? It would have helped, you know.'

'You were too fast asleep,' said Jack defensively. 'I did try to contact the front desk.'

'And what had they to say?'

'Nothing, because there was no one there. I let it ring and ring.'

'Jack, I don't know what to make of all that. Are you sure you heard the tap run before the toilet was flushed?'

'Of course, I am sure,' said Jack getting angry.

'Look, let's get dressed and go down and ask them at the desk if they heard anything.' Molly tried to sound sympathetic.

They made their way down the deserted corridor to the lift. The foyer, with its still silent fountain, was, in daylight, bright and colourful. They were greeted by a smiling young receptionist who answered their hesitant *'hable usted ingles?'* with a smiling, 'But of course.'

Molly then explained, 'My husband thought he heard cries in the night. More of a girl's scream, a scream, you understand a scream?' On getting a nod she continued, 'Was there a report of anyone being injured or attacked last night?'

The dapper young man behind the desk looked startled. Fingering his tie, he darted glances to his left and right as if seeking assistance from these two mad people. The English had a reputation for being difficult; but this?

'No señora, there has been no such report. I have been on duty since twelve o'clock last night and nothing have I heard. What time did your husband hear the sounds?'

'About three o'clock,' said Jack, adding firmly, 'and I rang the desk.'

'Oh,' said the young Spaniard, thinking this was going to be one of those days, and in the winter too. 'What number did you ring, sir?'

'Zero nine. It kept ringing and ringing,' Jack said accusingly.

'Ah,' said the relieved receptionist, 'that was the number for services. It is not attended at night in the winter season, sir. You should have just dialled one.'

'Jack, you idiot. You got the wrong number.'

'It was dark and I thought it was the number we rang yesterday evening. Anyway I didn't want to turn on the light when you were so fast asleep.'

'I suppose it was an understandable mistake,' said Molly, showing some solicitude.

'I cannot understand it, sir, there were only four rooms occupied in that section last night; you in 335, an old Spanish couple in room 336, a newly-wed French couple in room 334, they were on the first night of their honeymoon, and two elderly English ladies. Look, there are the newly-weds crossing the lobby towards the restaurant.'

They looked across the foyer, their eyes following a tall young Frenchman with his arm around a stunning brunette. At least, for Jack she was stunning. Molly's eyes narrowed. Her face was a study as she met the young receptionist's smiling eyes.

'Thank you very much. My husband must have been dreaming after all. Jack, we had better go in to breakfast.'

'I wasn't drea—' started Jack.

'Later,' she hissed as she trod on Jack's right big toe, and louder, 'Are you coming Jack dear?'

Eaten Pane

Yonkers was going to have a warm humid day. The temperature was already climbing into the eighties and it was still only half nine on a Saturday morning. The heat apart, my hair was too long for a wedding. At least that was my wife's contention.

Despite the deserted roads and footpaths the glitzy hairdressing salon was busy. Four ladies, early birds, were seated in the plush chairs attended by three carefully made up assistants, two blondes and a brunette wearing arresting black dresses, mother of pearl chokers and golden bracelets. Two other ladies were seated in large armchairs leafing through *Harper*'s and *Hello* as they waited their turn.

The carefully manicured receptionist, upgraded into a more expensive looking black dress, ensconced on her plush turquoise chair purred an insincere greeting, followed by, 'If you folks wait a half hour we can take you both in adjoining chairs.'

My wife looked at me with an impish gleam in her eye replying, rather too readily for my liking, 'Why not? My husband badly needs his hair cut. Darling, you can't appear at the wedding looking like that, think of the heat.'

The receptionist's expression confirmed to the other ladies that my hair certainly needed cutting. All the same, I was not going to have a hair cut in her futuristic unisex salon where I was the only man; not bloody likely.

Barber shops, traditional barber shops, had become an endangered species, hit first by the long-haired cult of the Sixties to be followed by the scented sculptured hairdos sought by today's Yuppie males. Traditionalists, or reactionaries, like me still clung to their old barber shops. There, good fellowship, stimulating conversation, or gossip if you will, and a feel for tradition still survives. I had been told they were alive and well in New York. Now seemed a good time for confirmation of this.

Before the trap could close I excused myself on the basis of having sighted a barber's down the street. I had caught a glimpse of a red and white pole, partially shielded by another sign, further down Main Street.

'Do come back if you can't find one,' said Mary solicitously.

'I will.'

She disbelieved me, knowing my aversion to unisex hairdressing salons. I sped out of the salon and up the street where I thought I had seen the pole. Sure enough, it was a barber shop.

Inside this haven were three familiar upright worn leather chairs, two vacant, the other occupied by an elderly man having his hair cut by a venerable barber holding a pair of stainless steel scissors, which were rhythmically clipping the air over his customer's head while he finished a story.

Entering further, I saw it had a long, worn, brown leather-covered bench fixed along the right-hand cream-coloured wall. Above the seat there was a padded strip of leather on the wall as a back rest. The tall barber chairs facing the other wall had a white Formica-type shelf along its length with a built-in white hand basin opposite each chair. Scattered along the shelves' length were the usual accoutrements of the trade, delph shaving mugs, hair sprayers, razors, brushes and combs, scissors, hand clippers and plastic containers of hair shampoo. Over the shelf, for the whole length of the wall, were a continuous series of mirrors held on to the wall with chromium covered screws. One of the chrome screw covers was missing. Good. The mirrors gave an illusion of space in what was really a narrow corridor of a room. It could be said the functional chrome fittings had seen better days. On one or two of the taps the chrome was worn down to the brass. Even the old black electric shaver the barber had been using had its innards kept in place with black insulating tape. Halfway down there was a pile of dog-eared magazines on a small mahogany table, topped by the massive bulk of Saturday's *New York Times*. The shop had all the characteristics of the Fifties. A delightful time warp, and for me a lifeline.

Before I could get my hands on the paper, the barber pointed his buzzing razor at the other chair, greeting me with, 'Mornin' sir. Ed is out front an' will be with you in a second.'

'Ed,' he hollered, 'there's a guy here who wants a hair cut.'

A short stocky man with a crew cut appeared, wearing a navy sweat shirt tucked into dark blue denims. He looked to be a young sixty-five or thereabouts, reminding me of James Cagney, the Hollywood actor who used to play a lot of tough guys. He fitted into the general ambiance.

Ed conjured up a chequered cloth with which, in a single flourish, he had covered my front and tucked under my chin even before I realised what he was doing.

'How will it be buddy?'

'Short back and sides.'

'Where you from?' he asked, sensing a stranger.

'Ireland.'

'Ireland,' he exclaimed, pronouncing it like many Americans do; 'Eye-er-land.'

'Did you kiss the Blarney stone?' he asked. It's not the first thing one expects to be asked.

'No,' I said, 'we Irish don't need to kiss it. Sure haven't we got the gift of the gab anyway.'

'I kissed it in '43,' he volunteered, bursting to tell any Irishman he met.

'1943,' I said somewhat surprised, 'wasn't that during the war? Were you over there on leave from England?' I asked.

'Nope. I mean I wasn't on leave. We was on duty. We flew inta Cork in a Douglas DC3 an' drove to Blarney.'

Intrigued, I exclaimed, 'But Ireland was neutral during the war. What were you doing flying in there?'

'Nope. We flew in some cargo to Cork an' left the next day. Don't ask me what it was. We was flying all over Europe dropping cargo. I remember flying to Holland an' dropping supplies on to the Dutch where they had opened, or blasted, the dikes leavin' places cut off by the sea.'

'Gee we had a great time travellin' all over, at Uncle Sam's expense; Italy, France, Belgium, England, Scotland, Holland, even Germany towards the end. I guess we musta been lucky – we never got hit. As far as I was concerned Uncle Sam could have spent a million dollars on our flying around Europe. It was like a vacation. We kinda hoped the war would go on longer. Now don't get me wrong Buddy,' he added quickly, 'we knew guys were gettin' killed an' it was better we finished them off sooner than later. Anyway it was only a matter of time, once we cleared the Germans outa Italy.'

'The Italians – they hated the war an' that guy Mussolini. At least that's what they told us everywhere we went. Our guys had a ball there. We were treated like heroes, sort of thousands of Humphrey Bogarts and Errol Flynns. You gotta believe it. We were treated even better than those film stars.'

He paused, and I could see in the mirror the open scissors poised in mid-air over my shoulder in front of his navy sweat shirt, with a wistful expression on his face. I sensed his mind was back in the Italy of the Forties. The spell broke. The scissors recommenced their snipping. 'The ordinary GIs from Idaho an' the Mid-West, some of them had never gotten out of their own county, never mind their State, had never seen anything like the reception they were gettin'. Dem Italian people were greetin' 'em like heroes an' film stars rolled into one. And when I mean people I don't mean men.'

'Why not men?' I asked.

'You musta been young then?' he asked.

'About thirteen or fourteen,' I replied. He nodded his head, as if I was still that age.

'Their men were all at war, or in prisoner-of-war camps. Most hadn't been home for years, an' it showed. Not in them, in their women folk. I'll tell you sometin', keep women away from it for a while and they are worse than the men. You gotta believe it. As sure as I am standing here they threw themselves at us. We were only flying in an' out but I can tell you those farm boys from Idaho... most of them didn't know what hit them. Not, I'll tell ye, that they were too slow at learnin'. They gave us presents of wine, flowers, even food, which they couldn't afford. They couldn't do enough for us. Not that our guys weren't generous too. Sure they were. It was wartime. We saw some real hardship. Our guys gave out food an' cigarettes, you know Camels, Chesterfields, chocolate and nylons. Did they make a hit wid those nylons, did they what? I have to tell ye we walked ten feet tall out there. It sure was great.'

For a second I had a vision of his five foot six growing to ten feet whilst he again hesitated with the cutting, the scissors blades held open in mid-air in his right hand as his mind zoomed back to the war in Italy in his DC3. Shaking free the memory he continued with his saga as he again shrunk back to size.

'People asked us, they didn't ask they pleaded, to come back after the war an' spend some more time in their houses. A lot of our guys married Italians an' brought them back to the US. GI brides they usta call 'em. Ever hear of them in Ireland?'

'Yes, I saw pictures of them in the newspapers when they were going to America,' I said.

It was really a rhetorical question, for he continued as if I had not replied.

'I never forgot the great times we had in Italy. Not that we didn't get treated well elsewhere, but Italy was somethin' special.'

'Did you ever feel tempted to go back?' I asked, sensing more and wanting to get my money's worth.

'I sure did but I hadn't seen my gal for about two years. We got married soon as I got back stateside. Then we had a family, an' you know what that means. They are all grown up an' married now. So about four years ago Cindy got so cheesed off with my stories about Italian hospitality she agreed to go there.'

'Well,' I said, 'how did it pan out?'

He was holding the scissors preparatory to the ritual of cutting the last few overlooked hairs, real or unreal. They hovered for a few seconds before agitatedly clipping again. He delayed giving me a direct reply for a moment.

'I had a buddy who was a gunner in a Sherman tank an' he wanted to go back to Europe after the war to see the places he had passed through. You gotta remember he didn't see much through the slits in his tank, rubble in one place is the same as rubble in another. But he couldn't recognise any of the places they had fought through when he returned in the Sixties, despite askin' questions everywhere he went.'

'One old guy in a French village in Alsace attacked him because some US tanks had shot up his wine cellar. He later discovered that they had bricked off half the wine store from the Germans, an' we had shelled the rest which he had hoped would be his nest egg for after the shootin'. My buddy couldn't even say if his guys were there or not, but he reckoned he'd better keep his trap shut from then on.

Hell, we was pushin' out the Nazis for them, and gettin' killed for our trouble!'

'But your visit to Italy?' I persisted, sensing a diversion.

'D'ye know Naples?' he asked.

'Yes. I was there in the late Fifties.'

'Well I guess it's been going downhill since. I called into a village near there where they had been real kind to us, insisting we come back after the war. Jeez, when I came back they couldn't even remember which war I was talking about. The lingo was a problem and we felt like one of those big ol' reptiles.'

'Dinosaurs,' I volunteered.

'Yep, I guess so. To tell ye the truth it was embarrassin'. We left for Naples where I had an address.'

'The cab, which wasn't cheap, offered to wait and bring us back, but when we got ripped off once by him on the fare out we figured someone would steer us right for the journey back. The street had changed, an' so had the address we had been given. The number we had was gone, but a guy told us he would take us to the family. He sure took us. With a knife as big as a bayonet, an' for everything we'd got, even our wedding rings. Jeez can you imagine it? There we were in the middle of nowhere without a dime an' we couldn't even speak the lingo.'

The razor buzzed away in the air like a giant demented wasp as he reflected on their predicament.

'Correction, it wasn't nowhere. It was like Harlem, an' that is somewhere you better believe you keep outa.'

'We went into a shop and an' old guy there remembered our part in the war, especially the GI's food kitchens an' nylons an' cigarettes. He got us a cab an' said we could pay for it at our hotel. He even said he knew of the party we were looking for. But Cindy, that's my wife, was not impressed – I guess depressed is a better word.'

'No one gave a goddamn about your lousy war,' she said, 'all they want is our greenbacks. We could live like a king in New York for what it cost us in Italy.'

'Boy,' he said with feeling, 'do they know how to rip you off. Cindy, she just wanted to get outa Naples.'

'We got to Rome thinking it would be better an' Cindy thought at least she could get to see the Pope. Folks there would be charitable seein' as where it was.'

'Well?' I asked.

'Well my ass,' he said rather savagely, 'Some shit stood on my toe in St Peter's Square; my money belt was cut an' gone before I knew it, and that was it. Some of our documents went too. Hell, if I want that kinda treatment I can have it for nothin' here in New York. Another buddy of a friend of mine went to Berlin afterwards an' had a great time. Can you beat that? And we flattened that burg. I know, as we flew in there. It's a funny world. But I'll tell you somtin', we had a great time in your country. That Blarney stone sure worked.'

I couldn't disagree. The hair cut was over and the $12 cost plus a good tip was a small price to pay. They sure wouldn't have been telling me about their war time adventures up the street. It even beat Cecil's in Ringsend.

The wife was settled into a light blue armchair reading *Vanity Fair* when I returned.

'I see you got your usual,' she offered. 'What was your barber like?'

'A cut above the usual,' I replied.

Monique

Tom Kavanagh didn't feel at all well. He was well used to smoke. Even the combination of Tiger Healy's Chesterfields, the Pig Nolan's Camels or the Head Winter's Prince Rupert pipe tobacco, whose smoke hung around the mess like a London smog, went unnoticed by him. Neither did he notice the creaking and groaning of *The Sycamore* as she headed into the easterly force nine gale. The four others who sat around the screwed down mess table, swaying in unison with the uneven motion of the ship, were totally preoccupied with their discussion. When the dry cargo freighter did hit a particularly bad wave their only reaction was to instinctively grab the side of the table so as to stay seated.

Tom was unwell at the thought of Captain 'Bligh' Byrne. If he found out about that bloody larch bark canoe in the ballast hold he knew what would happen. The Captain would have his guts for garters. Translated into action he would be a third mate for a long, long time to come. He had suggested the meeting to decide what they should do with the canoe. Tiger was a bit stubborn about it, yet too cute to let himself be accused by a junior ship's officer of being obstructionist. With sixteen stone spread over six foot three he was an impressive figure of a man who needed careful handling. Tom knew he didn't get his nickname, 'Tiger', for nothing. He was well aware he could order him to do what he wanted. Tiger would have to obey him. Thereafter, he and his friends could make things extremely awkward for Tom. The heavy-featured Pig Nolan may have looked stupid, all face and no features. But he wasn't, he was as sharp as a razor. He could easily have it leaked to the Captain that his third mate was a party to last night's shenanigans. Tom had suggested they should find a way to return the canoe to its owner. 'After all the Frenchie's livelihood could depend on it.' Tiger had not disagreed. His silence though confirmed he was not a man to forgive and forget. The more he drank the less he could forgive and he had drunk a lot. It was bloody awkward, thought Tom, gazing at the bulk-head lamp trying to penetrate the swirling smoke.

His mind drifted back to the series of incidents which brought them to the table. It had started with that bloody sneaky little bastard Squidgy, a crooked cook if ever there was one. The ship had left Rotterdam on 17th December with a cargo of cement for St John's, Newfoundland when, in mid-Atlantic, it ran into an unforecasted strong westerly headwind. This meant Christmas at sea instead of in Newfoundland, where the crew were looking forward to a bit of festive fun. That was bad enough but worse was to follow. Usually Christmas at sea meant traditional fare and liberal quantities of alcohol. To their consternation the soup was mulligatawny and the main course was rice and curried beef. To add insult to injury they were limited to a half glass of beer each, a small glass at that. Tom could clearly recall first the crew's disgust when the soup was served, followed by their stunned silence when the curry was placed before them.

For a minute the atmosphere in the mess was electric until the Captain roared, 'Where is that fucker Squidgy?'

Squidgy, a soulful expression on his face, sidled out of the galley, like the Dickens' character Uriah Heap, wringing his hands as if he was still washing them.

'You called, Captain sir?' he managed to squeeze out.

'Yes. I called you. What in hell's name do ye mean dishin' up this muck to my crew on Christmas Day? Do ye think we are a bunch of Indians?'

Squidgy's beady little eyes darted around the hostile faces in the mess and he visibly cringed.

'No sir, Captain. I think the ship's chandler in Rotterdam made a mistake. We got the provisions for the Indian freighter that was berthed beside us. We musta got theirs. Luckily I had some beer left in the ship's store.'

Captain Byrne was now in his 'Bligh' role. He eyed Squidgy speculatively. To Tom it looked as if it was a question of keel hauling now or later.

'Did ye not check what ye were gettin'?' he asked scornfully.

Squidgy's eyes darted around the room like terrified white mice until a thought caused them to stop at the Captain.

'Usually I do, Captain sir. Ye see I was off lookin' for your special... French wines,' he blurted out, hesitating as if he preferred to say no more.

'You did, did you now,' interrupted the Captain, in case he might say too much. Tom knew he liked Bollinger Special and whilst none of the crew were likely to know how expensive it was, one never knows. The Captain for all his sternness wanted to create some fellowship with them. Bollinger Special champagne, he felt, did not create the right image. Squidgy's ploy worked.

'You are a fool. Go back to your galley,' said the Captain in disgust. A relieved Squidgy scuttled off.

'Men,' said the Captain, 'he made a right cock-up of that. On behalf of the line please accept my apologies. However, in view of the mistake, and the saving in the cost of this,' he waved his hand in the general direction of the largely uneaten plates of curry, 'I will ask the third mate to give a special allowance to every man so that you can have a decent meal in St John's.'

There was a cheer from the men. Not too loud, thought Tom, as they didn't know how much they were going to get.

Tom knew there was little sympathy for Squidgy, who had got off lightly, seeing as he was generally regarded as being on the fiddle. Still, he figured, the Captain's examination of relative costs of the meals would probably reveal his little game.

Later the Captain called Tom aside and asked him to keep an eye on the crew after they went ashore, 'especially that fellow Healy, he could be a trouble maker. You know

Kavanagh, it's important for us to keep on good terms with the people in St John's.'

Tom got the message, 'In other words, Tom, I'll be looking to you to keep them in order.'

St John's was no New Orleans, but there was enough there to keep the crew happy. Several of them spent the extra money getting drunk, very drunk. Tom didn't see how he could do much to stop them. *How the hell can I*, he thought, *tell them to stop drinking. Some of them were drinking before I was born*. His primary concern was to keep them out of trouble, especially Tiger Healy, and the Captain off his back.

The trouble was that trouble and Tiger were bedfellows. On this occasion, Tiger, leaning against the bar, was well oiled and at peace with the world. That is until the little French Canadian, who was four sheets in the wind, lurched into his back. Tiger's full pint of beer spilled all over his chest and began dripping down his front. Tiger slowly turned around to view the perpetrator. He looked down at him, whereupon the little man pointed at Tiger's fly, said something in French, began slapping his thigh and laughing loudly. Tom had to admit Tiger looked as if he was peeing on the floor. In other circumstances he would have found it funny. Not now though.

Whilst Tiger was measuring the Frenchie for a coffin, Tom grabbed his arm and whispered, 'Tiger, for God's sake leave him be. Captain Byrne is behind you. We have an invitation to go to the bar down the road.' With that he pushed Tiger towards the door and motioned to the Pig to give him a hand. The other three followed them. They propelled Tiger so fast out the door he was on the pavement before he had time to object. There the cold air hit them like a knife, which helped to sober them up.

They made their way unsteadily along the quay until the Head Winters shouted, 'I see some canoes in the water. I bet one belongs to a Frenchie. See the name "Monique".'

Tom could see a number of larch bark canoes moored together in the water. The nearest had the name 'Monique' painted in white script on its prow.

Tiger brushed off Tom and the Pig and stared at the canoes.

'It's moored too far out,' said Jim Smith from behind, reading Tiger's mind.

'It bloody well is not,' growled Tiger and, before anyone realised it he had dived into the water. He swam over to the canoe and untied it from the others and wound its rope around his shoulder before he swam back. He reached some nearby stone steps with the rope and the canoe floating behind him. The Head and the Pig rushed down the steps and gave him a hand to get out of the freezing sea. They then unwound the canoe's rope from his arm.

'We'll put it in the ship,' said Tiger in a tone which broached no argument. 'That'll teach that little bastard.'

Tom, relaxed though not drunk, looked around anxiously. There was no one in sight and the freighter was only a few hundred yards away. He figured he had been lucky to get Tiger out of the bar and he would be pressing it if he objected to his decision.

The other three hesitated for a second, half expecting Tom to intervene. When he didn't they began pulling the canoe along the quay side until they had it between the quay and the side of the ship. Then Smith, the Pig and the Head had an alcohol-inspired discussion on how to get the canoe on board. They knew there was a watch at the top of the gangplank. First they had to get him out of the way.

It was the Pig who suggested that he bring up his half bottle of Chivas Regal to Whelan, the man on watch, whose bunk happened to be beside his. 'I'll get him to drink it in the fo'c'le. That'll keep him out of the way for a good quarter of an hour. You can come on board after I've got him in the fo'c'le. Use the winch to get the canoe on to the ship and store it in the ballast hold.'

This was agreed and the Pig made off for the gangplank. The others followed him when it was safe to do so and managed to get the canoe on board without difficulty.

Tom looked around for Tiger. He was way down the quay, still dripping wet and knocking back the remains of a bottle of whiskey. There was only thing wrong; a drunk in front of Tiger waving and pointing at him. Tiger said later he just mumbled 'Mon Dieu', which put Tom on his guard. The question was would he remember who he saw, and put two and two together when the canoe was reported missing? What was the legal term, thought Tom grimly? Accessory before the fact or after? *Anyway I am both.* To hell with it now, thought Tom, he might get a chance to return the canoe before they sailed. He didn't; and hence the present discussion. His concern was further fuelled by what the Captain had said to him.

'I hear some French Canadian fisherman had his canoe stolen last night. Did you hear anything about that?' Tom's pulse rate climbed while he dwelt on the significance of the Captain's question. It could be perfectly innocent, then maybe not. He managed to keep his tone normal when he responded,

'Not a thing, Captain.' That was it. There was no more. He did feel though there was more urgency about the future of the damned canoe.

The noise of the ship was deafening, yet for Tom there was a silence. The others were looking through the smoke in his direction with expectant expressions. He pulled himself together. They were obviously waiting for an answer to a question.

'Sorry, I was thinking. Did you ask me something?'

'Do you think the Captain suspects anything?' the Pig asked.

Tom saw a chance of a breakthrough. 'He might. It's difficult to say but he did look at me sharply,' said Tom.

'Well, we'd better be careful,' said the Pig, 'breaking the canoe into tiny pieces and throwing it into the sea could be risky. If someone saw the bits floating in the Atlantic he might guess what they were. A report could go to the Captain. Some of the others would just love to get us into trouble,' he added darkly. Tiger, now sober, was very concerned about the Frenchie who had seen him on the quayside. Tom was astonished he could recall anything. For some unknown reason, guilt maybe, thought Tom, he had a clear picture of him.

Tiger said, 'We cannot leave it in the hold forever.'

Tom awaited developments, knowing the rest expected him to say something. It was the Pig who responded first. 'Could we not heave it over the side tonight and let it drift on the current. It might even get to Ireland.'

Tom seized the opportunity. 'No, that won't do because we are travelling faster than the canoe could drift. If picked up too close to our position we could be under suspicion by the Captain, and everyone else too. We need to be more careful. Maybe we could put it overboard on the next voyage back across? The ship will be sailing from Rotterdam to Boston with some cement and it would appear by then as if it had drifted across the Atlantic. We will be quite close to Ireland and there is a good chance it will drift on to the shore there.'

Tom's suggestion met with general approval, except for Tiger who couldn't make up his mind if it was worth it to risk the wrath of the Captain for continued revenge on the Frenchie. As far as the Head, the Pig and Jim Smith were concerned Captain 'Bligh' Byrne was not a man to be trifled with.

Thus, on the voyage back to Boston Tom fixed it so that two of them were put on night watch. That same night, the canoe was carefully placed in the Atlantic not far from the Irish coast. Tom, watching from the stern, checked its disappearance into the dark night. He felt a very relieved man to see it was upright, riding the waves well.

For the remainder of the voyage, their careful monitoring of the news did not reveal anything about a Canadian canoe being washed up anywhere. Nor did Tom get any hint from the Captain that he was concerned about the canoe. So they waited and wondered.

They still had heard nothing by the time they got to Boston. The problem was that they could not ask anyone about it for fear of being associated with whatever had happened 'to that bloody canoe' as Tom referred to it.

Then, on the night before they left Boston, Tom was having a drink in an Irish bar with an overseer from the stevedoring company, when one of the barmen said to him, 'Did you see the bit about the Canadian canoe drifting across the Atlantic all the way to oul Ireland?'

'No,' said Tom afraid to say anything more.

'Here I'll show ye,' said the barman bending under the counter and producing an Irish paper.

There it was large as life, a picture of the canoe in perfect condition, with the heading 'Experts puzzled at find of empty Canadian canoe in Courtmacsherry Bay'. The piece went on to compare the drift of the empty canoe with the mystery of the *Marie Celeste*.

Tom's companion's protests had no effect. He had no option but to join him in a double Irish whiskey.

The story later developed into a controversy between experts, not on how the canoe got to Ireland, but on which current, and at what speed. A native Canadian anthropologist even claimed it proved that Ireland, and parts of Europe too, were colonised by his ancestors. The Canadian Government bought the canoe, paying its by now traced owner $10,000 for it. They then donated it to the British National Science Museum in London where the Canadian Ambassador, in an amusing speech, offered to give colonial status to the United Kingdom. The real experts, all five of them, said nothing.

Red

Red leaned against the wall, almost bent double, as he coughed his guts out. He felt knackered, not surprising seeing as he was smoking, in a freezing fog, his thirty-third Woodbine butt of the day. When he exhaled into the still air the smoke hung around his head causing him to inhale and exhale the same fog diluted smoke.

No wonder he was coughing. They weren't called coffin nails for nothing. He knew his bronchial tubes were not good, not that bad though, yet if he couldn't get out of this fog he would be a candidate for TB. He tried to penetrate the fog with his watery eyes. It was no use, if anything it was getting thicker, with visibility now down to two feet. Suddenly he felt the cigarette butt burn his thumb and forefinger. 'Damnit,' he roared into the fog as he dropped the butt.

He looked down to see where it had fallen. The fog was so thick that he couldn't even see the glow of the butt on the frozen ground. The only reason he knew it was frozen was because he had difficulty in maintaining his stance. Unable to reconcile the fact that his eyes were only about five feet from the ground, he persisted in looking down for its glow. At least, he had two butts left out of the fifteen Woodbines he had bought that morning. By his own reckoning he was somewhere around Ballsbridge. It had taken him nearly four hours to get there from Stillorgan. Sounded ridiculous, but so was the freezing fog. All he could do was to edge his way along railings, hedges and walls, slither over frozen pathways without really being sure of his direction. He had set out to walk to the night hostel, near Stephen's Green, in the hope he could get a bed for the night. Now it didn't look as if he was going to get a bed anywhere.

Red was starving. It had been a long time, at least eight hours he guessed, since he got that plate of Irish stew from Mrs Bradshaw in Stillorgan. Decent woman, she never gave him money but he could be sure of a dinner of some sort from her. He could still smell the stew from his beard, which only increased his hunger. He let loose another fusillade of coughs. This time it was the raw smoky acid in the air which started him off. The sound of his coughing seemed to be all around him. Funny thing about a fog, he thought, every sound seemed to have an echo or something.

What the hell was he going to do? He was weak from the hunger, had no place to stay for the night and didn't know where he was, and worse, where he should be going. God knows, he should know every inch of this place. He had tramped around it often enough. For certain, if he stayed out here in this he would be in a bad way in the morning. He could even be a frozen corpse. Red shivered in his heavy green ex-army coat, not sure if thinking about death only made his predicament more unbearable.

He knew there was an embassy somewhere around Ballsbridge with a civic guard in a shed at the gate. Maybe they could do something? Most of the civic guards knew him well, rather they knew him well by sight. The trouble was he didn't know where he was so how could he get to them? There was no point in staying here. He put his hands out in front of him again, shoulder high, and gingerly edged forward along the wall. If he tried to hurry he could slip and break something, which would be much worse, even disastrous. It was a rough wall, granite probably. His woollen mittens had no fingers which meant that, in the cold, the rough granite felt razor sharp. God knows, he should damn well know where he was. If the street lights had been visible he might have some idea. He looked up for the umpteenth time; even persuaded himself there was a glow from the lights, yet aware it could be wishful thinking. All he did know was that they go out at twelve o'clock, so maybe it wasn't that time yet. Then again, if he couldn't see them how could he be sure of even that?

He continued to sidle along the wall, arms outstretched like a sleepwalker, a very worried one. The ground was as slippy as hell. He was frozen, hungry and tired with neither food nor lodging for the night. All in all, his prospects were getting poorer by the minute. Red was no stranger to despair; this was plumbing the depths though.

Then he heard a familiar sound, a car horn. It was difficult to know whether it was near or far. He felt it was more likely to be on a main road, most likely the one from Blackrock to Dublin. The sound motivated him to increase his sidling speed along the granite wall. At least it was something to which he could relate.

He never saw her, not even when he felt some flesh and heard screaming right in front of him, a woman, a young woman by the sound. Red nearly died of the shock. His hands must be around her throat. At first he was too shocked himself to do anything, although his natural instinct could have been to stop the sound.

By now she was shouting, 'Help, help, murder,' followed by a piercing scream. Then he had an idea. It's funny, he thought, how things hit you at times, like St Paul on the road to Damascus. In this case more like Red on the road to an early grave. He held on to her throat for a few seconds longer than necessary, which merely increased the din from the girl; just what he needed. Satisfied he took his hands from her throat and shuffled his way around her until he got back to the wall on the other side of where she was still screaming. By the time he got there she had broken into sobs and cries for help. Not that Red hadn't sympathy for her. He had, a great deal, but his needs were far greater than hers.

He continued his slow progress along the wall. By now his fingers, sticking out of the woollen mittens, were frozen and bleeding from the rough wall. This, coupled with his shock at meeting the girl, or rather her throat, caused him to lower his hands, just in case there was anyone else coming against him. Red did not want to get a reputation for being another Jack the Ripper. Then he heard the sound he had been waiting for, the muffled sound from a civic guard's whistle. The problem was could the guard find her? More importantly, would he be able to find him in this peasouper?

The girl heard the whistle and started to shout, 'Over here, over here, by the wall.'

He could hear the shouts from two guards, 'Don't worry Miss, we're comin', are you all right, where is your attacker?'

They all sounded as if they were a few yards from him but he reckoned they could be anywhere, given the way sound travelled in the fog. Then he heard the girl saying 'over here' and the guard, talking in a normal tone, 'Are you all right, have you got a description of your assailant?'

'Red beard, big man, he grabbed my throat and wouldn't let go.'

Fine, thought Red, he needed a drag. He fished out his second last Woodbine butt. It was a bit small; better than nothing, he thought, as he pursued his lips and held up the match to the butt end, no sense in burning his nose with the flame. Red almost took a butt long drag. Christ, he needed that after all he had gone through. Funny thing, he thought, she could see my beard while I couldn't see her face. The combination of the second drag and the poisonous fog started off another uncontrollable fit of coughing. He made no attempt to contain it, quite the opposite, he encouraged it. Soon he was vaguely aware of the sound of the two civic guards asking who was there, as they slipped and slid in their hurry to get to him.

Red was in no hurry, his bed and meal ticket were on their way, for once he could agree with Scarlet O'Hara, his near namesake, tomorrow would be another day – at least for Red. Maybe jail wasn't the Ritz, but to night, as sure as hell, it had to be better than these frozen, smog-ridden streets.

Saturday Night

Rob, panting from his quick climb up the hill, pushed at the door of the old church. It didn't budge. Then he tried the heavy metal knob. It turned all right but the door still wouldn't open. He was too late. The church was closed for the evening.

He was unfamiliar with its opening and closing times as he normally went there only for christenings, weddings and funerals. His pop had said to him, when he stopped attending Sunday services, that he would go to church for each as he got older. At twenty-four he was going to occasional weddings and christenings; he certainly hadn't expected to be attending many funerals. He was now going to attend two, those of his elder brother and his nephew whose deaths might not have happened but for him.

He wandered around the side of the church, almost knocking down the hurrying little rector.

'Rob, Rob McCoy. I'm so sorry, my mind was miles away. I didn't expect anyone to come here at this late hour. I'm awfully sorry about what happened. I really cannot believe a thing like this could happen in our little community.'

'Thanks, Reverend Boyd, I wasn't paying much attention myself. The front door was locked so I was goin' to try the side one.'

'It's locked too. Signs of the times I suppose. Tell you what, I'll let you in and you can lock the door on your way out. Will you be all right on your own?' he enquired solicitously.

'Sure, sure Reverend, I just want to do a little thinking. I'll be glad to close the door. By the way, thanks for that.'

He followed the quick-paced rector around to the side door at his own longer more deliberate pace. When he caught up the rector was holding the weathered oak door open against its protesting metal spring. He offered him a wooden wedge.

'Rob, just stick this under the door when you are going in and pull it out on your way out. The spring'll lock it.'

He then hurried off.

Rob's footsteps echoed around the empty church which gave off an odour of mustiness and furniture wax. It had been built as a replica of a church in Normandy which Sir Douglas Bayley, the then local landowner, had seen on his honeymoon. He shivered at the drop in temperature when he entered in the church. No, that wasn't the reason. It was a warm summer's evening outside and it wasn't that cold inside. It was the solitude in the church and in himself. He was alone with two coffins holding two who were very precious to him. Jack's seemed huge beside his son's. Then Jack is twenty-eight and John was only seven. God it made no difference whether he thought 'is' or 'was', they would be the same age for eternity.

He glanced in the direction of the list of hymns on the wall and could recall their numbers – 12, 31, 26 and 18 – listed on the board without even looking at them. A lot of good any hymn singing will do them now, he thought.

He looked around the church at the altar, the pulpit, the shining brass eagle lectern and finally at the christening font where all three of them had been christened. Its atmosphere filled him with despair and despondency which seemed to filter through his whole being. *God how could you let this happen?* his mind cried out. *You're a fraud. Jesus Christ, you said love your neighbours. Did you do anything to prevent these killings? What had little John got to do with any of this? Nothing, and you tell us to love our neighbours. What if they hate us? If they don't love a harmless child how can they love, no tolerate, anyone or anything who disagrees with them? You let me be the cause. Christ, you have let them down, the two of them who went to your services every week. What good did it do for them? I'm alive and they are lying over there in their coffins. I ask you. Answer me.*

The church remained silent despite his brain-blasting questions.

Rob, alone in the church, sobbed uncontrollably in the gathering dusk as he stood in front of the two forlorn coffins. His tears ran down his cheeks on to his moustache and into the side of his mouth. He nervously picked up the salty tears with his tongue, only to feel even more disconsolate at the thought of the tearless bodies enclosed in their coffins. He turned on his heel and trudged out of the church, wiping the tears with the back of his right hand.

Rob carefully, and silently, removed the wedge and held the door to prevent it banging, not appreciating that he could disturb no one. As he left the church he somehow felt more at ease with himself. At least the visit had crystallised his thoughts into knowing what he must do.

He walked back slowly towards the front of the church, towards the moss-encrusted granite steps that lead to the iron gates. He paused there deep in thought. The little seaside town down below was spread out towards the sea-abandoned strand. The sun had set behind him, discarding its red print in the western sky. In the still air, sounds of normality drifted upwards as he surveyed the scene from the steps, normal sounds of children playing, birds bickering before settling down for the night and the heightened purr from accelerating cars. Was it really normal? Could normality cohabit with what had happened the other night? It had, that's what made it so difficult for him to understand. Then he noticed to his right, in some palm trees, a group of quarrelling magpies transfer their antagonism to a starling which had dared intrude on their territory. It fled for its life. He then tried, and failed, to pick up the roof of the Seaside Bar where it had happened. Somehow he was glad he couldn't. To his left, high in the brighter sky, he could make out the outline of a twin-engined plane approaching from the south, even before he could hear the sound of its engines. Gradually as it approached the noise of the plane's engines drowned the other surrounding sounds.

It called to mind his grandfather's, his mother's father, description of evil. He could recall the scene vividly now, starting with his overhearing a discussion between his pop and his grandpa. They were in the kitchen at the time when he had innocently interrupted their conversation.

'What is evil?'

'Your father knows what I am talking about, Rob,' his grandfather had replied. 'Let's say there's both good and bad in this world. Most of us, thank God, seldom encounter real badness, evil if you will. Sure we hear about it, even read about it, even see its consequences but it is met, face to face, by relatively few of us. I'll tell you though, if good and evil ever overlap then you will really understand what we are talking about. Do ye follow me, Rob?'

'No granddad,' said Rob mystified.

'Well let me give you an example, Rob. During the last war I was stationed in the south of England, near the Kentish coast, where we were expecting the Jerries to invade us. In between spells of duty I spent my time bird watching. As ye know, David,' he said turning to his pop. 'I was there during the London Blitz. Well, this night in June I was out listening to the nightingales singing. It was one of those still summer evenings when the singing of the nightingales is as clear as a bell. Entranced, I suppose that's the word for my feeling about their singing. Then I thought I heard a sound. Like the lowest possible note of a church organ. It increased gradually from the east until it got so loud it was deafening and the song of the nightingales was obliterated completely. By then I knew full well what that menacing sound was. What caused it? The Jerry bombers, Dorniers, Junkers and Stukas, those dreadful dive-bombers, together with their protecting fighter planes, Messerschmidts as I recall them, massing off the south coast of England before making their final run over London. There they would drop their horrible cargoes, killing defenceless men, women and children. I can tell ye I shivered in that warm summer's night at the thought of the death and destruction this massive force was going to inflict on the unfortunate Londoners. I hope, Rob, you never hear the terrifying screech of those Stukas as they dive to unload their bombs. When they were all assembled over the coast they headed north-west for London with their deadly loads. Their sound went as it came until it was gradually replaced by the singing of the nightingales. Soon we were left with their pure uninhibited lyrical singing, as if nothing had ever happened. The contrast between the two brought out, for me at least, the evil of the Nazi regime. You can imagine the peace and tranquillity which surrounded me that night, only for it to be replaced with death and destruction from that same sky. I hope, Rob, that in your lifetime you never meet with anything like that.' His grandpa never referred to that night again. For Rob there was no need, as if it was seared into his memory.

He reflectively rubbed the sole of his shoe off the edge of the granite step watching the now silent plane disappear to his right. He now realised his grandpa's story was told from the safety of the Kent coast, not from the carnage in the centre of London. It had been different for him.

Last Saturday night he was at a loose end and decided to call over to see Jack, Pam and especially John, his nephew. He was playing with John when Jack came home later on looking very tired. So much so that Pam remarked, 'Jack, you look worn out.'

'To tell ye the truth, Pam, it's as much frustration as tiredness,' he replied, 'at what's going on at that Roman Catholic church over yonder. We in the RUC are supposed to prevent the Loyalists from stopping them from going to their mass.'

Rob could see he was stressed out. 'Why are they bothering to get involved?' he asked Rob.

'The Government has made a decision that they must have freedom to worship. I suppose they would do the same if the Republicans tried to stop us. Anyways, we're doing what we were told to do. Sure, its being goin' on for the last few Saturdays and we're getting it real bad from the crowds of Loyalists who are being bussed in there from outside. I didn't see one local among them. These last weeks they have taken to trying to force their way through us to get at the Papists. The result is we're gettin' the brunt of their carry-on. I'll tell ye, it damn nearly got out of hand tonight. Instead of the usual name calling, Pope lovers, Fenian lovers, traitors and the like, they started to fire stones at the Roman Catholics. Naturally we had to stop them. It got very bad I can tell you. Our Inspector was great though. He stood up to them an' told them if they didn't give up he'd have the lot in jail.'

'Why don't they bring in the army if it's got that bad?' asked Pam.

'Sure, Pam, we've got to be seen to be handlin' it ourselves, and we did, in spite of stones, name calling and threats.'

'What sort of threats?' asked Pam anxiously.

'Aw, sure no different than any we got before,' replied Jack dismissively.

When Pam had gone into the kitchen Jack whispered to Rob, 'I'll tell you Rob, it was dog rough there this evening. They were no ordinary protesters. I've seldom seen an uglier lot of bowsies. One of them even threatened to do for me and a couple of my mates.'

After they had eaten, Rob could see Jack was still very keyed-up so he suggested they go out for a quick drink to a nearby pub. Pam knew Jack was tired and needed rest but when she was assured it would be a very quick pint she relented.

'It's the Seaside Bar, only a few minutes walk from here,' Rob told her.

'I thought you always went to The King's Head, Jack?' said Pam. 'Wouldn't you be better goin' there then?'

'You're right, most of our lot go there because it's near the station.'

'The Seaside is nearer to us. Sure isn't it a grand quiet place with no nationalists.'

'Make up your own minds, remember Rob you promised to be back early,' cried Pam after them.

'That makes it The Seaside,' said Rob firmly.

'If ye insist,' said Jack, too tired to argue.

The Seaside was not so named because it was near the sea but because it had a large mural covering one wall which depicted the nearby seafront of the little town. It had a thatched roof with low ceilings and oak beams, all of which gave it a homely atmosphere. It was fairly full with locals when they arrived so they went to the vacant space at the far end of the bar. It was evident to Rob that by the time Jack had drunk half his pint he had begun to relax. At least, he felt he'd achieved what he'd set out to do and could return to Pam with a totally relaxed husband.

There was a continuous trickle of new arrivals before a large group of strangers came into the pub. Although Rob couldn't see them at first he could hear rowdier voices coming closer as they made their way towards their uncrowded end of the bar. Some of them were complaining loudly that they should have stuck to their original plan to go to The Coach Rider. Jack was sitting on the stool opposite Rob with his back to the approaching newcomers. Their noisy ordering of drinks left the whole bar conscious of their drink preferences. In the process the bar lost its quiet atmosphere, the net result of which was that there was a noticeable hurry among the regulars to finish their drinks and sidle out.

'Sorry about that,' said one of the group, a huge man with red, blue and gold royal crown tattoos on both forearms, apologising when his elbow hit Jack's drinking arm. He turned around to inspect the damage when he blurted out, 'I know you. You're the fucking RUC bastard who stopped us at the Papist chapel.'

Jack ignored him and addressed a question to Rob.

'I'm speaking to you Fenian Lover. This is one of the bastards who threatened us,' he shouted to his friends. 'I asked him whose side was he on?' he shouted.

Another of the group shouted over, 'Well, whose side are you fuckin' well on anyway? Tell us, go on. We won't tell anyone else?' The rest sniggered at this.

'I wasn't on any side. I was doing me job,' replied Jack softly.

'He was only doing his job,' mimicked another ferret-faced one.

'Ye weren't ordered to push me, now were you fuckin' Papist lover?'

Jack ignored him again. 'Were you now Papist lover?'

'Look, I'm having a quiet drink with me brother. I don't want to talk about it. It's over,' replied Jack.

'Look, I'm having a quiet drink with me brother,' mimicked the ferret-faced one.

'Well, we don't want Papists drinking in a decent pub, now do we?' shouted the tattooed man.

More concerned now, Jack said, 'Look, I'm telling you I have a job to do. That means obeying orders or I lose me job.'

'Ye hear that? He's loyal to the crown but not to his own people.'

'You're not fit for the fuckin' job,' cried a thick-set man.

'Fit for nothing,' cried another. 'Maybe you'll retire?'

'Or be retired,' said the tattooed man, softly this time. 'You've no uniform to protect ye now, Fenian lover.'

'Nor other RUC bastards,' cried a little man, as broad as he was long.

'Let's go, Jack,' whispered Rob.

They both got up and, to Rob's surprise, walked out of the pub unmolested leaving the others in the bar.

'Don't run Rob, just walk quickly. Those are not finished with us yet. Thank God we haven't far to go. Pity I haven't got my radio on me.'

They turned right, then left into another street which led into their own street, leaving them less than two hundred yards from Jack's house.

Rob looked behind. To his relief they were not being followed.

'It's okay now, John, we've made it.'

Hardly had he spoken when a blue van passed and stopped about thirty yards ahead of them. The rear doors were flung open to release the group of men they had left at the bar. The ferret-faced man stayed near the van with what appeared to be a machine gun cradled in his arms. The rest carried a variety of iron bars, knives and heavy sticks. The tall man with the tattooed arms was sporting a vicious looking hunting knife.

'Now, weren't you two in a bit of a rush?' said the small square man. 'This might slow you down,' he cried as one of the others, standing behind Jack, struck him across the legs with a metal bar. Rob stepped forward to catch him as he staggered to the ground roaring with pain, only to be hit from behind by the same bar. He too shouted in pain as his legs gave way, only to receive another blow on the side of the head from a truncheon in the hand of one of the others. He fell, whereupon two of them pinned him to the road, tied his hands and feet and stuffed a piece of dirty cloth into his mouth.

Although racked with pain and semi-conscious from the blow to his head, Rob, from his position on the ground, could see Jack was being held in a kneeling position, with his hands tied behind his back. One of them held him by his hair with his head pulled far back. The tattooed man raised his large brown bone handled hunting knife and shouted, 'This will remind you not to support Popish bastards, ye fuckin' traitor.'

He made as if to slash Jack's throat; instead he slashed the right side of Jack's face. His companion, holding Jack's hair, roughly pulled the left side of his face over for the man with the knife to get a better angle to slash that side of Jack's face. Another, wielding a butcher's knife, again made as if to cut Jack's throat causing Rob to spit out the cloth and scream, '*No, no.*' He didn't go for his throat but for both his arms which he proceeded to slash through his shirt, from shoulder to wrist.

Their roars of pain caused doors to open, cautiously at first and then neighbours began to emerge whereupon the man with the gun shouted at them to close their doors and windows or be shot.

John must have slipped away from Pam because he came running down the street crying, 'Daddy, Daddy, leave my Daddy alone.'

He ran up to the man who was holding Jack by the hair and started to hit and kick him. Unable to push him away he called out to the others, 'Get this little bastard away from me, Georgie.'

The man with the bar pulled him away and was bitten in the hand by John. In an alcohol-fuelled rage he brought the iron bar down with force on John's head. The boy simply crumpled senseless to the ground. Rob winced, fearing for his nephew's life. His cry for help merely induced raucous laughter from the group.

Meanwhile the tattooed man wasn't finished with Jack. He ripped off his shirt and marked 'UVF' on his back and chest with his knife. Rob tried to struggle to his feet but was held down by his captors one of whom whispered in his ear, 'Stay still and your brother might live.' Rob did as he was bid. He could sense the tattooed man was itching to continue with his knifing.

The sound of sirens in the distance caused the ferret-faced man with the gun to shout, 'Let's go. Quick.'

They ran for the blue van and piled into the back. When Rob's jailers had gone he tried to struggle to his feet. Weakened by the blows and with his feet bound he simply collapsed on to the road again. The tattooed man with the knife hesitated about leaving, his eyes blazing, with madness it seemed to Rob. He turned back towards Jack and plunged the hunting knife into his body again and again, screaming, 'Take that, and that you Fenian bastard.' He stopped for a few seconds breathing heavily. Then he grabbed John's hair, lifted his head with his left hand and cut his throat which caused blood to shoot out in spurts over both his killer and the road.

Rob cried out, 'Oh no, no, you filthy rotten fucker.'

The tattooed man, still panting and covered with Jack's blood, walked over to glare down at him. Their eyes met, anguish in Rob's and the madness of lust in the other's. Rob knew for what seemed an age that his life was balanced on the sharp edge of that large hunting knife. The spell was broken by the van's horn and commands from the ferret-faced man, 'Harry, come on, leave them be.' He slowly turned away from Rob like a man in a trance and ran towards the moving blue van where his cheering companions hauled him into the back.

Rob shivered at the memory. He could recall every single feature of Harry, his denim jeans, dark blue sweat shirt, close cropped fair hair, thin-lipped mouth, mad pale blue eyes and the sight of Jack's life blood all over him. His tattoos would forever make him subconsciously feel cold fear at the sight of a crown, any crown.

He looked back at the church now shadowy in the gathering dusk as he nervously tugged at the side of his moustache and thought, *If only I had gone to the other pub... If I hadn't gone to see Jack that night I would not be here and they would not be dead in there.*

The sounds of the children were replaced by two girls laughing followed by jeers from their boyfriends. At least his visit to the church, whilst it might not have had the intended outcome sought by his pop, had focused his mind on what needed to be done. If it took him the rest of his life he would find that fuckin' murdering, tattooed Harry. First, he would carve those tattoos off each of his arms with a bone-handled hunting knife. Then he would match, cut by cut, the wounds he had inflicted on his brother Jack.

Winning

Glenn was deep in thought. At one time he only played to win. Now, he didn't even want to play. That was it, winning bored him. The realisation nearly took his breath away. Until he had thought it through, winning was life. Sure he lost sometimes, neither willingly nor often, but only after a hard fight against an opponent who was in a higher league. Anyway a good fight added spice to winning. Everyone in the camp looked up to him as the best tennis and baseball star in the three camps. Being the best at tennis, champion for the last three years, in the three copper camps in the middle of the Atacama desert was no big deal though. He could continue winning, unless he broke a leg or something, as long as his contract lasted. He supposed lack of any real competition was the reason for his present deliberations.

His reflections were interrupted by silence. Normally there was a crowd for the singles' final with the usual background talk interrupted occasionally by shouts of encouragement. Now he could hear a pin drop. Shriver's service ball came thundering down the clay court before he could gather his wits. The silence was broken by scattered applause and yells. Judd Keaveney's baritone voice, from the umpire's chair, rose above the clapping. 'Shriver has won the second set by six games to four and the score now stands at one set each.'

Goddamnit, my mental meandering has caused me to lose the blasted set, thought Glenn savagely.

He looked over at his own supporters. They looked stunned. As well they might seeing as he had beaten Shriver in last year's semi-final without losing a game. *I'd better get back into this otherwise I'm sure not gonna be popular with Gus and the guys.*

He won the first game in the next set, his service, with three aces and a smash from a weak return to his last serve. The pattern was much the same for the rest of the match. He dropped four games in the next two sets to win the title for the fourth year in succession.

Congratulations flowed from all the camp supporters with Gus, the team captain, in his southern drawl expressing particular satisfaction. 'Gee Glenn youh sure cleaned him up in those last two sets. We was worried when he won the second. What happened? Youawl looked like a fellah who had lost the complete rhythm of his game?'

'Well, Gus, you said it. I lost my concentration. I was thinkin' Gus that I should stop playing for a while and give some of the others a chance. I don't want to sound bigheaded but stateside I was playing in a much higher league than anyone else in the camps. I know it's good to win such a great trophy, but four successive singles' cups is enough.'

'For cryin' out loud Glenn, youh think if any of those other camps had a player of your calibre they wouldn't play him? Would they what. It's the luck o' the draw Glenn,' said Gus firmly.

'I know, Gus, but ye see I played for the college and no one here played at that level.'

'Look youh here, Glenn, if they got a player better than you don't think they wouldn't play him as long as they could. Youh gotta believe it.'

Glenn decided to say no more and just to enjoy the open air victory party being held in his honour. The Anaconda company's support for sport was total. After all there was little else to take their minds off copper in the middle of the world's most arid desert. The vice-president, Doug Amer, who was responsible for the three camps, was a tennis freak which made the tennis final into the annual sports event of the year. Glenn was still a little uneasy about winning so easily, almost to a point of guilt. There was a talented Chilean guy, Sergio, working with him who, with a bit of coaching, could be the best tennis player around. He had given him a few lessons. In order to take the pressure off himself he decided to coach him more intensively, to see if he could win the trophy next year.

It was Baldomero Prado, Sergio's father, a good athlete in his day and a member of the Nazca tribe of desert Indians, who had told Glenn about the Indian tribes who were supposed to have lived in the desert thousands of years ago. Glenn was fascinated, at the same time doubting Baldomero's story, as he looked around the arid desert. 'I can't believe it,' he said to him, 'sure nothing, and I mean nothing, grows there now. For God's sake even Iqueque only has a little rain one year out of about seven, and it's near the sea. The Atacama is the driest desert in the world with no life there.'

Baldomero told him, 'Glenn, years ago, grandfather told me that part at least of that desert was once fertile, covered with trees and vegetation. It was a fertile oasis inhabited by settlements of Indians who were farmers and hunters. That is all part of our tribal folklore. You must know it doesn't take that long for good land to turn into desert. Look at the Sahara, in our own lifetime it has gradually crept southwards. What's a few hundred years in thousands of years?'

'Well if you say so, Baldo,' said Glenn, not entirely convinced, but using the family version of his name to soften his doubtful tone.

'You know the Pan American Highway. It starts in Chile at Arica.'

'Sure I do,' said Glenn, wondering what was coming next.

'Well there is a spur road from the highway which leads to a part of the desert, no more than five by ten kilometres wide, where there is reputed to be evidence of habitation, settlements maybe.'

'But nothing lives out there, Baldo,' said Glenn, still not convinced.

'Arrowheads do. Now would they be there if there was nothing to shoot at Glenn? You know that desert is so dry, it never gets rain. Even if you drop a sandwich there it will not rot. We know food can lie there for many years. There is nothing there to eat it, except the occasional four-wheeler,' said Baldomero, flashing his white teeth with an impish smile.

'Okay, Baldo, I'm sorry but I have been out there, in a four-wheel drive, and I find it hard to believe anything ever even grew there. What I would like to do is carry out a search myself in that area, if that's possible?' said a now very interested Glenn.

'It won't be easy. The area sounds small but I know others who have tried and failed. On the other hand grandfather showed me two arrowheads which he said were found there, one agate and the other quartz. Here, Glenn, pass me that piece of paper and I'll sketch out where you might look. I warn you that it may not be that accurate,' said Baldomero, beginning to map out the area.

From that day onwards Glenn was totally preoccupied with the desert. Whatever interest he had in sports noticeably dwindled.

'Glenn, the guys are wondering about the game Tuesday week?' It was Gus.

'Sorry, Gus, I haven't played for some time. Can I give it a miss?'

'Well we kinda miss you. Youh awl heard about our last game against camp three?'

'Yeah I heard. We lost. I'm sure sorry about that.'

'I know you're kinda keen on the desert these days. What are youh lookin' for out there?'

'Arrowheads. Indian arrowheads.'

'Yeah don't say. Funny place to be lookin' for arrowheads, seeing as there is nothing there to shoot arrows at,' said Gus, scratching his head. Glenn could see Gus wasn't saying what was really in his mind – that Glenn had gone a little crazy.

'If you could excuse me for the game I'd appreciate it, Gus. Ye know how it is?' he said, more for something to say than anything else, as he could see quite clearly that Gus was at a loss to understand what had happened to him. He could have lived with sunstroke, but wandering around the desert at every opportunity?

In the weeks that followed Glenn found his former popularity was diminishing fast. They were beginning to regard him as a bit of an outsider. People didn't hail him as much and he was beginning to be offered only the occasional drink. Clearly he wasn't one of the boys any longer.

This didn't entirely displease Glenn because he wasn't being pressurised to play. On the downside he was getting concerned. After three months searching the desert, he had found nothing and lost quite a few friends. There were some compensations though. The awesome sunrises and sunsets in the desert were something he would always remember. The backdrop of the Andes gave the rising of the sun an edge which Glenn thought was almost counterbalanced by the colours in the setting sun. Variations in colouring and shade in the silence of the Atacama gave a new meaning to atmosphere. For Glenn the grandeur of the Andes in the rising and setting sun generated an almost tangible spirituality. That sensation, however, didn't overcome his craving, for that is what his search had grown into, to find an arrowhead. Otherwise his credibility in the camps would go down the Swanee. They would have good reason to regard him as crazy.

One evening he was leaning against the bonnet of his jeep, admiring the start of the sunset, whilst moodily wondering which area he would pick for his next search. As befits such a mood he was kicking the desert with the toe of his right boot. To this day he doesn't know what made him look down. It was about an inch long and sort of off white. He could recognise the tiny rectangular stone as graphite. Without any shadow of a doubt it was an arrowhead.

In all his sporting successes Glenn had never experienced anything to equal the exultation he felt at that instant, when he realised what was at his feet. He looked around the arid landscape, disbelievingly before his gaze was again directed to the arrowhead. He half expected it to have disappeared like a mirage.

It was still there and, with his whole body trembling, he rushed his right hand down to the ground to grab the little arrowhead.

It was real all right.

He placed it on the palm of his left hand, felt it with his right thumb and forefinger. It had perfectly uniformed serrated edges, proving beyond all doubt it was an arrowhead designed to cut the veins and arteries of its victim. He marvelled at the precision of the workmanship which had produced such a delicate, and deadly, weapon.

Glenn was ecstatic. His exultant roar and dance of triumph spread over the silent desert. Probably the first such sound since the Indian hunters killed their prey right there. It proved it hadn't always been a desert. Arrows would be useless in present conditions. He began to visualise the area as it was then; covered in vegetation and trees with areas devoted to maize, potatoes and carob.

Probably llamas were their farm animals. There were two things which puzzled him. How come a salt water valley could be so fertile and could it really be true that there was a reference to camels in one record of the valley of the Attacams?

One thing was clear. The area must have been covered in dense vegetation. How else would they have lost their precious arrowheads. He felt it again with his fingers and marvelled at the workmanship. It was perfectly uniform. How expert they must have been to achieve such uniformity. He felt the serrations again on each side of the arrowhead. Their precision was such they could have been done by a modern machine. Quartz could fracture easily as it was chipped into shape, which meant the craftsmen had to have a delicate touch. He couldn't visualise modern man with their sophisticated tools achieving anything like the same result.

The journey back to camp was one of the happiest of Glenn's whole life. If he told anyone in the camp about his find he couldn't expect they could possibly share his enthusiasm. Offhand only Baldo, maybe Sergio too, could share his joy. If the others couldn't share it then he felt he should say nothing for the present.

Baldomero was due to visit Sergio in a few weeks' time. When Glenn rang him he was delighted about his find and suggested he go out to the same area to see if there were more, as their folklore indicated their ancestors hunted in given areas. Baldomero suggested that Glenn on his next visit should try to visualise if there had been a lake or a river in that part of the desert. He also asked him to post one of the arrowheads to him which he would in turn forward to a professor of the University of Chicago who was expert in this area and a good friend of his.

Glenn couldn't wait for the following Saturday to come around. If Baldomero was right, there must be more arrowheads out there.

'Glenn youawl's in great spirit this evenin'.' It was Gus who had joined him at the bar for a drink. 'Seeing as youh are heah how about joining the team foh the next ball game? Yeah, we miss youh, Glenn.'

'I'm sure sorry, Gus, but with my contract finishing in about six months I wanna spend as much time in the desert as possible.'

'Yeah I suppose so,' said Gus, not really able to understand what had come over Glenn. 'If I can be so bold as to give youh a word of advice, Glenn.'

'Sure Gus, any advice from you would sure be appreciated,' replied Glenn, unsure what was coming next.

'Whall just to tell youh that Doug is keen to get you back into tennis so if youawl is thinkin' of an extension it might be a good idea to start playin' again. Youh see ma point?'

'Thanks, Gus, I hadn't looked at it from that angle,' said Glenn, understanding the message. 'To tell you the truth I hadn't given much thought to the end of the contract. I've been too taken up with my visits to the desert. What about Sergio, he's comin' along just great?'

'Not as well as you. Besides it's not the same without youh, Glenn.'

After that they talked in generalities but Glenn figured making up mind time was looming, no tennis no contract.

Glenn left the camp on Friday night, intending to sleep in a tent attached to the jeep. That would give him the whole weekend to search the desert area surrounding the spot where he had found the arrow. He examined the map very carefully to see if in fact water had been there. He drove the jeep on to any higher ground in the area for the same reason. He was not entirely convinced it could have been a lake but it was the best way of checking it out that he could come up with. Glenn took a centre point on the map and decided to go in widening circles until he had covered the whole area, including any notional lake shore.

After four hours of careful searching he had found nothing. He felt he was now searching around the shores of what could have been a lake. If Baldomero was right he should be coming across something. Rather than overtire himself he decided to eat, so he erected an awning at the back of the four-wheeler and took out his food. He didn't know what caused him to look at the tracks behind the wheels. The piece of quartz wasn't an arrow. On the other hand it didn't appear to have been shaped by nature. It was like a ring that had one segment removed and a sort of shoulder on part of its circumference. He picked it up, satisfied himself it could be man-made and noted one of the points of the interrupted circle was as sharp as a needle. He carefully recorded time and place before placing it in an envelope.

After his meal he continued his search. Later on, about half past three to be precise, he saw them, not one, but three arrowheads. Glenn found himself trembling with schoolboy-like excitement as he bent down to pick up each one, all within a half hour. This time two were black agate and one was quartz. Moreover they were not of uniform design or shape. All three were within fifty feet of one another. Baldo was right, this must have been a recognised Indian hunting area. How many years ago had he said? At least two thousand.

Glenn noted the agate head was different in that the bottom of the triangle was 'D' shaped, presumably to fit into the wood leaving more arrow exposed, thus giving greater penetration. The quartz was very small and he suspected it was used for hunting birds.

He stood there in the empty desert, trying to guess what might have happened. A group of Indians on a hunting trip who had shot at some pray, birds or animals. Had they only wounded them? Was that the reason their arrows were not recovered, or had they simply missed and their arrows ploughed into the undergrowth, lost until the undergrowth was gone. Now that he had found four arrowheads he felt relaxed enough to speculate. Glenn was now at peace with the world, not exactly whooping for joy but humming with contentment.

That night Glenn slept in his tent for longer than usual which denied him his favourite view, the Andes at dawn. After breakfast he decided to narrow the gap between one circular walk and the other as he had a hunch the hunting area was small. After all Baldomero had said the Indians reckoned it was only five by ten kilometres. Now his examination of the ground was more intensive and his hunch paid off as he found two more quartz heads before dark. Again one was different in design. Instead of a 'D' shape at the bottom of the triangle it had a rectangular-shaped spur. All the better to stick into the wooden shaft of the arrow. He was either seeing a development of the arrow design or the work of another craftsman. The next two weekends weren't so productive as he found only two more. He didn't mind now that he had got some. To be holding a direct link with history, two thousand years plus, was intoxicating for Glenn. Before then two hundred years was about the limit of his history. He was in two minds as to whether he should spread the good news in the camp or not. His cocoon of happiness did not completely isolate him from the limbo of stilted conversation into which he was now cast by his former admirers. He didn't think they would be impressed by the sight of eight arrowheads of unproved age. It'd be time enough to consider saying anything after Baldomero arrived.

'Glenn, I have good news and bad for you. Which do ye want first?' said Baldomero with an impish grin.

'Gimme the bad first, Baldo,' said Glenn grimly.

'Your heads are not two thousand years old at all,' he said still smiling.

Glenn's heart sank, he felt as if a smiling Baldo had crushed it, and the bastard was still smiling.

'You want to hear the good news, Glenn?' said Baldo, still grinning like a cat.

'I suppose so.'

'My professor friend radiocarbon tested your arrowhead and it came out at six thousand nine hundred and fifty-five years old, or thereabouts.'

Still suffering from the bad news, Glenn asked, 'Say that again Baldo?'

'Seven thousand years, that's how old you arrowheads are. Glenn you have pushed back history by several thousand years and stood Chilean anthropology on its head. The workmanship on those arrowheads has stunned the historians up there. Glenn, you are a celebrity, famous.'

'Wait a minute, Baldo. You're kiddin' me again.'

'My dear Glenn, I had my little joke, what I have just said is true. A representative of the university, my professor friend, wants to come down here to see you and to be shown where you found the arrowheads. I suppose he will want to see the rest. And, he suggests you release this story to the *National Geographic*, he has a friend there. I can tell you grandfather would be delighted, because they were largely relying on folklore for the origin of their arrowheads. Now the tribe's history goes back far beyond anyone's expectations.'

'God, I donno what to say, Baldo, except thanks to you. If it wasn't for you this would never have happened.'

'Have you told anyone in the camp?'

'No. I was waiting till you arrived before doing anything.'

'Well, you better tell them now before the press and the others arrive.'

Glenn spoke first to Gus, one of the few who had made it his business to maintain contact with him.

'Ye mehan that's what youh was doin' out there in that desert. Lookin' for ancient arrowheads. Wahall I'll be damned, Glenn, youol son of a gun. An' the *National Geographic* will be here, in this camp, to interview youh. That sort a makes youh famous. More than winnin' the tennis match or the ball game. Folks here are sure gonnah be proud of youh. Did youawl tell the vice-president?'

'No, Gus, you are the first,' replied Glenn to a visibly pleased Gus.

Telling Gus meant the word would spread like wild fire around the camp. Many did not appreciate the significance of the find, but the fact that Glenn was about to be interviewed by the *National Geographic* and NBC was sufficient to have everyone shaking his hand. Doug Amer, the Vice-President, came down specially to his office having been told by Gus.

'Great news, Glenn. We wondered why you got caught up in the desert, now we know. When these TV people come we must have a celebration. This is a big occasion. By the way have you given any thought to a new contract?'

'No,' said Glenn, mindful of Gus's warning about his future if he gave up tennis.

'Well it's there for you. I need hardly tell you we want to keep you on the payroll, Glenn. You have a bright future in Anaconda. We want the company to have a share o' that gutsy determination you applied to games and to your search in the desert.

'A winner anywhere, Glenn, that's you.'

Disgruntled

'How do you mean he grunts?' said Helen.

'You know, he just grunts if I say anything to him. Generally when he's looking at the TV or reading. He never gets out a proper sentence, or even a word. I suppose you could call it a sound coming up from the throat and out through the nose. He doesn't even open his mouth. How else can I describe a grunt, for God's sake Helen?' Phil's tone clearly displayed her exasperation at having to try and define her husband's Frank's, grunt.

Helen and Phil went back a long time so she was well used to Helen's analytical approach to almost everything in her life.

Helen meanwhile was tapping the fingers of her left hand on her shapely right knee. As a small girl Phil recalled Helen's German father doing exactly the same thing when he was thinking. After twenty years of marriage Helen, unlike Phil, still retained the looks and figure of a twenty year old. If they had a night out together, men would concentrate their attentions on Helen, most of them assuming she was unmarried. Not that Phil was jealous, she was just extremely jealous of her friend's figure and beauty. Despite her occasional efforts at dieting she never could follow Helen's disciplined approach to diet and exercise.

Helen's fingers ceased tapping. She had come to a conclusion.

'Does Frank's grunt indicate he was listening, or just acknowledging his having heard your voice?' she asked.

'He never appears to remember what I have said, so he can't be listening.'

'Stuart used to do the same to me,' said Helen, reflectively picking up some unseen particles from her skirt. 'He used to give a catarrh-like grunt; a sub human sound I called it at the time.'

'You mean he has stopped?' exclaimed Phil, her voice going up a couple of octaves on the word 'stopped'.

'Oh yes, he stopped all right. There is a cure for everything, provided you keep trying. Sometimes Phil, one must up the ante to find a drastic remedy,' said Helen firmly.

'I have tried Helen, really tried very hard. We even have had words over his grunting, but you know Frank. He is too laid back to get worked up over a little thing like that.

On one occasion I even pretended the kitchen was on fire. Would you believe he just grunted, louder than usual I grant, and continued reading the paper? Later on when I tackled him about it he said, "Sure I knew you were only joking." I am surprised Stuart never said anything to Frank about stopping, after all they play golf every week.' The words came tumbling out of Phil, indicating her frustration with Frank's attitude.

'I hardly think Stuart would mention his cure to Frank, particularly on a golf course,' said Helen dryly.

'Phil,' continued Helen, 'I know you are a bit worked up over Frank's oink. I can only tell you how I cured Stuart.'

Phil was used to Helen's use of obscure words to make a point but, unwilling to show ignorance, she made a mental note to look up 'oink'. Just now she was more interested in Helen's remedy.

'How precisely did you solve it?' she asked.

'You of course know, Phil, that I take Mother away for an occasional weekend?'

'Two or three times a year,' offered Phil.

'Well, four times to be exact, one for each season,' corrected Helen. 'As you will recall the weather last summer was poor. But for the weekend we had planned to go away they forecasted continuous sunshine. So this prompted mother to suggest we continue over until the Monday evening; normally we return on a Sunday evening. Naturally I felt it necessary to tell Stuart about our later return. I found him slumped in the study reading a newspaper with the TV going full blast. He had just come in from the office and had got a glass of cold beer to cool himself off. The heat was almost unbearable. "Stuart," I said, "Mother and I will stay on until Monday night." He just grunted. I knew he wasn't listening and would be wondering why we had not returned come Sunday evening. Then he would proceed to accuse me of not telling him.'

'I can just imagine it, Helen,' said Phil feelingly.

'Anyway,' continued Helen, 'I again spoke to him, "Stuart, remember we will not be back until Monday evening." There was another grunt, more elongated this time, as if to reassure me that he might have heard. He hadn't of course, so I took myself up to the bedroom.'

'When I came down Stuart was as I had left him. I said, "Stuart, I am off to collect mother." This didn't even merit a grunt so I said, "back on Monday, darling." That got a grunt, so I added, "Stuart darling how do you think I look?" That merited two more grunts from behind the paper which I could have interpreted as unseen approval. Then I repeated in as icy a voice as I could muster, "How do I look Stuart?"'

Phil knew just how cold a tone Helen could adopt when she was annoyed. So apparently did Stuart.

'He shook the newspaper, without looking up, and muttered, "Great Helen, just great."'

'At least I had now got his attention, Phil, although he hadn't looked at me, so I said, in the same tone, "Stuart, darling you never even looked at what I am wearing." He slowly lowered his paper to glance over the top. Then his two arms with the paper crashed on to his knees as he exclaimed, "Helen, you can't go out like that!" He was now bolt upright in the chair. Have you heard of eyes popping out of the head? Well, all I can say is that Stuart's were exploding out of his.'

Helen paused for maximum effect. Phil was now totally captivated and burning with curiosity. 'What on earth came over him?' she gasped.

'Now that is a very appropriately phrased question Phil. It wasn't quite what came over him but what was not over me. Nothing. I stood naked before him, except for my black high-heeled evening shoes, you know the pair, and my long black evening bag under my arm. I had grabbed Stuart's full attention. "Christ Helen," he said, "have you gone crazy, going out like that?" he said trying to sound normal. Little did he realise how strangulated it sounded to me.'

'"Why no, Stuart, I am not crazy. Did you not hear me say just a few minutes ago that I was going to change into something suitable for this awful heat?"

"I certainly did not," said Stuart, very self-righteously.

"I suppose not when you hardly ever listen, darling."'

Phil could contain herself no longer. 'Good grief Helen you are joking,' she almost whispered.

'Far from it, Phil. I was deadly serious. What else could I do to cure him. You tell me? Anyway,' she continued, 'Stuart was a bit unsure of the situation. I need hardly add that I fed that uncertainty. He jumped out of the chair, grabbed my elbow and led me back to the bedroom. He even chose a light summer dress for me to wear before helping to pack my suitcase. He then offered to drive me to mother's flat. I refused of course, whilst still acting the part so he could not really be sure if this was a ploy or if I had really flipped my lid, a sort of heat stroke. All I can say, Phil, is from that day to this Stuart responds immediately I speak to him. I realise he thinks I was fooling but I know from the look of him, he cannot really be sure.'

Helen looked at Phil's flushed face, thinking she would look much better if she lost some weight. Helen's remedy fascinated Phil but she couldn't imagine following her example, it was all right for Helen but not for her.

'Helen, I'm not sure I could go through with that. Anyway, it's the wrong time of year,' she added lamely. There was a mirror on the wall in front of her and what she could see of herself only confirmed her unsuitability for such an escapade. 'I'm not sure if I have the best figure for it, Helen. Maybe I should give Frank one more chance before I go for a really radical remedy.'

Helen said nothing. Phil broke the silence by adding, 'After all, Frank is not like Stuart. It may not have the same reaction on him. It would be just like him to tell me to go and get dressed. Besides, if Frank and Stuart ever spoke to one another about it we would never live it down. Are you sure Stuart never spoke to Frank about your cure?'

'Yes, Phil, I am quite certain he never did, nor ever will.'

Fifteen Days on the Pog

Esclarmonde hobbled over to the edge of the fortress and looked down on the besieging forces some seven hundred *pieds du Roi* below her. The fortress of Montsegur, in which she stood, was perched on top of the Pog which itself was surrounded by the Pyrenees.

It was the first time in ten months she could look down with safety. Safe, she thought, now that is an odd word for her to use in the circumstances in which the *bons hommes* were placed. She was sure the French knights, their men-at-arms and their paid mercenaries, were relaxing. They could feel very safe. She shivered, it was still cold on the first day of March. 1243 had started off as a bad year and it could now only get worse for most of her Cathar co-religionists. Esclarmonde knew she needed time to think.

She could just about hear the sound of the besiegers' instruments being wafted in the still air from below, their clarity probably due to the surrounding mountains. They had something to celebrate. That sound was drowned by another from the barbican end of Montsegur where the Basque mercenaries were playing their weird musical instruments made, she was told, from wood and the stomachs of sheep. At least it was preferable to the constant swish of stones from their stone guns haphazardly seeking the lives of those in the fortress, or should it be called their temple. The plaintive wail of the Basque instruments caused her to shiver again, not from the cold this time, but from the thought of what the future held for her friends and their families. Her sister Arpais had once said that this wasn't music but a sound to frighten their enemies. It was succeeding.

They had fifteen days to decide to recant or die, during which time they would celebrate their Bema festival. It would be a time, the last time for many, they would be together. To be burned or recant, that question was preoccupying many of the good people in Montsegur just now. Esclarmonde had been taught that she should not as a Believer, a Cather or a 'pure one', fear death. Did not the perfecti teach her that all material things, including those below, came from the evil spirit, Satanas. Thus our souls were imprisoned within our fleshly bodies. If she received the *consolamentum* her soul would be freed to go to the Realm of Light. Easily said, perhaps easier for her with her crippled limbs than for the others.

Her mama, Corba, had spoken to her and told her that over the next two weeks they would pray together and thus be guided by the Holy Spirit. Esclarmonde suspected her mother wouldn't recant even though her father, Raymond de Pereilha, was one of Montsegur's governors. Her mother, the Marquesia de Lantar, was by French standards an important person. She supposed her family would be treated well if they gave in to the inquisitors' demands. Her father, she felt would not want their religion to end here on the Pog, never. Her two sisters what about them? Phillipa's husband, Pierre-Roger de Mirapoix, she knew would not wish to end up on the pyre, nor would Arpais's husband, Guiraud de Ravat. Whilst they supported the *bons hommes* they were not of them. Her young brother, Jordan, had been included in the hostages held by the French, to ensure the terms of surrender would be met in full. His decision had been made for him. Esclarmonde sighed when she thought of the decisions facing her family over the next fifteen days.

There were many, she knew, many old respected perfecti and perfectae who could not recant under any circumstances. After all was not Montsegur their home where they would study the Holy Writ until their souls were freed from their mortal bodies? Bishop Bertrand Marty had spoken to her on the fourth day, 'My child, you have suffered enough. I think you should go with your sisters.'

'My Lord Bishop I will await my mother Corba's decision before considering that,' she had replied. Bishop Bertrand said nothing, just frowned and nodded his head several times.

It was clear that all the perfecti were completely at peace with their decision, whereas others were very distressed at the inevitable consequences of that decision.

The debates and discussions exercised a great deal of the time of the men-at-arms and their families. Some days later as she made her way towards the far end of the fortress, to the citerne for water, she overheard one group's animated discussion.

'If we take the *consolamentum* we will be saved for ever. We will be leaving this evil which now surrounds us,' said one woman.

'And we will be burned at the stake in a few days' time if you do not recant. The inquisitors will test our commitment to their church. You know what that means? We have to think of our children. We cannot have them burned for our own beliefs. Who will look after them if we die?' said a man, possibly her husband, thought Esclarmonde.

'They have promised to give us a full pardon, even for those who massacred William Arnald and the other six inquisitors at Avignonet,' said one of the men-at-arms.

'They call us heretics. It is they who are the heretics. Are not our perfecti the purest humans on the earth, truly they are *bons hommes* and good Christians whose spirits are close to Christ. Are they not better Christians than the corrupt and worldly Roman clergy?' Esclarmonde recognised the speaker as Bruna, a wife of one of the men-at-arms.

'I wish I had never come here,' said another, 'my wife says she will take the *consolamentum*. You all know what that means, death at the stake. It's breaking my heart.'

They were so engrossed in their discussion they paid no attention to Esclarmonde who was standing nearby. She however could take no more as their problem was too close to that of her own family. She moved on through the crowded fortress which was now filled with a mixture of joy, fear, sadness and for many, dread.

Her father, who had been the great leader of the defenders for the whole period of the siege was now full of dread. He knew her mama, Corba, was slowly coming to a decision to take the *consolamentum*. Her grandmama had already been made a perfecta in 1234 by Bishop Bertrand Marty. She had given all her worldly possessions to Philippa, her sister and stated, 'I will not abjure my beliefs. If my soul has to meet my God through the stake then so be it.' Others had given their belongings to various friends and relatives. She had heard of *sous melgoriens*, salt, pepper, wax, clothing, grain, and clothing being given away. Her grandmama had explained that she would have no further use for her worldly possessions and she was not going to let the French take anything from her other than her useless body.

The days seemed to fly past and towards the end, particularly after the festival, it was becoming clear who had made what decision. Esclarmonde had prayed with her mama and she had decided, midway through the fifteen days, that she could not recant. Her mama decided to take the *consolamentum* on the second last day. It was a terrible decision for her to take as she would now be leaving her young brother Jordan, of whom her mama was particularly fond. Esclarmonde tried her best to comfort her family. Strange, she thought, that she, a cripple, should be the member to comfort the others. It was difficult for them to understand the joy which their decision engendered. It was not a martyrdom, but a release from evil for their souls. They would enter eternal happiness and pray for those others whose worldly imprisonment would continue. It was no good, they were inconsolable and in a way she could understand their grief. But it would be wrong for her to deny her eternal soul from joining the Good Deity in Heaven.

Her father asked her to reconsider her decision not to recant. It pained her deeply to have to say, 'Dearest Papa I cannot bring myself to imprison my soul for eternity, for that is what I would be doing. You know I love you all dearly, and I know you will take the *consolamentum* some time in the future. Then our souls will be united in happiness.'

'So be it Esclarmonde, whilst it grieves me, I understand your wishes. For my part, if our religion is to survive we must ensure the survival of some, the credentes, and more importantly the *bons hommes*. I will make further arrangements for the remainder of our treasures, gold, silver, documents and money, to be taken from here so that we can continue our work.'

'I know Papa. We must ensure the rest of our brethren will be given the opportunity to save their souls from the further evil into which they are now being forced.'

The night of 14th March was one of trauma for all the people in the fortress. She realised how close they had all become during the hardships of the ten-month siege. They all joined in prayer together, particularly the Our Father which was special for them. Soon they tired and were silenced into troubled sleep or wakefulness.

Esclarmonde had a very untroubled sleep that night now that she knew her soul would be freed. Yet she could not help fearing the pyre being prepared down below by the French. She was comforted by the seventeen brave men and women who had taken the *consolamentum* amid tears of joy and sorrow that evening in the certain knowledge that they too would now face the fire the next day.

The following morning, all those who were to recant, or did not need to do so, were led out of Montsegur for the last time. She and the other perfectae and perfecti were left behind with a guard and some inquisitors. Later, more soldiers and mercenaries of the French king came and roughly shackled them together for the steep climb down to their death. They allowed Bishop Marty to head the long line. There was no objection when her grandmama indicated she wanted to be between her daughter and her granddaughter. The steep narrow track meant they had to descend in single file down the mountain, with solders lining the way and pushing on those who were slow, irrespective of age or injury. Some of the soldiers laughed when all three of them slipped and fell on the slimy track.

Bishop Bertrand Marty had estimated there would be two hundred and forty-three good people in the long line. From time to time she could see the line below and above her. The impatient shouts of the men-at-arms and the sounds of their beatings could be clearly heard in the morning air; yet she did not hear a complaint or moan from the good people.

It must have been Bishop Marty who started the Lord's Prayer, at least it started from the front and gradually was taken up along the line to her mama in front, to her grandmama behind and on up the line until the whole Pog appeared to be resounding to their prayer. Finally, they were above a field where some besiegers were gathered to her left surrounding their friends and relatives who had left before them. To her right she saw a huge square pile of countless faggots, straw, and what looked to her like pitch. Around the pyre, for that is what she knew it to be, there were stakes and poles apparently forming a barricade which would prevent anyone getting in or out.

Her mama saw her looking at the scene and said, 'Dearest Esclarmonde, fear not. The Holy Spirit will give you strength to leave all this wickedness. We may appear to be dying but it is to eternal life we are going. Our martyrdom will live for ever as an example to those who will follow us that good can overcome evil.'

'I know Mama, I am not afraid,' she said.

She tried to see if she could make out her family as she descended to the level of the field. She could not and was glad. They had stopped saying the Our Father and she could hear the chanting of psalms by Roman clergy dressed in cream robes. Were they inquisitors, she wondered, trying to persuade themselves they were praying for us? At that instant her grandmama said, 'It is an insult to have those whores of Babylon mouthing their heretical psalms near us.'

As the long line of *bons hommes* came to the palisade they could see men-at-arms with lighted pitch torches at the ready. They were taken off ten at a time and tied to the sides of the pyre; some others, their hands tied, were pushed up on top whilst those who could not climb, the sick and the wounded, were simply thrown up on top, irrespective of whether they landed on others already there. More faggots and straw were flung on top on them.

A knight tied the three of them together, but before doing so he begged them to recant. Her grandmama responded, 'Young man, we thank you for your kindness, but our religion teaches us that you are delivering our spirits into everlasting life from this repulsive world.'

The young knight simply shrugged his shoulders and said nothing. Esclarmonde could see he was upset. She felt sorry for him and said, 'Do not worry, we will pray for your salvation when our souls are delivered to the good God.'

At a signal from one of the inquisitors, torch-bearers approached the pyre and she saw them set fire to it, starting at the two corners within her view. Before the smoke could increase, the others set fire to other parts with several pitch torches simply being flung on top. In the clear, almost still, morning air the only sounds at first were the clink of armour and the chanting of psalms; gradually they were overtaken by the sound of burning from behind her, followed in turn by moans from her friends affected by the flames. At the front the smoke gradually increased until it began to shut out the light. It then made them choke and cough. Soon she could feel the heat and hear the roar from the fire behind. She couldn't breathe, the smoke was choking her lungs, causing her to cough which only made her take in more of the burning smoke. Her mama and grandmama held her hands and they attempted to pray. It was no good. Her grandmama's hand slipped from hers and through a gap in the smoke she saw she had fallen forward. The heat from the fire made her gasp for more air that was no longer there. She began to panic wishing to get away but the combination of searing pain in her lungs and the intense heat caused her head to spin.

The voices she could now hear (how could she hear them above the flames?) were soft and gentle. Esclarmonde felt a feeling of peace flow through her whole being. She was ascending up above the pyre. Below she could see blackened bodies and twisted limbs whilst around her were translucent figures, the most beautiful figures she had ever seen. A gentle hand was leading her ever upwards. Instinctively she knew it was her mother's.

Esclarmonde now knew for certain her soul was free from the gaol of her body, just as a butterfly sheds its larval cage which binds it to the earth. She was entering the Realm of Light.

Marriage – Taj Mahal Style

It was obvious to his friends that Ahmed was worried. He, more than they, enjoyed their morning coffee shop discussions, largely because his visits were interrupted by frequent business trips away from Manama. This morning he also looked forward to a soothing smoke from the nargila.

Here Ahmed was among friends, not just business friends, but those he had known since childhood. Together they could have uninhibited, highly enjoyable discussions on topics ranging from the Gulf War to their children's demands in a too rapidly changing world. A no holds barred open forum where Ahmed felt a singular sense of fellowship. To his friends he was a clever, articulate debater whose innate sense of humour kept their discussions from getting out of hand. Some, aware of Ahmed's safety net attributes, would deliberately push their point to the limit, knowing he would rescue their debate from going too far. To a foreigner their discussions sometimes sounded as if they were about to come to blows, until Ahmed's measured tones brought them back from the edge. Thus their best, and most pointed, debates coincided with his presence.

Abandoning their current discussion on Balfour and the Palestinians for a moment, Abdul Hussein, seeing Ahmed's black Mercedes pass by, observed, 'It must be a family matter which is disturbing him.'

His friends' startled glances at this *non sequitur* caused him to add, 'Ahmed, I mean. His car has just passed by.'

'What makes you think that?' asked Khalil Haddid, predictably, thought Abdul, since his friends knew he thought about little else other than his furniture business. Some even credited him with having sawdust for brains.

'Have you noticed lately how he tends to withdraw from our discussions whenever a family topic comes up?'

'He does not even join in our debates with his usual enthusiasm,' observed Nabil Mehrez, 'even though his business is going very well, especially since the second son joined him. The last time he was like this, not quite as low spirited though, was when his eldest son, Rakan, decided he wanted to study medicine in preference to joining the furniture business.'

'We had better not ask him if there is anything wrong. He may tell us himself in due course,' said Abdul, putting an end to the speculation.

They were right. Ahmed was worried. Abdul had guessed correctly when he said it was family. His daughter Fatima had just announced she wanted to go to the university to take a law degree, just after a young man, Khalid al Khedris, had called to his house to ask for her hand in marriage. To complicate matters further Ahmed had intended to have her betrothed to her third cousin, Rashid al Abbari. He was an outstanding businessman whose father was a very good friend. Maybe Rashid, being a few years older, was a little too stiff for Fatima, reflected Ahmed. But she would have the full support of both families. Unfortunately, whilst there was an unspoken understanding between himself and Rashid's father, Nabil, he had not told Fatima, nor the two families. Although he had never spoken directly about it to Nabil, they had talked around marriage and it was in both their minds. Now this proposal from Khalid al Khedris had come out of the blue and Fatima had told him that she was unwilling to accept young Khalid as a husband. She wanted to take a law degree. He knew he could order her to marry him, but he was not inclined to do that as it would also shut the door on Rashid as a possible son-in-law. Nor was he anxious to see her buried away for at least four years studying law. She could be too old for a suitor when she qualified, with both her current suitors gone elsewhere. The fact was that Khalid's proposal had been made and she could bring dishonour to the family if she, or rather he, turned it down without good reason. Announcing she is going to university after receiving the proposal would indubitably be misinterpreted, especially by the al Khedris family. Moreover it would look bad in the eyes of nearly everyone, who would regard Khalid as an eminently suitable husband for any girl.

It is a mess, he thought grimly, as he waited to turn his car into the car park across the road. It had brought far too much tension into his heretofore happy family environment. Fatima was an only daughter which made her happiness all the more important, not only to himself but also to his wife Mai. They had a very close mother and daughter relationship. Any attempt by him to exercise a father's authority, other than in the interest of Fatima's happiness, was not realistically an option.

In the Arab world, tradition was most important, to such an extent, as his friend and supplier from the USA, Bill Ryan, pointed out to him last week, he was a prisoner of that very tradition.

'Ahmed my friend, you are in a real catch-22 situation,' Bill had said to him in his Pittsburgh study, 'if you order her to marry Rashid you will please him and his family only to antagonise the whole al Khedris family, and God knows how Fatima will react. Yet if she goes to the university you will lose out by appearing to be too weak.' Seeing Ahmed's expression Bill spread out his two broad hands, halting his friend's reaction. 'I am merely expressing what other people might say, not I, who after all has been your friend for twenty years.'

Ahmed knew Bill was, as always, trying to help him. He acknowledged their friendship. When they first met Ahmed was just starting to expand his business and wanted to source a large order for furniture from the United States. For a sum in excess of what his bank was prepared to cover, Bill, whom he had just met through a mutual acquaintance, had given him extended unsecured credit during their first year. Ever since they had done business with the minimum of guarantees. Their mutual business's had evolved with Ahmed becoming a substantial customer of Bill's, whose furniture currently sold throughout the Middle East by one or other of his outlets.

'Bill, you know our traditions better than most. Have you any ideas?'

'You're not asking the best man, you know.'

Ahmed understood only to well what Bill meant. He knew too that sometimes a person who has gone through his own family traumas can best advise others. American family life, reflected Ahmed stroking his beard, with its wilful children, broken marriages and lack of religion was a crazy lottery at best. Bill, despite his emphasis on family relationships, had had his unfair share of trouble, or rather his family had. Jack the eldest got a well-paid job in the Bank of America and was transferred on promotion to Sacramento, where he met this girl, an actress. Then he rang his parents telling them he was marrying in three days' time, as his wife was about to go into a play. This meant they would have no honeymoon if the wedding was not brought forward. The marriage exploded like the star she craved to be. She ran off, after eighteen months, with a well-known older actor, thinking her career would rise under his influence. It did not. He dumped her for his co-star within two years.

Bill's daughter, who started going out with boys when she was twelve, Ahmed could not imagine that in an Arab family, married a Russian businessman, who was quite wealthy, but whose whole existence apparently revolved around making more money, to the exclusion of everything else. She hardly ever saw him, not surprisingly, as he was already married to another women in San Diego. She was so upset, when she did find out, she went off to South America to work with the Peace Corps where she married a

French Canadian teacher, 'old enough to be her father,' said Bill bitterly.

Frank, the youngest worked with his father, still unmarried at thirty much to the concern of Bill and his wife, Sue Anne.

Freedom could create its own problems, thought Ahmed. At least Bill, unlike most Westerners, appreciated the merits of arranged marriages. He would be an excellent person to give him some advice on what he might do about Fatima.

'Ahmed, to work out any solution you need to get her out of the family and local environment for a short spell, otherwise it can get out of hand for everyone. Unlike me, at least you have an opportunity to do something. Bear in mind Fatima's happiness should be just as important as family honour. Maybe they even go hand in hand, Ahmed?'

Bill had given him the germ of an idea which, on the plane back, he developed into an action plan.

A gap in the traffic brought him back to the present. He quickly pulled the large Mercedes 500 over to the cleared site which had become the coffee shop's unofficial car park. He parked the car and stepped out into the oven like heat of the noon day sun. Brushing the creases out of his white kaftan, he dodged across the side road, deaf to the cacophonic din from the horns of impatient drivers. Once over, he entered the air-conditioned coolness of the coffee shop. Out of habit he took a deep breath, taking in the familiar pungent odours of strong coffee, mint tea and, of course, tobacco. His friends, seated in their usual centre table under the blades of the big brass ceiling fan, gave him a warm greeting. He sat down in one of the black leather-covered chairs to the left of the mosaic fountain. They had moved there when they became aware that a wider and unwanted audience had been created from their words being reflected off the blue patterned wall tiles in the corner. The rest of the room had simply stopped talking when they were in full debate.

His friends were pleased to find his humour had improved since his return from the United States. They now knew today's discussions would be lively. Ahmed gulped down the first cup of dark coffee poured out for him by the waiter. Praise be to Allah, that tasted good. He motioned for the nargila to be placed beside him. The waiter carefully placed the red charcoal on the tinbak. He put the mabsam in his mouth and took a deep breath, feeling the smoke go down into his lungs. Ahmed was ready for the fray.

By the time he got back into his sunbaked car he felt purged of any tensions. So much so that when he reached home his wife Mai immediately noticed the change, which in turn released the tension that had recently pervaded their household. Ahmed knew what he was going to do. First, he would outline part of his plan to Mai, conscious of her closeness to Fatima.

'Mai, you remember the conversation I had with Bill?'

'Of course, about going away with Fatima to see if you could both talk things through. I suggested you do it on your next trip. I think we learned from Bill to stay close to our children.'

'My annual Indian trip, buying textiles for the factory, has been fixed for next week. I have decided to take Fatima with me. My business will only take a day or so, leaving us time to visit Delhi, Agra and Jaipur. That will give us an ideal opportunity to talk.'

'That is a good idea,' said Mai, relieved that something constructive was at last happening. She had been concerned lest Ahmed made a unilateral decision, a wrong one, from which there would be no appeal.

'I would suggest, Ahmed, you both have your serious talk at the Taj Mahal, making it your last stop. Fatima should be more receptive there.'

Mai had always treasured their visit to the Taj when they were young.

'Please remember, Ahmed, she wants to get a better education. At the same time I think young Khalid would make a good husband. He comes from a very nice family. If it's not to be Rashid then he would be an excellent alternative – that is if you can get her to put off going to university.'

Instinctively, Mai did not favour Rashid as a husband for Fatima. He was older and too staid for a young impetuous wife. However, she had kept these thoughts to herself.

'Mai, I think it better you should speak to Fatima about India. If she felt she was being coerced by me into going the exercise could be abortive.'

Fatima did not need much persuading, especially as her mother told her that a visit to the Taj Mahal was the chance of a lifetime. Besides, Fatima knew it would have been churlish to have refused her father's invitation. She had heard Bill's expression that there was no such thing as a free meal. The Indian visit would not be free.

When her father had finished his business in Delhi he showed Fatima around the city, which included a visit to the Quw-wat-ul Islamic mosque and the massive Qubt Minor, rising over seventy-two metres into the sky. 'One of the finest Islamic monuments ever,' said Ahmed proudly, 'as strong as a good marriage – built to last.'

Fatima ignored the reference. Ahmed, irritated at his own misjudgement, went on to describe the fourteenth-century Alai Darwaza as being the first truly Islamic building in Delhi. He was determined to say nothing more about marriage in any shape or form until they got to Agra.

Fatima gradually saw that her father was not intent in relentlessly pursuing the marriage topic. So she began to relax and enjoy herself. He was a fund of information about India, particularly any Islamic aspect of Indian architecture or history.

Ahmed had a friend in Jaipur, Mr Sharad Aneja, who arranged for them to get into the City Palace with its treasures, carpets and, above all, the Peacock Courtyard which they viewed from the private Chandra Mahal, where the Maharaja still lives.

At the nearby Palace of the Wind, or Hawa Mahal, from whose multitudinous windows the royal ladies viewed the teaming traffic in the street below, a difference of opinion arose between Mr Aneja and her father over the origins of the Pink City.

'It was in honour of the English Prince Albert's visit which caused the city to be covered in pink, and you still keep repainting it that colour. I thought India had gained its independence,' said her father provocatively. It was obviously a type of game between friends, thought Fatima.

'Ahmed, my friend, how wrong you always are in this matter. It was not done for the royal visit at all, but many years earlier and then claimed for such by foolish journalists, English I say, who wished to impress their own countrymen. Why then should we Indians not keep it like that, it's good for tourists to go to the Pink City. Is it not unique in this world? Am I not correct, Fatima?'

Fatima, sensing they never wanted a definitive answer to their dispute, ducked the question by asking another. 'It is very beautiful, but surely the Maharaja did not have all those wives – there must be hundreds of windows up there?'

Mr Aneja was taken aback by the question, which served Fatima's purpose. 'Of course not, the windows are for all the ladies in the palace to view the street below. The Maharaja would not have that many wives.'

Ahmed did not wish to go into a discussion on Hindu and Muslim marriage practices just now, in case it affected his own plan. He suddenly looked at his watch saying, 'My dear Sharad, are we not cutting it fine if we are to see Amer Fort before returning to Rambagh Palace?'

'Of course, Ahmed, we had better go now.'

Fatima relaxed. She was grateful to her father, who had obviously sensed her anxiety at the turn the conversation could take, and irritated with herself for dropping her guard. Her father made no attempt to raise, obliquely or directly, the issue of her future while they were in Jaipur. She was grateful to him for that and so, after the initial tension, she was now totally enjoying her trip. Not so Ahmed. He was becoming more uneasy. Time was running out. In a day and a half they would be leaving Agra, and the Taj Mahal, for home. He had carefully planned their itinerary to reach Agra when there was a full moon, so that the impact of what the building was all about, love and marriage, would set the scene for his plan. If it didn't work he was back to square one, too unpalatable to even contemplate. For her part Fatima, inspired by her mother's memories and photographs, was too excited to sense her father's tension.

Nothing could have prepared her for the reality. Not even her first sighting, through the haze from the rooms in Agra Fort where Shah Japan was imprisoned by his son Aurangzeb. There he had to live out the rest of his life with only the view of his wife's distant mausoleum on the far bank of the river Jumna. The poignancy of the unfortunate man's final years of tantalising separation merely heightened Fatima's anticipation.

'We will visit the Taj tonight, Fatima, then go back tomorrow morning for a daylight viewing before going home.'

Ahmed was feeling more optimistic as he sensed the magic of the Taj was beginning to work. He could feel a greater rapport had developed between them, which must augur well for the success of his plan.

At dusk he led Fatima to the horse and carriage which was waiting for them outside the hotel. Fortunately the mist had lifted. This made for a clear starless night inhabited solely by a huge moon which caused the Taj and its surroundings to glow in its half light. From the main entrance they walked towards the ornamental pool and gardens fronting the Taj. Her first sighting took Fatima's breath away. Even Ahmed was still in awe of the spectacle before them. There was an ethereal air to the marble building, as if it was floating on air, a haunting image of perfect symmetry truly reflecting the eternal love of the Emperor for his deceased wife, Mumtaz Mahal.

'All for love Fatima. He built that exquisite jewel in her memory. Never has love been so perfectly remembered for so long by so many generations in this world.'

'Father, it is exquisite, beyond anything in my dreams. How shall I ever forget this evening? I now know why Mama was so enthusiastic. Thank you, Father, for your kindness,' she said, touching his sleeve. She fell silent, transfixed by the luminous masses of white marble interspersed with semi-precious stones.

'Fatima, let us go back to the marble seat, over there where we can contemplate the magnificence of this work of art. It was there your mother and I sat so many years ago.'

They walked back to the seat, both now under the spell of their surroundings. Fatima sat down determined to remember the view perfectly. She would never forget one single detail of the scene. After a few minutes she spoke in a low voice, slowly and hesitatingly at first, as if thinking aloud.

As she spoke he noticed how the moonlight enhanced her beauty. She was wearing a white, flower-embroidered blouse and long black skirt which matched the darkness of her hair. It was uncanny, thought Ahmed, as he shivered in the warm night air. For a moment he had relived his last visit here with Mai. Fatima was so like her. He listened carefully to what she said.

'Dear Father, I know I have been a source of sorrow to you and to Mama, for which I am truly sorry. Please forgive me. The last thing I want to do is hurt you both, or cause any unease for the family. But I would like, no it is more, I have an urge to go to university to study law. If I do not go now I could spend the rest of my life regretting it, which could affect my relationship with any husband. It is possible I may not like it and give up, but it is vital for me to find out. I hope you do understand, Father.'

Ahmed hesitated before replying, careful not to destroy the mood. The scurrilous thought occurred to him that he must buy Bill a present for creating this opportunity.

'Fatima, I appreciate what you have just said. I know I never told you. I should have, but I had in mind that you would marry your cousin Rashid. Unfortunately I never mentioned it to him, or directly to his father. Just as well. Young Khalid's proposal came out of the blue, as did your announcement,' and, sensing that word was provocative he hastily amended it 'your desire to do law. Regrettably you did not make that clear to us earlier, because it could look now to Khalid's family as if it was a spurious reason for turning down his proposal. I have to say he is a perfectly good spouse for you, coming from a very good family. The question now is what to do...' He tailed off, raising his two hands in the air with an air of helplessness.

They were silent for a few moments before she said, 'Father, I have known Khalid since childhood. He is a very nice person, but let him, or Rashid, wait four or five years until I qualify. You can then decide which I should marry.'

'Unfortunately that is not a clear option now. After all you have a proposal on the table. Maybe there is a possible solution though.' He paused as if clearing his thoughts.

'What, Father?' whispered Fatima anxiously.

'Let's say I give you permission to marry Khalid on condition he agrees to your going to university for the first year of your marriage. After that he, or between you, if you wish, can decide if you shall continue. He will of course have to realise that your university term will be residential. If he refuses then the same proposal can be put to Rashid.'

Fatima said nothing for a while. They both sat in silence which, to an onlooker, seemed as if they were enraptured with their surroundings. In fact, their surroundings no longer existed for either of them.

Ahmed felt pleased with his suggestion. After all he had given it considerable thought. As head of the family he had to appear to act positively, at least to outsiders, and most of all to Khalid's father. He felt sure Khalid would turn down such a bizarre proposal whilst he was quite certain Rashid would agree to it. If Khalid did accept his proposition then that was better than Fatima just going to the university, second best to be sure, but it would get him out of his embarrassing predicament. He was a good young man with a bright future and from a very acceptable family. He looked around, feeling pleased with himself, once again conscious of his surroundings.

Fatima sighed, obviously coming to a decision. 'Father naturally I would prefer a more straightforward solution. I equally appreciate I should not continue to cause concern to you or Mama. Therefore I agree with your suggestion. Will you speak to Khalid?'

Allah be praised, thought Ahmed. The end of their relatively brief conversation resulted in a palpable deflation of their tensions, which in turn lead to their chattering like two children as they made their way towards the marble steps in front of the mausoleum. They substituted their shoes for cotton sandals before entering the Taj, the result of Shah Jahan's twenty-five years' labour of love.

Ahmed was pleased with the outcome. Thanks to the Holy Prophet, Fatima had agreed. For a moment, when she paused at his suggested solution, he had felt a tightening of the chest, whereas now the pleasure of this visit was equal to that of his last with Mai. The visit, he now realised, highlighted the love he felt for both, plus just how important was their collective peace of mind.

As soon as he returned he saw Khalid and outlined his decision to agree to the wedding on condition Fatima attended university for the first year. He stressed she would be required to be in residence during term. Her continued studies thereafter would be a matter for himself, as her husband. Khalid listened carefully to what Ahmed had to say. To his credit, thought Ahmed, he did not appear to be put out by the unusual terms. He merely requested twenty-four hours to consider it.

'Take as long as you like, my son,' said Ahmed magnanimously, feeling quite pleased the way things had gone.

He left for the coffee house, where his friends were pleased to see him back from another journey. 'It was undoubtedly a family matter since he brought Fatima with him to India,' said Abdul. 'It must be resolved, given his high good humour.' The rest nodded their heads knowingly.

When Khalid did not return after twenty-four hours Ahmed suspected his family had dissuaded him from going ahead with such an unusual marriage. It wasn't that he was slightly delayed. He was several hours late. He had plenty of time to accept, therefore he was not going to accept, reasoned Ahmed.

He was wrong. At the thirty-first hour he came back with a purposeful expression on his face. A good-looking boy, thought Ahmed to himself as he wondered how he would back out. The sentence was long, delivered in a steady monotone, as if he had rehearsed it for some time. Ahmed has guessed right on that one at least; he had spent considerable time thinking about his reply.

'Sir, please excuse my not responding earlier to your proposition put to me yesterday but, as you will understand, it was necessary for me to speak to my family who also found your proposals most,' and here he hesitated for a word, obviously not the one his family had used, 'unusual, but I truly love your daughter Fatima, so in a lifetime what are a few years?' Not waiting for answer he continued, 'If she wishes to study for a degree I shall not stand in her way, although naturally I would prefer it if she was with me every day. Sir, I will be more than willing to abide by your terms. One minor matter though. As the university commences in a few months' time I would be deeply appreciative if the wedding could take place soon. That way we will have time for a honeymoon.' He was nearly out of breath with the rush of words.

Ahmed had to adjust to the unexpected, so he concealed his feelings under an air of joviality. 'Of course, of course, my son, we will start making the arrangements right away. Indeed this very day.'

He picked up the phone to ring an anxious Mai, and at the same time hoped he was concealing his surprise. Now that there was a resolution he felt surprisingly relieved. At least Fatima was getting married. He was too mature and experienced a man to brood on partial failures, or partial successes.

Mai too sounded relieved, which was all to the good. Maybe, after all it was for the best, though he hoped his coffee house friends would not make inquiries about why Fatima was going off to college after she was married.

The wedding was a great success, largely due to Mai's determination to make it so, and indeed to the support she got from Khalid and his family. Everyone said they had never seen a more radiant bride, or a happier couple. Fatima, to her father's surprise and gratification, said they were going to honeymoon in India and Nepal. 'I want Khalid to see the Taj Mahal, Father.'

A week later, holding hands, they sat on the marble seat.

'Fatima dearest, I still wonder if we were fair to your father?'

'The same thought was running through my head, dearest. As you know we sat on this same seat that night. If anything had happened to keep us apart I would have died. You know that, dearest. I could sense Mama knew that too, although she never spoke to me about my feelings for you until a few weeks ago. But she knew. That is why she hinted to me that Father wished to have me marry my cousin Rashid. I think she saw him as a bit old and staid. Apparently she always ended up their interminable discussions by saying to father, "Ahmed, remember Fatima's happiness is most important for us." If I had not said I wanted to do law, Mama knew I would probably end up by marrying Rashid. We, you and I, could not take that risk. But I will have to go to university, at least for a while. I cannot let Father down.'

'Your father is a wise and kindly man. I will be forever grateful to him for the way he has received me into your family. If our first is a boy let us call him Ahmed.'

'By all means my dearest. If she is a girl can we call her Mumtaz?'

Off the Piste

Heather lowered herself into the middle seat of three, fastened her seat belt before adjusting the seat to its upright, take-off, position. Then her elbows laid insidious claim to a reasonable proportion of the arm rests on either side, while she made sure to avoid any contact with the two adjoining passengers. Satisfied, she stretched out her legs under the seat in front, glad she was at last about to leave Borovitz. Her right foot had touched something solid, probably metal tubing from the seat in front. Her thoughts were interrupted by a 'sorry' from the man on her right. He smiled as he shifted his position and readjusted the jacket across his knees.

He wants to talk, thought Heather, so she muttered 'okay' without looking at him. To head off any further conversation she leaned back on the headrest and closed her eyes. The young man said no more, obviously he had taken the hint.

Her thoughts were again interrupted by the girl on her left's giggly conversation with the young fellow across the isle. Curious, thought Heather, she had an accent just like Liz's. It was a pity she had to leave Liz in Borovitz. On second thoughts, maybe Liz had mixed feelings about her departure. After all she could now give her full attention to Hans. Nice fellow; funny, if he hadn't appeared on the scene she probably wouldn't be sitting on this plane now. It really was one of life's vicissitudes; Hans first, then mulled wine followed by... It didn't bear thinking about.

She had been on several skiing holidays with Liz, first in Austria, then France followed by Italy. This year she had decided to persuade Bill to take up skiing. His change of job put paid to that plan. Bill, aware of her fondness for skiing, suggested she go again with Liz, who had been pressurising her anyway to go to Hungary. 'It's cheap and unspoiled,' she had said. They had hardly booked into their small hotel before Hans and his friend appeared on the scene. Heather was too eager to develop her relationship with Bill to indulge in any holiday romances. Bill, for his part, had laughingly said she would be safe with Liz. She saw his point. Liz was stunning. Not that she, Heather, was not good-looking also. She was, but for some reason men always made a beeline for Liz. Karl, Hans's friend, was just plain ugly and resignedly moved elsewhere when she gave him the brush off.

Threesomes never worked, reflected Heather. It didn't take her too long to become aware she was an intruder. That was why, in the restaurant at the top of the piste, she pretended she wanted to go down that five kilometre piste on her own. Admittedly her inspiration may have derived from the near bottle of mulled wine with which Hans had plied her. 'Eeet is good for the blud, Header.' Bloody hell, Heather reflected, it was good for more than the blood, and bad for something else; the bladder. She noticed a group of army trainees who were getting ready to ski down under the watchful eye of a bored sergeant. *No point in being left behind that lot,* she thought; *they are bound to be slow.* She quickly bade farewell to a relieved Hans and Liz before taking off.

Maybe it was the mulled wine which gave her a unique feeling of exhilaration on that piste. At any rate for the first two kilometres or so Heather was in heaven. She was brought down to earth however when she got an urge to have a pee. Where though, a piste is not exactly littered with loos? Halfway down she could stand it no longer. She noticed a copse a couple of hundred metres down to her left. The other skiers on the piste were far enough away, and travelling too fast, to pay any attention to her.

Once she had decided to make for the copse, her arrival there became all the more urgent. She hurriedly peeled off to her left. As far as she could see, the next skiers were a good distance behind her and there was no one ahead of her. The trees did not give her the cover she would have liked, although that was a minor matter now that her brain had signalled to her bladder that relief was at hand. What she had not taken into account was the steepness of the terrain around the copse.

Once there, she managed to secure reasonable screening from those on the piste by anchoring the front of her left ski against a tree trunk. Secured against drifting downhill over the soft snow Heather rolled first her pants and then her briefs down over her legs. This manoeuvre effectively tied her legs together. She had just started when a shout to her right caused her to look over. There were three of them, men, possibly facing a problem similar to hers. The shout was from the first who had gone past before he realised what she was doing. The second, now under notice, exclaimed to the third, 'Jesus, Robin do you see what I see.'

He mustn't have been looking where he was going as he skied straight into a tree. Heather heard the loud crack followed by a string of curses. The sound of a bone being broken was not an unfamiliar sound to her. She had last heard it on a hockey field when a player broke her tibia. Here in the snow it sounded like a gun shot.

There was another sound behind her. It sounded like, indeed was, men's voices singing a marching song. What the hell was going on in her quiet little copse? No one sings a marching song in the snow. She turned her head to look, twisting her body as she did so. It was just enough to release the ski on her left foot from the foot of the pine tree. Frantically, she tried to stop herself while she tugged to get her pants up. It was no good. She was moving so fast on the steep snow that navigation through the rest of the trees became top priority. It did not prevent her hearing the silence when the singing suddenly stopped. One minute the copse was ringing with the marching song, then there was an eerie silence. Silence, apart from the swish of her skis as they gathered momentum away from the trees and down the steepening slope.

Heather was trapped in a crouched position, her sticks trailing behind with her pants down around her legs. It was curious, she noted afterwards, she never felt cold in the below zero temperature.

The silence continued for a few more seconds only to be broken by loud cheers, whistles and shouted remarks in Hungarian by the army men behind. Heather thanked God she didn't know the language. Her fervent wish was that this was all a dream and she would wake up under a nice warm duvet. Wishful thinking, reality dictated that she was now locked in a crouched position, skiing at an ever increasing speed with a bare backside exposed to an astonished group of army trainees. Further, if she did not stop soon she was going to end up not too far from the end of the piste, where there were bound to be a body of curious onlookers.

Off piste the snow was so soft that Heather figured if she fell into it she could be in worse trouble trying to get out. She was gathering speed and soon she would be out of control. There was really only one thing to do. Fall backwards on to her skies so that the front of the skies would point upwards whilst the back, with her weight on them, would dig into the snow and halt her progress. With any luck she would be held up by the skis. Thankfully, there were no more trees with which she had to contend.

Heather sat down on the skis and shivered as she felt the cold snow on her thighs and bottom. She tugged madly at her clothes and managed to pull up her pants without getting too much snow into them. Her haste and embarrassment had insulated her against the worst effects of the cold.

The soldiers had the decency to follow from a distance and once she was up and going they took off to her left, having recommenced their song. A melody she would take to her grave.

She shivered in her seat in the plane at the very thought of that song. Normally, she could say the rest of the journey down was uneventful. For Heather it was anything but as she had the distinct impression everyone was looking at her and smirking. Not so, when she arrived at the end of the piste the onlookers were engrossed in watching an ambulance depart, presumably with the broken leg. It was odds on her fame had preceded her, certainly to their small hotel. People there were too solicitous and of course they gave the game away when she was asked if she wanted to leave her ski pants in the drying room. Heather had had enough and decided to seek refuge in her bedroom. She was still there when Liz came in much later.

'Is it true what I heard in the village Heather?' enquired Liz. Heather didn't even bother to ask her what she had heard. She knew, and replied vehemently.

'I am never again going to drink mulled wine, or any other liquid on top of a ski slope, and that is for certain. Oh God Liz, I am so embarrassed. I must be the laughing stock of the village.'

'Oh it will be a one day's wonder. After that they will have something else to preoccupy them tomorrow, Heather.'

'I doubt it, Liz. Will you do me a favour? I want to get out of here as fast as I can. Do you think that travel agent friend of yours can do anything for me?'

Liz tried to get Heather to stay, but she would have none of it. The agent managed a swap with someone who was glad of a few extra days and Heather was delighted to get a seat on a plane the following day. *What a blessed relief,* thought Heather.

The rise in tone brought her back to the plane. She was being asked something. She opened her eyes. The hostess was leaning over with a food tray in her hands. 'Would you like dinner Madam?'

'Yes, yes, of course thank you very much,' she muttered before she realised what she had said. She would have preferred to have been left alone in a semi stupor with her thoughts. She took the tray and played around with the food, eating the salad and leaving the plastic-looking chicken and vegetables.

The hostess came back with a tray for the guy beside her. He was having some difficulty in getting himself upright in his seat. Heather moved her right arm off the armrest as he placed his two hands on each arm rest and heaved himself into an upright position. Just as he did so he let out a curse as his jacket fell on the ground.

He saw Heather's look of curiosity and volunteered, 'It's my leg. It's in plaster. I am going back to the Blackrock Clinic to have it examined.'

He smiled and hesitated, waiting for the usual question. As Heather was slow to respond he continued, 'I know, I know you are going to ask me how it happened. You are not going to believe this but... by the way,' he was looking intently at her now, 'did I meet you somewhere before?'

When Heather started to reply in the negative he interrupted, 'No, no don't say anything. I never forget a face, especially one as pretty as yours.'

When she opened her mouth, unsure as to what she should say, he raised his two hands and said, 'Please, please give me time... until the plane lands. I'm sure I will recall where we met by then. I'll tell you what, I'll give you ten punts to one I will place you before this plane lands in Dublin.'

Heather just nodded bleakly. *What else can I do*, she thought, *only pray I win that tenner.*